"Sexy, scathing, de.   ...ing."
—Gretchen Felker-Martin, author of *Manhunt* and *Cuckoo*

"This book's coming in hot! King-Miller brings a delightful appetite for rollicking weirdness, queerness, sexiness, and chainsaw prowess. An absolute blast."—Hailey Piper, Bram Stoker Award–winning author of *Queen of Teeth* and *A Light Most Hateful*

"Sharply written and filled with richly drawn, complex characters that I genuinely cared about, *The Z Word* is one of the most innovative and deeply affecting novels I've read in a while. Playful, acerbic, and utterly engrossing, it's astonishing to realize that this is Lindsay King-Miller's debut. I'm ravenous for more!"—Eric LaRocca, author of *Things Have Gotten Worse Since We Last Spoke and Other Misfortunes*

"A gripping read about actual community and the dangers of corporate Pride that bites down on you like a wild animal and doesn't let go."—Mattie Lubchansky, author of *Boys Weekend*

"Lindsay King-Miller's timely Pride-versus-corporate-politics parable vibes like *28 Days Later* helmed by a rainbow Romero."
—Clay McLeod Chapman, author of *What Kind of Mother*

"Packed to the brim with drag queens, complicated relationships, and buckets of blood, *The Z Word* is scary, funny, gross as hell, and ultimately deeply touching. The zombie apocalypse has never been queerer—or more fun."—Matthew Lyons, author of *A Black and Endless Sky* and *The Night Will Find Us*

"Funny, disturbing, and refreshingly compassionate, *The Z Word* is a grisly blast from cover to cover."—Calvin Kasulke, author of *Several People Are Typing*

the

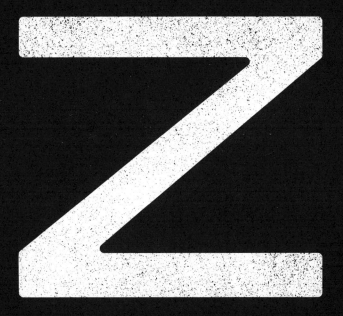

Z

word

LINDSAY KING-MILLER

QUIRK BOOKS
PHILADELPHIA

**For the queers who threw
the bricks, and the ones
who carry the torch**

Library of Congress Cataloging-in-Publication Data
Names: King-Miller, Lindsay, author.
Title: The Z word / Lindsay King-Miller.
Description: Philadelphia : Quirk Books, 2024. | Summary: "During a Pride
    celebration, Wendy notices the beginning of an infection that seems to be
    turning people into zombies. She and others from the local queer community
    must team up (despite interpersonal tension) to try and stop the outbreak,
    discover its source, and survive"— Provided by publisher.
Identifiers: LCCN 2023036099 (print) | LCCN 2023036100 (ebook) |
    ISBN 9781683694076 (paperback) | ISBN 9781683694083 (ebook)
Subjects: LCGFT: Queer fiction. | Zombie fiction. | Horror fiction.
Classification: LCC PS3611.I5897 Z33 2024 (print) | LCC PS3611.I5897
    (ebook) | DDC 813/.6—dc23/eng/20230906
LC record available at https://lccn.loc.gov/2023036099
LC ebook record available at https://lccn.loc.gov/2023036100

ISBN: 978-1-68369-407-6

Printed in China

Typeset in Sabon LT Pro

Designed by Andie Reid
Production management by John J. McGurk

Quirk Books
215 Church Street
Philadelphia, PA 19106
quirkbooks.com

10 9 8 7 6 5 4 3 2 1

CONTENTS

CHAPTER 1 6

MIKE 28

CHAPTER 2 33

CHAPTER 3 47

CHAPTER 4 55

CHAPTER 5 65

CHAPTER 6 78

CHAPTER 7 89

CHAPTER 8 103

SAMANTHA 111

CHAPTER 9 116

CHAPTER 10 128

CHAPTER 11 134

CHAPTER 12 153

IRIS 158

CHAPTER 13 165

CHAPTER 14 175

COURTNEY 196

CHAPTER 15 206

CHAPTER 16 218

CHAPTER 17 231

LEAH 246

CHAPTER 18 249

CHAPTER 1

"Don't they have anything besides this hard seltzer bullshit?" I fume to nobody in particular. Only a handful of people are foolish enough to be sweating their asses off out here on the front porch, instead of inside, where they would still be sweating their asses off but also dancing or flirting or getting laid.

"I think the good drinks are in the kitchen," says a young, heavily bearded white guy sprawled on the porch swing. "The planning committee got, like, ten cases of this stuff donated, so they're trying to offload it." I recognize him vaguely from the few Pride planning committee meetings I attended last summer and fall. I think his name is Mike.

"Right." I sigh, pick up a seltzer and inspect it—Seabrook Black Raspberry—then drop it back into the sea of melting ice. I'm sure if I go inside, I could find something better in the fridge. Our hosts, Samantha and Aurelia, are craft beer lesbians. But Sam and Aurelia are also nonmonogamous lesbians who are, apparently, an hour or less away from a threesome with my ex-girlfriend Leah. I was inside for five fucking minutes before I caught a glimpse of Aurelia caressing Leah's neck. No beer is worth that.

A handsome butch woman, maybe in her fifties, is sitting on the front steps of the one-story adobe house. She pulls a flask from her jacket and holds it out to me. "You want? I always bring my own." Her voice has a lilt that might be the slightest vestige of a Spanish accent.

"What is it?" I'm hesitant about hard liquor. There was an incident involving Jack Daniel's one New Year's Eve, and it hasn't sat right with me since. But I don't want to turn down an overture of friendship.

"My own," she repeats. "Ultra-local, small-batch, artisanal moonshine."

A spasm of wings blurs past my face. I yelp and flinch, slapping the huge palo verde beetle with the back of my hand. The glossy, thumb-sized bug spins off course and lands on the concrete near my feet, squirming on its back.

"Ugh," I shudder. I slam my Doc Marten down on the beetle with an audible *crunch*.

"Nice shot," the silver fox says. "I hate those little fuckers."

I lift my foot to check the results of my assassination attempt. Half of the beetle's body is nothing but a dark smear, and I'm glad the porch light is too dim to see its color.

"Now you definitely deserve that drink," says the butch.

I take a whiff of the flask's open neck. Jesus, it's strong. I can smell it even over the scent of my own nose hairs singeing. "Wow," I say when I can breathe again. "I don't think so. I don't want to burn my tongue off the first night of Pride weekend."

"I guess my tongue is stronger than yours," she says, smiling wickedly. "Beau, by the way."

I smile back, willing myself not to be awkward. "Wendy." Beau has streaks of pearly gray in her thick black hair and the kind of crow's feet that suggest she does a lot of laughing. She's around my height and broad-shouldered in a short-sleeved button-down shirt. Beau might be my mother's age, but she's hot. And if Leah's getting laid tonight, I should too, just to make it very clear that her actions have no impact on me. "How do you know Sam and Aurelia?"

"Dykes on Bikes," she says. "There's not an official San Lazaro chapter, but we have a Facebook group. I found Aurelia there when I was looking for a mechanic in the family."

Aurelia works on Leah's bike sometimes, too. *That's not all she's going to be working on*, I think involuntarily. Jealousy and attraction fizz together in the back of my throat. I'm about to ask Beau what she rides, maybe with some innuendo thrown in, when I hear a skittering sound. I look down at the floor of the porch and swallow a scream. The palo verde beetle is moving. Its carapace is shattered, but still it's managed to flip over. Its intact front legs scrabble over the cement as it struggles to drag itself out of the wreckage of its own guts. Some unidentifiable but oozing part of its anatomy stretches, then snaps.

"Son of a bitch," Beau yelps. She slams the bottom of the flask down on the beetle and twists it viciously. There's a squelching sound. When Beau lifts the flask again, something drips from its bottom.

"Okay, I'm definitely not drinking that now," I say.

There's a honk from the street and a car pulls up to the curb. It's neon green with a hot-pink logo airbrushed on the hood: PIZZAPOCALYPSE. The driver who climbs out is probably in their early twenties, a few years younger than me. They're tall and lanky, with long, tangled, sun-bleached hair and an oversized polo shirt with the same logo as the car.

"Pizza's here!" Mike cheers. The driver waves like a celebrity greeting adoring fans, then grabs a stack of pizza boxes from the front seat. It towers in their arms, slipping alarmingly to one side as they saunter across the gravel that passes for Sam and Aurelia's front yard.

Beau opens the front door and sticks her head inside. Loud music and the smell of sweat spill out onto the porch along with bright light from the living room. "Who's paying for the pizza?" she yells into the din.

"Can I help with that?" I ask the delivery driver, less out of altruism than because I'm certain they're going to drop the stack at any moment. Up close, I can see the driver's killer jawline and a smattering of freckles on their high cheekbones. I also notice a pin with the words THEY/SHE on the collar of their polo shirt, the baby blue and pastel pink of the trans pride flag clashing with the shirt's neon colors.

"Oh, I'm totally good," they reassure me. "I work out." I swear I hear the pile of boxes creak as it sways. The driver is so stoned. I can smell the pot smoke over the stomach-rumbling garlic smell of the pizza.

"Are you guys always open this late?"

"We're always open," they say. "Hunger can strike at any moment, and Pizzapocalypse is here to answer that call." The words sound like a joke, but their tone is weirdly serious. I'm not sure whether they'll be offended if I giggle.

Aurelia steps out onto the porch, holding the door open with one hand and proffering a neatly folded stack of bills in the other. "Hi, Sunshine," she says to the driver. "Didn't know you were working tonight. Want to come back after you clock out?"

"I never clock out," says Sunshine inscrutably.

Aurelia looks amazing, tall and curvy, wearing a Harley-Davidson muscle tank. I'm so distracted staring at her that when

Sunshine dumps the stack of greasy cardboard boxes into my arms, I almost drop them. Sunshine takes Aurelia's money and sticks it into the fanny pack at their waist without counting it.

"Oh, hey, Wendy," Aurelia says, belatedly realizing who I am. "Thanks for grabbing those."

"No problem," I say, and head for the kitchen. The crowd parts around me. The tang of sweat and alcohol is strong, but underneath there's a spicy, homey smell, a mix of patchouli and home cooking. I came here for dinner once, with Leah; Sam made pierogis, with Aurelia's maduros for dessert. No one's invited me over for dinner since Leah and I broke up.

I try not to look around for Leah. Unfortunately, I find her without looking, since she's the only person in the house with bright blue hair, and she's also perched on the kitchen counter, two feet away from where Aurelia directs me to deposit the pizza.

"Hi," I say, because that's slightly less awkward than pretending I don't see her. Leah is a lushly proportioned woman with a round, pale moon face, and tits and belly and thighs to spare. She's wearing tight jeans and a strappy tank top, displaying the colorful tattoos on every bare inch of skin below her collarbone. I know the ink continues down her back and ribs, spilling onto the curve of her hips, and I want to trace it with my tongue. I want to bury my face in the crook of her neck and breathe in the smell of her.

"Hey, Wendy," she says, perfectly casual, like she's never bitten my shoulder hard enough to draw blood when she came. "I didn't know you were gonna be here."

"Yeah, um, they invited me, so," I say insightfully. There's grease on my palms from the pizza boxes; I want to wash it off, but to get to the sink I'd have to maneuver past Leah, basically walking between her legs. I wipe my hands on my skirt instead, leaving a stain I instantly regret.

"Wendy!" I'm hit from behind by the full force of Samantha, wrapping her arms around my waist and squeezing hard. I turn around and hug her back. Sam's short and stocky, lined with solid muscle she uses to flatten chicks on the roller derby track. She hugs hard, leaving me breathless, almost gasping at how long it's been since anyone has put their arms around me.

"I'm so glad you're here," Sam says, and I believe she means it. "We haven't seen you in way too long."

"Thanks for having me," I say.

"Of course," Sam says. "You were on the committee."

I see Leah's eyebrows arch delicately at that, and I know she's remembering that I stopped showing up to meetings when we broke up, without ever telling people I was quitting.

"I didn't really do anything," I say.

"That's not true," says Aurelia. Her tone isn't as warm as Sam's; she's always more reserved. But I glow a little inside when she says, "You wrote that grant proposal for the main stage." It was a small grant, just a few hundred dollars from an arts organization to pay some of the performers. I pulled an all-nighter the night before it was due, frantically deleting and rewriting while gulping black tea, terrified of letting the festival down. By the time the awardees were announced, Leah had broken up with me and I wasn't around to enjoy my success.

"So what are you up to now?" Sam asks. "Still writing grants?"

"Oh, uh, no," I say. "I was never really a grant writer, I just had a fundraising job in college." I don't add that I hated every minute of it. The truth is that I quit working at the coffee shop where Leah and I met, and since then I've been scraping by with an assortment of gigs and odd jobs. I don't want to admit that to

Sam and Aurelia, two smart, capable, responsible adults whom I desperately want to like me, even if they are hooking up with my ex.

They're waiting for me to say something else, so I shift the focus back to them. "It seems like you've done an awesome job on the festival. It's way bigger than last year, right?"

"Yeah, it's great," says Sam wryly. "All it costs is our souls."

I nod and avoid looking at Leah. Apparently the partnership with Seabrook is still a sore subject. I remember some of those early arguments around the folding tables in the public library meeting room, back when I was still part of things.

"The soul is a fiction invented by the patriarchy to control our behavior," Leah says. "Free booze is real."

"Definitely a stretch to call hard seltzer *booze*," Sam says, but she grins and slides past me to wedge herself against the counter between Leah's legs. I try not to stare at them as Leah leans forward and rests her chin on the top of Sam's head.

Aurelia grabs a slice of pizza loaded with peppers and olives, folds it in half, and takes a bite. "Well, it's a done deal," she says, ever the peacekeeper, even with her mouth full. "We can talk in postmortem about whether we want to keep the sponsorship for next year, but for right now we might as well enjoy it."

"At least we got the new health center out of the deal," says Leah.

"And *you* get a fancy new job," says Sam.

I try to keep the surprise from my face. "You're working for Seabrook?" I ask Leah. It's true that she facilitated the sponsorship deal, but working for a corporation like that outright seems very out of character for the Leah I know.

But of course, I don't know her. Not anymore. And maybe I never knew her as well as I wanted to believe.

"Not for the brewery," she says. "I'm the community liaison for the new LGBTQ community health center." It sounds like she's reading off her business card, not speaking to me directly. I wonder if she has business cards now. Does she keep them in her boot next to her pocketknife?

"Congratulations on selling out," I say. I mean for it to come out light and teasing, the way Sam sounded a minute ago, but my voice sounds the way I feel: hot and irritable and seething with envy. I hate that something this big changed in Leah's life, and Sam and Aurelia knew about it, and I didn't. I hate that my story with Leah stopped six months ago and theirs just kept going. And I fucking hate hard seltzer.

Leah's eyebrows shoot up, but all she says is a mild "Thanks."

"They actually have some cool stuff planned," Aurelia says. "Free STI testing, counseling groups, a queer prom . . . you'd almost think San Lazaro was a real city."

"Yeah, Leah's really pushed them to put their money where their mouth is," Sam says.

"So we should be grateful that our whole community exists at the whim of our corporate overlords," I say. Aurelia and Sam glance at each other, wide-eyed, and I know I should back off, but the feeling of having Leah's full attention for the first time in months is irresistible. There's a spark in her hazel eyes that I know is anger, but it doesn't look too different from passion.

"Yeah, Wendy, it's not perfect," she says. "It's a compromise. Not everyone is ready to walk away from something that matters to them the second they hit a conflict. Some of us actually want to work through the messy stuff." And there it is: we've gone from talking about Seabrook to talking about *us*.

My anger dissipates in an instant, leaving only cold sadness behind. The combined pressure of all three of them staring at me is too much. "Sorry," I mumble. "See ya."

Why did I try to pick a fight with Leah? Was I trying to make her feel bad for breaking up with me? She's right: I was the one who smashed what we had. It was precarious, like a delicate snow globe balanced on the corner of a table, and I shoved it over the edge because I was so sick of waiting for the shattering sound. Leah grew distant and I feared losing her, and to make myself feel better, I fucked someone else. If I'm heartbroken, I deserve to be.

Someone follows me through the crowd as I hurry out of the kitchen. "Wendy, wait." I turn, my stomach leaping with a moment of irrational hope, but it's not Leah; it's Aurelia, still trying to smooth everything over. "Hey, she didn't mean—"

"No, I know," I say, forcing cheerfulness. "It's all good. I'm just going to go dance."

Aurelia looks like she wants to say something else, but she bites her lip and seems to change her mind. "Okay."

Instead of dancing, I walk down the hall to the bathroom, close the door, and sit on the toilet seat, resting my head in my hands. The party sounds from outside rise and fall like waves. I think about crying, but I don't.

Six months. It's been six months since I nuked my relationship with Leah just so she wouldn't get the satisfaction of being the one to dump me. Apparently I haven't gotten any smarter during that time.

After a minute, I stand up and wash my hands for no real reason. In the mirror over the sink, my face looks sad and tired and older than I want to feel. My eyeliner is smudged, and my post-breakup pixie cut desperately needs a trim. I wonder how many Pride parties I've spent feeling envious and left out, wishing I could break through the membrane between me and the other, better party that seems to be happening all around me. If anything, this year feels worse than usual, because these people are all Leah's friends. I can't meet anyone's eyes without wondering what they've heard about me.

As I walk down the hall from the bathroom to the living room, letting the current of the party carry me past tide pools of conversation, I'm distracted from my self-pity by a small commotion. A tall, dark-skinned Black guy in black lipstick and a crop top lurches into the front room, half carrying a petite girl with lighter brown skin and a shaved head. "Can anyone here drive?" he asks.

"No," someone yells, "we're all gay."

"Fuckin' come on, is anyone sober?" He gestures to the girl slumped against his arm. "She's three-quarters to blackout. Somebody needs to take her home."

I never got around to finding something I wanted to drink, and am about to volunteer when someone else says, "I got it."

Of course it's the last person I wanted to see tonight, looking effortlessly gorgeous as usual. Jacquie, the grenade I tossed into the middle of my life six months ago, is pretty in a quiet, androgynous way, the kind of woman who still gets described as a tomboy even though she's nearly thirty. Tonight she's wearing a Seabrook T-shirt with the sleeves cut off, her light brown hair in a ponytail.

A flash of resentment burns on my tongue when I see her, which is entirely unfair. I was the one who chose to sleep with Jacquie while I was still dating Leah. None of what happened is her fault. Still, I try to fade into the crowd so she doesn't see me.

Jacquie steps forward and takes the smaller girl's arm. The girl sways, almost stands upright, then collapses against Jacquie. "Hey, Emmy," Jacquie says soothingly. "Do you have your house keys? I'm going to drive you home, okay?"

Jacquie to the rescue, I think wryly. She's always the first in line to take care of everyone else's needs, whether that's driving a drunk girl home or hooking up with a self-destructive mess who's convinced her relationship is doomed and wants to skip to the end. She'll get eaten alive someday if she doesn't figure out how to say no to people.

Emmy half opens her eyes and scowls blearily. She straightens up, pushing herself off Jacquie's arm. "Don't wanna go home," she slurs. "'M just a little . . ." She trails off.

"I think you need some sleep, honey," says Jacquie, reaching out like she's going to rub Emmy's back.

Emmy's eyes flash open and she knocks Jacquie's hand away, hissing like a cat. Then she claps her hands to her cheeks as if in dismay. The skin around her eyes stretches and distorts, and I realize she's dragging it down, digging her fingernails hard into her own flesh.

Around Emmy and Jacquie, people step back. "What the fuck?" someone murmurs.

"Sleep," Emmy says nonsensically, her eyes glittering. Jacquie reaches out again, and Emmy shoves her in the sternum, sending her stumbling backward. Emmy snaps her jaws in the air, as though trying to bite something the rest of us can't see. "Sleep," she says again, drawing out the vowel so it twists and crackles. I've never seen a drunk person act like this. Emmy must be *beyond* obliterated.

"Listen," Jacquie says, and I hear her placating tone fraying around the edges, but before she can finish her sentence Emmy leans over and vomits explosively on the floor.

Everyone jumps back. Emmy doesn't look around for a trash can or a sink; she just curls her body forward and retches, not even attempting to cover her mouth. Bile pours out of her like a faucet. I smell stomach acid and blood mixed with the tang of alcohol. My own diaphragm roils, but I clench my jaw and breathe through the urge.

Someone must have alerted Samantha and Aurelia, or maybe they just heard the noise, because they appear in the doorway from the kitchen, looking horrified. Aurelia's eyes go glassy and she claps a hand over her mouth.

Emmy finishes heaving and stands there, her face grayish. Jacquie's still reaching toward her, one hand frozen in the air, her face caught between sympathy and disgust. For a moment, no one moves.

Finally, Jacquie inches forward again. "Okay, Emmy, we're going to get you home," she says. "And whoever cleans up this mess, you're gonna buy them several drinks at the festival on Sunday. Can we agree on that?"

Emmy curls her lip in irritation, and I'm worried she's going to swing at Jacquie again. But then she sighs, and her whole body sags. She'd hit the floor if Jacquie didn't step forward to catch her. This time Emmy doesn't push Jacquie away.

Sam rubs Aurelia's shoulder, then disappears back into the kitchen. I still don't see Leah anywhere, which is a small relief in all the chaos; I don't think I could handle being in the same room as Leah and Jacquie at once.

"Thank you," says the tall guy to Jacquie. "I'll clean up here. Will you text me and let me know when she's home safe?" Jacquie nods and turns toward the door, all but dragging Emmy alongside her.

As the guy surveys the mess on the floor, hands on his hips in exasperation, Sam comes back with a roll of paper towels and some cleaning spray. She says something quietly to Aurelia, who nods and follows Jacquie and Emmy out the door.

"I'll help you clean up," I offer, no longer trying to blend into the walls now that Jacquie's gone.

"Thanks, dude," says the tall goth guy. "I keep telling Emmy she shouldn't try to keep up with me, but she was like, you can't get drunk on fizzy water."

"That was so bad," said Sam. "She's gonna feel wretched in the morning, too."

"What's Aurelia doing?" I ask.

Sam chuckles, folding paper towels into a stack almost as thick as it is wide. "I asked her to go make sure Jacquie's okay to drive, but mostly I just wanted to get her away from the barf before she has a sympathy upchuck. She's delicate." I feel a pang of envy at the effortless sweetness, at the idea of being known and understood so well.

"Oh, I just about ralphed too," says the tall guy. He uses the paper towels Sam hands him, grimacing all the while. "Gross, gross, oh my God, gross." I run to the kitchen, grab the trash can from under the sink, and hold it out for him to deposit the horrifying detritus.

This guy, I realize now that the commotion has abated, is stunningly good-looking. His eyes are huge and deep brown, and his cheekbones are ridiculous. Plus, he's at least six four. He doesn't exactly look straight, with his expertly applied lip liner and Sisters of Mercy T-shirt cut off at the rib cage, but then I'm not straight either. Maybe we could meet in the middle. *Keep dreaming*, I chide myself.

Sam is spraying the floor with cleaner, dousing the acrid smell with chemical lavender, when Aurelia returns. "Thank you so much for dealing with that," Aurelia says.

"How's Emmy?" asks the tall guy.

"Wrecked," Aurelia says. "Jacquie's going to have to carry her up to her bed." She looks faintly repulsed, and I get the feeling Emmy's total cognitive dissolution grosses Aurelia out almost as much as the vomit. I've seen Aurelia have a beer or a shot on occasion, but never enough to get even a little sloppy. She's the most collected person I know.

"Assuming Emmy doesn't deck her when she tries," Sam says. "I never knew she was such a mean drunk."

"She isn't usually," the tall guy says. "I don't know what was up with her tonight."

"Oh, Pride makes everyone act weird," says Samantha. "You run into all your exes in the span of five minutes and it just explodes your brain." She's not looking at me when she says it, and I can't tell if it's pointed or not.

Mike, the guy from the porch with the impressive beard, dashes up to us, looking concerned. "Hey," he says to Sam and Aurelia. "Someone's either fucking or breaking up in the bathroom, and they locked the door."

"Oh, for fuck's . . ." Crisis mode activated, the two hostesses follow Mike down the hall, leaving me standing there with a trash can full of vomit and paper towels, smiling nervously at the most beautiful man I've ever seen up close.

"Um," I say. "I guess I'll just . . ." I turn and head for the kitchen. The tall guy follows me. As I replace the trash can under the sink, he washes his hands, running the water so hot I can see the steam.

I could slink away into the crowd, but I force myself to say something to him. "You definitely deserve another drink after dealing with that. Can I get you something?"

"Not a Seabrook," he says immediately.

I laugh. "I'd never insult you by offering one of those. Want a rum and Coke?"

"Is there Diet Coke?"

I rummage through the bottles on the counter until I find the one he wants. "One diet rum and Coke for the champion of kitchen floors everywhere," I say as I hand him the red plastic cup.

"They had diet rum?" he asks. I just blink at him. He shrugs, grins, and says "Thanks" again before throwing back most of the drink in one long swallow. I watch the long column of his throat as he gulps.

"I'm Wendy," I say as I pour myself a vodka lemonade.

"Logan," he says, leaning against the counter. I can see his hip bones above the waistband of his jeans.

"So, Logan, what brings you to this fine party?" I ask as he licks fake-sweet soda from his lips. My attraction is throttling my social awkwardness in real time. I suddenly feel like I could make small talk for hours.

"I kind of live here," he says. "I'm crashing with Sam and Aurelia until I find a new place. Plus I'm on the planning committee with them. I'm the token drag queen."

"Drag queen?" I look him up and down again, not bothering to be subtle about it this time. It dawns on me that his face looks familiar; I just didn't recognize it with so little makeup. The height, the goth aesthetic . . . "Holy shit, you're Dahlia DePravity, aren't you?"

This time his smile is wide enough that I can see a hint of a dimple in his right cheek. "One and the same," he says.

"Oh, wow. I can't believe I didn't recognize you. You're amazing." At the last drag show I attended, a month or so before Leah and I broke up, Dahlia DePravity did an aerial silks routine to a Siouxsie and the Banshees song. I was completely captivated by her long, muscular legs, bare feet gracefully pointed. He's wearing black jeans now, but knowing those legs are underneath makes the plain denim much more interesting.

The dimple deepens. "Go on," he encourages. "Say more nice stuff about me."

I laugh. "Seriously, you're really talented. And hot, but you obviously know that."

"I'm hot or Dahlia's hot?" It took him a few minutes to catch up, but he's now giving me the same look I'm giving him. This is the part of socializing I'm actually not terrible at. I'm not gorgeous, but most people aren't holding out for gorgeous, and I can usually quell my anxiety long enough to get someone into bed. It's the other, less tangible forms of connection I've never been able to figure out.

"Both," I say. "I'm not picky. I mean, I am, but not about that."

He winks at me. It's a little weird to see someone wink in real life. "An equal opportunity enjoyer, huh? I feel that." His gaze flicks down to my thighs and now I'm glad I wore a skirt.

"So how's the planning committee been?" I ask. "Working with the corporate sponsors and everything?"

"I didn't really have anything to do with the Seabrook people," Logan says with a shrug. "I was just there to work on the finale. I'm a logistics bitch. I got our fireworks permit and made sure the drag queen float has a good spot in the parade."

"Is that how you ended up staying here?"

"Yeah, kind of. I actually knew Aurelia before I met Sam, it's a funny story . . ." He launches into a convoluted tale about his former roommate, a truck with a flat tire, and a batch of weed brownies left in the oven too long. It's not, in fact, a funny story, but standing here watching his lips move is entertainment enough for me.

"What's their guest room like?" I ask. So far Logan doesn't strike me as particularly attuned to subtlety, but the look he gives me says he's followed this particular train of thought to its destination.

"Not bad," he says. "You want to see it?"

As I'm following Logan down the hall, a door swings open. Leah emerges from a bedroom that must be Aurelia and Sam's, her cheeks flushed pink and her blue hair far from its usual sleek tidiness. Our eyes meet, and something claws at the inside of my chest. Her gaze ticks from me to Logan and back, and a small, mean smile tugs at her mouth. My heart thundering, I wrench my eyes from hers and follow Logan so closely I almost beat him through his bedroom door.

It's barely a guest room, more like a combination of office and storage room, with a tool bench, a small desk and ergonomic chair, and a futon squeezed into one corner. That's all I have time to take in before I'm grabbing Logan and pulling him in for a kiss that suddenly feels desperate. I taste the waxy sheen of his black lipstick and the spicy sweetness of rum and Diet Coke. His tongue is hot and eager against mine.

I groan into his mouth and kiss a line down his neck. My hurt and anger toward Leah sublimate almost instantly into a different kind of arousal, and I'm mouthing at Logan's collarbone, trying to forget everything except the taste of his skin.

"Can I?" he asks, tugging on the hem of my tank top. I murmur something affirmative and he pulls the shirt up and over my head. He reaches behind me and struggles with the clasp of my bra, so I help. The look of appreciation on his face is gratifying. "You've got such great boobs," he says. "I'm totally jealous of your boobs."

Rather than ask him what adult human being describes a sexual partner's body parts as "boobs," I guide his hands and show him how I like to be touched—rough and urgent. He takes the hint enthusiastically, and I gasp. "You like that, huh?" he whispers. "What else do you like?"

I run my hands over his chiseled torso and undo the button on his jeans. "I like to get fucked," I say recklessly.

"Damn, me too," Logan says. "Maybe next time. Unless you have a dick with you?"

I shake my head. The truth is, I don't even own a strap-on anymore. Leah took them all when she moved out; she was the one they'd bonded with. "Oh, well," he says. He wraps his long fingers around my wrist and slides my hand down, over the obvious bulge at his groin. "I always bring mine."

My neck aches from straining upward to kiss him. "Get on the bed," I say.

He tumbles backward onto the futon and looks up at me hungrily. I reach for the zipper on my skirt, but Logan shakes his head. "Keep it on," he says. "I want to fuck you in your skirt and boots."

I pull my skirt up over my hips and make a slow, teasing performance of sliding out of my underwear. Logan rubs the heel of his hand over his crotch. "You're so hot," he says. He unzips his pants and shoves them down. "Are you going to ride me?"

"Yeah," I say. "But I'm not wet enough yet. Help me out?"

"Can I watch you do it?" Logan says, leaning back on one elbow while his other hand lazily strokes his dick. It's a nice dick. I haven't been this close to one in a while. "I want to see how you jill off." Okay, I'm just going to pretend I didn't hear that one.

Murmuring a silent apology to Aurelia and Sam, I grab their office chair and position it beside the futon. Reclining the way he is, Logan has a perfect line of sight directly between my thighs as I spread them.

Something slams into the door from the other side. I can't tell if it's someone knocking on purpose or a body stumbling drunkenly into the wall. There's the sound of someone screeching with what might be anger or laughter. "Fuck off," Logan yells in that direction. "We're busy."

A muffled voice on the other side of the door echoes, "Busy, busy!"

"Fucking weirdos," Logan mutters. To me, he adds, "Don't stop."

So I don't stop. I make slow circles with my fingers and let my head tip back, not restraining the moan that rises to my lips. It feels good. I like being watched. I like making a production of my pleasure. I like hearing Logan's whispered curses and the rough, quick sounds of him jerking himself off.

"So fucking sexy," he murmurs. "Will you put a finger—"

"God, yes," I interrupt. After "boobs" and "jill off," I'm not sure I'll survive hearing his chosen synonym for *cunt*. Biting my lip, I ease first one, then two fingers into myself. I run my other hand up my neck and into my hair, make a fist, and pull.

"Yeah," Logan says, and in my head I hear another voice. *Yeah, you like that, don't you? You love the way I fuck you. Say it. Say it louder, baby.* Squeezing my eyes shut, I can almost feel her fingers tangled in my hair, yanking my head back, biting my throat, my nipples. Throbbing around her hand, four fingers deep, twisting—Leah, Leah—

"Come on, just like that. You're so beautiful."

I open my eyes. Logan.

"It's so sexy when you . . ." he starts, but I cut him off again.

"Shut up and fuck me."

Logan reaches for the jeans he flung to the floor and fishes something out of a pocket—a small, rainbow-striped square of foil. "Oh my God," I say, surprised into giggling. "Is that a fucking Seabrook-branded condom?"

"There were a bunch of them on the table by the door," he says. "I probably have a different kind somewhere. You want me to look for one?"

"No," I say. "Just put it on."

I push him back into the futon and straddle his hips, guiding him into me. I'm gloriously wet and it's smooth and sweet and perfect. "Is this okay?" I whisper, and he says "Fuck yeah," and then it's all hot skin and gasping and his hands wrapped around my waist, holding me in place as he thrusts up, fast and punishing.

"Wendy," he whines in my ear, "you feel like heaven."

"Flip me over and fuck me harder," I say, because I still feel Leah's name on the back of my tongue. Logan wraps his arms around me and rolls, giggling like a little kid. Then I'm on my back, my skirt still up around my waist, my feet still shod in green Doc Martens crossing at the small of his back. He braces his arms on either side of my head and slams into me with everything he has, shoving me across the futon inch by inch with every thrust. By the time my head is knocking against the wall, I'm almost not even thinking about Leah anymore.

I moan and wail like a porn star, partly because it really does feel amazing, partly because being loud turns me on more, and definitely not at all in case Leah is within earshot. "Yeah, you like that?" Logan pants in my ear. "Are you going to come for me?" He doesn't wait for an answer before he starts repeating it like a mantra. "Come on, Wendy. Come for me."

Is he serious? On my back, from vaginal penetration alone?

I'm feeling great, but I am nowhere near orgasm. This is fore-play. Apparently, however, Logan expects it to be the main event. "Why don't you come first," I purr, trying to sound sensual instead of irritated. "Then you can get me off."

"Yeah, yeah, yeah," he huffs into my neck, his hips piston-ing faster and faster as his rhythm starts to falter. His breath comes fast and shallow against my skin. He whispers something that might be my name, and then he convulses above and within me, the muscles in his jaw standing out as he grits his teeth and spasms. I squeeze his body tightly between my thighs, stroking his back and neck. Pressed this close together, I can hear his pulse slowly returning to normal.

"Damn," he finally says. "That was . . ."

"Yeah," I say, stroking his sweaty hair. He rolls off me, and I sit up.

"Just give me a second," Logan says, still breathing hard as he drops his head to the pillow. There's a pause as he shifts and settles, and then he very quietly says, "Oh, fuck."

"What?"

"It broke."

For about three seconds I don't know what he means by "it," and then my stomach twists. The condom. The goddamn motherfucking rainbow-wrapped, Seabrook-branded promotion-al condom.

"Oh," I say. My guts are twisting into a French braid, but I make myself take a deep breath and let it out slowly. "Okay. Well, I guess we can deal with that tomorrow."

"All right," he says, too easily. "Do you still want me to—" He makes a gesture that I might have found crudely attractive five minutes ago, but that holds absolutely no appeal now.

"No thanks," I say. My libido has taken an abrupt nosedive.

"Word," Logan says, and rolls over, burrowing into the pillow.

I sit there quietly, listening to his breathing as it slows. The sound of the party down the hall is a dull background sound, the roar of the ocean. Above it, bright and clear, I hear a cry that fills me with an instinctive flash of joy, followed by a slow, sinking grief. It's Leah, of course, and she isn't thinking about me.

MIKE

Mike is so much drunker than he meant to be. Probably dehydrated—the heat inside the house is stifling, turning his head into a bass drum. Sweat pools in his armpits and at his hairline, drips down the crack of his ass. He can't tell what song is playing but he fucking *hates* it.

He wishes Pedro was here. He pulls out his phone, as though there's a chance it might contain a text from Pedro, which he already knows it doesn't. Everyone here is in the process of hooking up. Sam and Aurelia and Leah are slobbering on each other in the kitchen, and Leah's ex was making eyes at that goth dude, and apparently Jordy and Keith are back together, at least for the next two hours. Only Mike is pathetic and alone. No one's even looking at him. Not that he'd do anything about it if they were—he's not a cheater. But it would be nice to be seen. Noticed. To feel a little less invisible.

He opens his texts with Pedro and sees the last one he sent. *I'll miss you tonight*, read but unanswered. Looking at it sends a pang of humiliation through him. Pedro doesn't even fucking *care*, Mike thinks. And then a foreign, hideous thought: Pedro could be with another guy right now.

Shit, why not? As the image blooms in his mind, like a drop of blood staining a glass of clear water, he can't believe he's never worried about it before. Pedro lies to everyone in his life, keeps Mike a secret from his family, from his job, from his friends. Hiding the truth is something he does well, even though he claims he hates it. If he can do all that, why couldn't he be keeping something from Mike, too?

Rage, red and animal, swells in Mike's chest. The stink of his own sweat chokes him. He's in *love* with Pedro, and Pedro pretends they've never met. Won't even add him on social media. Who treats someone they love that way?

Maybe Mike isn't really Pedro's boyfriend. Maybe he's the guy on the side, and Pedro has another man he goes home to at night, a man he's with right now. That would explain why he didn't want to go to Pride with Mike. Maybe he was afraid he'd run into someone who knows his real boyfriend. Blow his whole double life wide open.

Mike tries to type *Where the fuck are you?* into his phone, but his fingers are clumsy and slippery and the letters that appear on the screen don't correspond to what he meant to write. He deletes, tries again. Sweat stings his eyes, and he rubs them with his knuckles. The keyboard swims in front of his face, refusing to resolve into something he can understand. He jabs his finger at the phone again. *Where.* Just the word *where*, that's all he needs to write. *Red*, his screen tells him.

Squeezing his eyes shut tight, Mike shakes his head. This is stupid anyway. The urgency of a moment ago is fading, and he sticks his phone back in his pocket, embarrassed. Mike trusts

Pedro. He's a good person; it's not his fault he has to hide their relationship.

As fucked-up as things have gotten in Arizona these days, no one could fault Pedro for staying closeted to protect his career. People might say any kind of shit about a gay man who teaches elementary school. And it's not like Mike didn't know what he was getting into when they started dating. Pedro was clear that he wouldn't be coming out any time soon, and he gave Mike plenty of chances to decide that was a deal-breaker. None of what Mike feels right now is Pedro's fault.

No, he realizes, the people he *should* be angry at are the ones who made Pedro feel this way, the ones who made it impossibly dangerous to be a queer adult who works with children. All the fucking Bible-thumpers, and the opportunists who exploit their fear and disgust in order to grab for more power. Like that Randall bitch up in Phoenix, telling everyone that drag queens are coming for their kids. "Lying assholes," Mike says out loud, and remembers that he's still slumped on the couch at Sam and Aurelia's when several heads swivel around to stare at him in surprise. Mike just scowls back until they all look away.

His body is a cacophony of insistent and contradicting needs, but one blares louder than the others. He needs to piss. Could go outside and pee off the porch, but Aurelia would probably bitch him out for that. She's fuckin' uptight, he thinks. He likes Aurelia, usually, but tonight the thought of her scowl if she caught him peeing in her yard makes him irrationally angry. *Cut back on the estrogen before you become an even bigger cunt*, he imagines saying to her.

A nasty laugh bursts from his chest, startling him. What a fucked-up thought. He would never say that to *anyone*, much less Aurelia. He's not usually a mean drunk. Being at a Pride party without his boyfriend is fucking with his mood in ways he never expected.

Mike pushes himself off the couch, feeling like a pinball on a tilting table as he staggers through the crowded house. He walks into a wall and goes with it, bouncing off, crashing into the opposite wall, ricocheting back and forth down the hallway. His shoulder hits a door, hard, but the pain feels rounded off and far away. Someone yells at him from the other side of the door. For a brief red moment, Mike wants to kick the door off its fucking hinges and tell whoever it is to say that to his face.

Christ, it's so hot in here. Pain thrums like a second heartbeat at the back of his neck. How much *did* he have to drink? He finally finds the bathroom and half falls through the open door, barely catching himself on the edge of the sink. That red spike of anger pierces him again, and Mike thinks about putting his fist through the wall, but the urge abates.

Instead, he does what he came here to do. Piss comes out hot, so hot it *hurts*, and Mike slams a fist into his thigh to keep from yelping from the pain. What the hell is wrong with him tonight? He stares at himself in the mirror as he zips up. His face looks alien, somehow threatening. A low, growling impulse from somewhere south of his rib cage wants to *rip it off*. Then his stomach twists and snarls, and he leans over the toilet bowl and pukes into his own piss. That comes out hot too, stinging his throat. He spits and spits into the awful swirling mess.

Finally, Mike straightens up and splashes cold water on his face. The walls seem to flex, to sweat, like a living, breathing thing. Mike needs air. He leaves the bathroom and makes his way back through the crowd, shouldering people out of the way harder than he needs to. Fuck this party, he thinks. He wishes suddenly and ferociously that he'd stayed home. He wants to be somewhere cool, somewhere quiet, just him and Pedro.

It takes him three tries to turn the knob and open the front door. A faint breeze hits his face, but it's not enough. It's just as hot out here as it was inside, even if the air is fresher. Distantly, he thinks he hears someone say, "You okay, man?" The word *okay* sounds weird and Mike says it out loud a few times. It's just two letters stuck together. It barely even means anything.

Somewhere too close, cicadas are buzzing. The noise makes him vibrate from the inside, sharpens the pain in his skull. He feels sunburned, heat radiating off his too-tight skin. His head sways from side to side, like a bear tracking a smell. There's something out here he needs, if he can just . . .

Finally he sees it: the cooler, swimming with half-melted ice and cold aluminum cans. He sticks his hand in up to the elbow and grunts low in his throat as actual *steam* rises from his skin. Fuck yeah, this is what he needs. Something cool to drink, something to quiet the cicada screech echoing behind his eye sockets. Mike grabs a can of Seabrook and presses it to the back of his neck, scoops up two more in his other hand. Then he staggers off the porch, missing the last stair and almost falling, but not dropping his cans. He needs to get away from all this noise.

For a long second, Mike doesn't remember where he is. He spins in place, searching the swell and ebb of the horizon for anything that looks familiar. Finally, his gaze crashes into his pickup truck, so black it blends into the night sky, so dusty it's part desert. It looks terribly far away and Mike's not sure he can cross the distance, but he makes his feet move in that direction anyway.

Pedro, he thinks. The truck can take him to Pedro.

But by the time he drags himself into the cab, he can't remember where he wanted to go.

CHAPTER 2

I wake up wedged into the gap between Logan's futon and the wall. I'm sweaty and my right foot is asleep, apparently because Logan crossed his ankle over mine in the night. I can't decide whether I find that endearing or annoying, but the pins and needles in my toes tip me toward irritation. Sunlight knifes through the blinds with early-morning sharpness, and beyond the guest room door the rest of Sam and Aurelia's house is quiet.

I sit up and run my fingers through my hair. I'm wearing only my underwear from last night, tacky between the legs with various fluids; there's a purplish bite mark on my left breast. My body is a collection of aches, mostly the pleasant kind acquired through fucking, but my head pounds in a not-at-all-erotic way. Worry swirls in my stomach, amorphous and sour, and for a moment I don't know why. Then I remember the broken condom.

Logan turns and snuffles on his pillow. It's the only pillow, and he slowly pushed me off it over the course of the night until I was lying flat on the futon. I feel a flash of mixed fondness and irritation. He's still gorgeous, even sleep smudged and drooling a little. I wonder if I'll see him again. I hope so.

But not now. I need to get moving before he wakes up. I don't want to be perceived this morning. I don't want to talk to anyone. I want to exist in this early-morning quiet, my grimy veil of invisibility, until I can take some Plan B and stop panicking.

I slide off the foot of the bed without waking Logan, then feel around on the pile of black clothes that makes up the guest room's floor until I find my jean skirt and tank top. Dressed, I open the door as carefully as possible and cross the hall to the bathroom.

The carnage of last night is obvious in here: a streak of what looks like vomit on the toilet seat and a latex glove in the sink, in addition to the collection of empty beer bottles and Seabrook cans stacked on the rim of the bathtub. I squat to pee, not touching the dirty porcelain, then rummage through the medicine cabinet, hoping I'll find Plan B stashed up here in a corner somewhere. Don't lots of uterus-having people keep it on hand just in case? Apparently not Sam. I do find a clean washcloth that I use to wipe under my arms and between my legs, though the latter feels like wasted effort when I pull my sex-grimed underwear back up. After a second's deliberation, I take the underwear off again and stuff it in the trash can, pushing it down until it's no longer visible.

Finally, I smear toothpaste on my finger and scrub at my gums. As I'm spitting into the sink, the door opens.

"Umm," I say, which is about the most cogent thing I can manage with minty drool running down my chin and my ex-girlfriend staring at me.

"Sorry," Leah says. She takes a step back, pulling the door closed. My heart skips stupidly. I hurry to rinse my mouth with tap water and open the door again.

"Sorry," I say, echoing her without meaning to. "I mean, you can go ahead. I was done."

She can tell when I'm flustered, and she wouldn't be Leah if she let me off the hook easily. "You're up early. Restless night, huh?"

My face gets hot. "I might have slept better if you and your girlfriends weren't being so loud."

"Didn't used to bother you," Leah says lightly. Then she walks past me into the bathroom and closes the door in my face.

I storm down the hall and find my purse on the coat rack. Beau is stretched out on the sofa, snoring, one arm flung over her face. I envy the simplicity of the hangover she'll no doubt wake up with.

The blue-white heat of the July sun feels good on my skin for an instant after I step outside, then immediately becomes unbearable. Sweat prickles at my hairline and between my thighs, and I regret discarding my underwear.

Sam and Aurelia's front yard is a semicircle of gravel with a few cactuses in planters. It's currently littered with cigarette butts and beer bottles and what I'm pretty sure is a puddle of vomit. There are still several cars parked helter-skelter on the driveway, including a black pickup truck behind my own beat-up hatchback, arranged perpendicular to my car so that there's no way for me to back out.

"Fuck," I say under my breath. I don't recognize the truck, and I hope its owner didn't drunkenly Uber home last night, leaving me indefinitely stuck here.

Walking up to the truck, I see that there's someone inside it. After a moment I realize it's Mike, the guy with the beard from last night, passed out with his face smudged on the steering wheel. From the litter of Seabrook cans on his passenger seat, it seems like he decided to party solo until he blacked out.

I knock on the window, politely, shave and a haircut. He doesn't respond. I knock a little harder, this time with the side of my fist. Mike still doesn't move, and for a moment I have dire thoughts about alcohol poisoning or choking on vomit. "Hey," I yell, banging on the metal of his driver's side door. Mike shifts in his sleep, lip curling in what looks like a sneer but would probably, if I could hear him, be a belch. He's alive, which is a relief, but his eyes still don't open.

"Dude!" I hit his door again, but it's useless. My skin feels too tight in the hot, dry air, and the sound of my fist on the car door echoes in my aching skull.

With a sigh, I turn and walk back to the house. Beau is still asleep on the sofa, and Leah is nowhere to be seen. I resist the urge to linger and listen at the door of Sam and Aurelia's bedroom, and instead go straight to Logan's room. The door is slightly open, as I left it, but I knock on it gently anyway.

Logan is still sprawled on the futon, and I have a vivid, shivery sense memory of the taste of his skin. A low ache in my belly and between my legs, like a cramp, reminds me I never got off last night, but I push that thought out of my mind and slip through the door's narrow opening into the room.

"Logan," I say softly, sitting down on the futon beside him. He snuffles and rolls over. I tap him on the shoulder.

"Huh?" He looks back at me, still two-thirds asleep or so. Squints, rubs his eyes with his knuckles, visibly struggles to focus. "Hey, you're up."

"Yeah," I say, feeling slightly embarrassed. "I was actually going to hit the road, but there's a little problem."

"Problem?" Logan blinks up at me. I notice again how deep his brown eyes are, framed by dark, soft lashes.

"My car is stuck," I say. "Someone's parked behind me, and he's passed out in his truck, so I can't get out."

Logan pushes himself up to sitting. "Yeah, okay. So you need me to get him to move?"

"If you can, that's great. Otherwise I was hoping you'd give me a ride."

"Sure, I can do that." He stretches, and I try not to get distracted by his shoulders. Or his pecs. Or . . . "Where do you live?"

"Not back to my place, actually, at least not first thing." I try to relax, fight the urge to grit my teeth. I desperately wanted to take care of this on my own, without asking for help, without ever discussing it out loud. "Can you drive me to a pharmacy?"

"On a Saturday morning? Why?"

My mouth feels dry. Has he completely forgotten? "I was hoping to pick up some Plan B."

"Oh." He nods, then considers, then says "Oh" again, with more emphasis. "Right. I spaced. Sorry."

"It's all good," I say with a levity that sounds strained even to me. "Just want to make sure I handle it."

"Yeah. Right. Totally." Logan stands up, completely naked. Reflexively, I look away. Seeing him naked now feels entirely different than it did last night. Today I feel sticky and intrusive. "You want to wait in the kitchen?" he asks, and I nod gratefully.

At the kitchen table, still piled high with pizza boxes, I scroll through my phone. My social media feeds are full of photos from last night, people laughing and dancing and flirting, all of it joyful and seemingly effortless in the way I've never figured out how to replicate. As far as I can tell, I'm not in any of the pictures. Emmy's not the only person who overindulged, I see; almost every shot includes people in the background who look on the verge of puking, or are slumped against walls like they're too shit-faced to stand. Lots of the photos feature rainbow-logo Seabrook cans, and Seabrook is reposting with abandon on its own pages.

And of course, in picture after picture there's Leah, Sam, and Aurelia: laughing, dancing, arms around each other, the glowing embodiment of all things Pride. The whole party—the whole community—revolves around them. My stomach twists. I chalk it up to drinking too much last night and needing breakfast.

"Oh, hey, Wendy," says Aurelia in surprise. I didn't even hear her enter the kitchen. "Did you sleep here?"

"Yeah," I say, and don't explain further. She cocks an eyebrow at me, a gesture of invitation, but I don't know what to say. I can't start talking to her about Logan when he might walk into the room at any moment, and I can't ask how her night went because the answer would eviscerate me. Her usually immaculate hair is a mess, and I know who fucked it up.

Aurelia keeps looking at me, expectant and confused, until I look back at my phone, feeling like an asshole. I want to be friends with her so badly, but I can't seem to find the words that would make that possible. Or maybe it's not a question of words. Maybe I'm just not the person I would need to be to feel at home here, to make casual conversation at the kitchen table with the woman who's fucking my ex. I scroll through photos without seeing them, wishing I could fold myself up smaller and smaller until I just disappeared.

Fortunately, Logan emerges a moment later, wearing a casual daytime goth ensemble: black cutoff shorts and a black band T-shirt, the name written in a font so ornate I can't even decipher it. "You ready?" he asks me. "Hey, Aurelia," he adds as an afterthought.

Aurelia nods at him. "See you later," she says, pointedly directing the comment to Logan instead of to both of us. I suppose I deserve that.

Logan's car is in the alley behind the house, protected by a fence from the chaos in the driveway. The spot where it's parked is currently in full sunlight, which means the interior of the car is three degrees cooler than spontaneous human combustion. I climb in, trying not to touch anything, making sure my skirt protects the back of my thighs from the superheated vinyl of the seat. In the close heat of the car I can smell my own body and I'm uncomfortably aware that I don't have underwear on.

"Which pharmacy you want?" Logan asks.

There are only two drugstores in San Lazaro. One is downtown, the other on the far east side. Neither is particularly convenient to our current location. "East side," I decide.

We drive in silence, less out of interpersonal awkwardness than because the blasting air conditioning is too loud to speak over. I'm grateful to it for the barrier to conversation as well as for lowering the temperature to a balmy 95 or so. There's not much traffic this morning; apparently everyone is still sleeping off last night, or simply hiding indoors from the sun.

Eastside Drug is one of the few businesses in town open twenty-four hours, but when we pull up, it looks oddly empty. The neon OPEN sign is on, but there are no cars in the lot and no movement in the windows. I glance at Logan but he doesn't return my look.

Although the heat inside Logan's car was suffocating, stepping out into the unmitigated sun feels like a slap to the face. I hurry to the door without waiting for Logan, who follows me at a sleepy pace. The door is locked. Despite the OPEN sign, there's a hand-scribbled piece of paper taped to the door that just says

BE BACK.

Those words, written so hastily the ink is smeared, give me a strange feeling. Without a subject, the sentence could be read as an assurance, but also as an entreaty. And there's no time specified—does it mean "Be back soon"? "Be back eventually"? The back of my neck prickles, sweat going cold on my skin.

Logan rattles the door handle, then cups his hands around his eyes to peer through the glass-paneled door. "Weird," he says. "The lights are on. It looks open, but . . ."

"What's that?" I catch sight of something out of place. Logan moves back and lets me press my face to the door.

Beside the far wall of the store, at an angle that's hard to see from the door, a shelf is tipped over on its side. Plastic pill bottles and cardboard boxes are strewn across the floor. I can just catch a glimpse of a spreading puddle on the carpet, something dark—cough syrup, maybe. Beyond the toppled shelf, one of the refrigerator sections that line the walls is open, its glass door hanging askew.

"It's a mess in there," I say. Logan follows my gaze and nods.

"Maybe the pharmacist went out to get cleaning stuff," he says.

"Yeah. That makes sense." In fact his explanation doesn't sit quite right with me, but I can't explain what feels off about it, so I don't try. I look for another moment at that spreading stain, which might be purple or red, and then I turn away.

"Downtown?" he asks when I slide back into the heat inside the car, just as bad as the heat outside but a slightly different texture, bludgeoning instead of flaying.

"Is that clock wrong?" I say, gesturing to the dashboard where green numbers display a few minutes past noon.

"Don't think so."

I check my phone, which agrees with Logan's car. "Huh. It feels earlier than that." I look around at the empty parking lot. Where is everyone? There's always something a little eerie about southern Arizona in the summer, when people stay out of the sun and the streets feel deserted.

Logan looks at me expectantly, and I remember that he asked a question which I haven't yet answered. "Downtown would be great," I say. "If you've got time."

"No problem," he says. "Nothing going on today until Hellrazors tonight."

I had almost forgotten that it's still Pride weekend, and there's a big drag show tonight. "Are you performing?"

"I'm the emcee." He glances at me, then flicks his eyes back to the road. "You going to be there?"

For a moment, I picture retreating to my apartment, taking my morning-after pill in the heat of the afternoon, and going to bed while the sun is still up. I imagine the quiet, the darkness, the simple relief of being alone. It would be easy to disappear. Maybe I could try making friends again in another six months.

But then I imagine Leah at the drag show, looking around and not seeing me, smiling smugly to herself at the proof that I couldn't hang. More social media photo galleries without me in them, more stories of Pride debauchery in which I'm not even a minor character. I'm tired of disappearing. I'm tired of proving Leah right: that I don't care, that I don't contribute, that I can't be bothered. I want to make a place for myself. "I'll be there for sure," I say, then repeat it to convince myself. "For sure."

"Word," Logan says. Then he asks, "So do you have any STIs?" His tone is so relaxed and conversational I don't process the actual words for a solid ten seconds.

"Oh my God," I say, staring out the window. "You can't just

ask someone that."

"Of course you can. The condom broke. We have to have the conversation," he says. "It doesn't have to be a big thing. Having an STI doesn't make you a bad person. I'm not some kind of asshole who would, like, be an asshole about it."

"No, I mean . . ." I shake my head. "I'm sure you're not. Sorry." A frank discussion about sexual health feels much more intimate than anything I did with Logan last night. I should be grateful to him for bringing it up, but instead I'm vaguely resentful. He's acting like we matter to each other, and it's making me feel guilty, because his well-being was never part of my calculations.

"Well, I get tested every three months. My last test was a month ago and it was negative. I've slept with one guy since then, but we only had oral sex and we used protection." He's so matter-of-fact and it makes me want to jump out of the car while it's still moving.

"Okay. Thanks," I say. "I don't have anything either." He's waiting for more, but I just stare out the window. I don't tell him that I got tested after I slept with Jacquie, trying to do one responsible thing, much too late, as my relationship with Leah crumbled around me, and he's the first person I've had sex with since then. It's too much, too revealing; he'd sense the bottomless pit of my sadness and need, feel himself slipping on its edge, and flee.

"I just want you to know you can talk to me about stuff like that," he says. He tries to give me an earnest, searching look, but has to look back at the road before it really has time to sink in. "I . . . Wendy?"

My heart plummets like a stone into a well, and it's not because Logan is trying to have a heartfelt conversation about trust and boundaries while the heat is fusing my ass to his passenger seat. There's a little royal-blue hybrid parked on the other side of the street, except it's not parked, really; it's only halfway pulled over, rear end still hanging into traffic, so cars in the oncoming lane have to edge around it to avoid crossing the center line. I recognize that car. Once, in a memory that will never fade no matter how much I wish it would, I had sex in that car, twisting uncomfortably to wedge my torso between the steering wheel and the girl in the driver's seat, my free hand gripping the head-rest behind her, thinking of someone else the whole time.

It's Jacquie's car, swerved off the road and abandoned. The passenger side door isn't even closed all the way.

"Shit, Logan, stop the car. Stop!"

Instead of screeching to a halt in the middle of the road like I would have done, he pulls over to the curb and parks. "Wendy, what's—"

I'm out of the car and running into the street before he has a chance to finish. Someone honks. I don't even bother to flip them off.

My mind flails, racing through the options. Jacquie doesn't live anywhere near here; I've only been to her house once, but I remember the general area. Maybe she crashed with a friend in the neighborhood after driving the drunk girl home last night. Maybe she's hooking up with someone new; there's certainly no reason she would tell me if she were. But the weird angle of the car and the open door make me feel panicky, my breath coming too fast and shallow.

The key is still in the ignition, though the car is off; the battery is probably dead. That must be why no one has stolen it. Then it occurs to me that maybe they did, and this is where it was abandoned after a joyride.

There are no obvious red flags in or around the car, no broken glass or signs of struggle. I try to push out of my head the image of Jacquie injured, stumbling out of her car and passing out in some remote arroyo.

Logan's hand on my shoulder makes me jolt. "What's going on?" he asks.

"This is Jacquie's car," I say. When he looks at me blankly, I clarify, "The girl from last night. The one who drove the drunk girl home, remember?"

"Oh, Emmy, right." He looks around as though he expects to see one or both of them emerge from one of the houses lining the street. "Does she live around here?"

"Jacquie doesn't. Does Emmy?"

"No. She's up by the mall." He points behind us, in the direction Jacquie's car was driving before it swerved. I grimace. Not only did Jacquie not make it home last night, she might not have even made it to her first destination.

"Did you hear from Emmy since last night?" I ask. Logan checks his phone, but he's already shaking his head.

"I'll text her now," he says. "You want to check with Jacquie?"

I bite my lip, hesitating. Jacquie and I don't exactly have a texting-to-make-sure-she-got-home-safe relationship. Assuming she's all right, she won't be thrilled to hear from me.

I look at the car again. That passenger door hanging open, like a jaw hanging slack. The darkness inside a throat waiting to swallow.

I take out my phone and pull up my text thread with Jacquie, trying not to look at any of the previous messages we've exchanged. All of them are explicit, and all dated before my break-up with Leah. I hurry to type something innocuous and shove my phone in my pocket again.

Logan and I look at each other for a few moments, waiting. Neither of our phones buzz.

"What should we do?" I ask. The thought of calling the cops crosses my mind, but I don't suggest it.

He chews on his lower lip. It's dry and chapped, flecks of last night's lipstick still clinging to the dead skin. "Ask around, I guess? We can go back to Sam and Aurelia's and see if anyone there heard from them after they left."

I nod. We make the drive in tense, sweaty silence.

Mike's car is still in the driveway, trapping mine against the fence that separates the front yard from the back. Once again, I approach his driver's side window. He's still apparently asleep, now with his head tipped back. A crust of something vile clings to the corners of his mouth. Worry creeps up my throat. It's terribly hot, and must be hotter in the cab of his truck, with no air conditioning turned on. Could he have gotten heatstroke?

"Mike," I shout, too freaked out to worry about sounding polite.

Mike's head snaps up and he glares at me balefully. His eyes are painfully red. Instinctively, I jump back from the window. I jump a second time when he whips his head forward, crashing his forehead into the glass between us with an audible crack.

"Holy shit," says Logan.

Mike shouts something I can't make out with his windows closed, but I can hear his voice well enough to know that it's distorted with rage. This is not a hangover or heatstroke. Whatever's wrong with Mike—and clearly there's something wrong—is altogether stranger.

He yells again. I'm pretty sure I see his lips form the word *hello*, but that doesn't make sense. Why would he be screaming "hello" over and over, the word flying from his mouth like a threat?

As he shouts at me, he fumbles in his passenger seat, searching for something. My heart throbs with sudden, incoherent dread. It's Arizona; even a gay man might have a gun in his pickup truck.

I'm relieved to see Mike find his keys and shove one into the ignition. My relief fades when his engine roars to life and he slams the truck into reverse, tires spitting gravel and dust as he lurches backward. Mike's bloodshot eyes lock on mine. Then he spins the steering wheel, and the car leaps toward me like an animal pouncing.

I throw myself backward, slamming an elbow into Logan's solar plexus because I didn't realize he was so close behind me. We both land on our asses, coughing from gravel dust and exhaust and shock. For a moment I'm afraid Mike is going to reverse again and I won't be able to get out of the way in time. Instead, he burns rubber, adding a nasty, acrid smell to the day's oppressive heat, and screeches off down the road.

CHAPTER 3

Logan scrambles to his feet, but I just sit there for a moment, waiting for the flood of adrenaline to subside. My pulse is racing like a frightened jackrabbit. My chest hurts. The back of my throat burns. Slowly, carefully, I stand up and brush myself off.

"Well," I say, my voice shaking, "at least I can move my car now."

"Motherfucker," Logan says, and continues muttering curses and blasphemies as he follows me to the door. By the time we get there, Sam is already opening it from the inside, her eyes big.

"What the hell was that sound?" she asks.

"Mike trying to mow us down with his truck," I say, forcing a laugh I don't feel. Beneath the crushing heat, I feel bone-cold and scared. I don't understand the fury I saw in Mike's face, the unhinged aggression. I wonder if sleeping half the day away in the hot car did something strange to his brain.

"Holy shit, are you kidding?" Sam gestures us inside.

"Maybe he woke up and realized he was late for something," Logan says. I'm not sure if he's attempting a joke or an actual explanation of Mike's behavior, but either way, it falls flat.

"Are you guys okay? Did you get hurt?" Sam asks. She holds out her arms like she's welcoming me in for a hug. For a flicker of a second, I feel as soft as warm wax in the glow of her concern, and I'm tempted to lean into her and cry. But as I step through the door into the living room I see Leah and Aurelia sprawled on the couch. Aurelia is leaning back against Leah's chest, and they're both looking at something on Aurelia's phone. Beau is nowhere to be seen; she must have woken up and left while Logan and I were out.

"No thanks," I say, trying to clamp down whatever momentarily loosened in my chest. "I should get going."

"Wait, Wendy, the other thing," Logan says. The bizarre run-in with Mike chased everything else from my brain momentarily, but now I remember that we came back here to find out if anyone has heard from Jacquie.

But I don't want to say Jacquie's name in front of Leah. I don't want to see the way she'll look at me, hear the veiled insinuation in whatever questions she asks. I shoot a look at Logan, hoping he'll take charge of the conversation.

"Have any of you guys heard from Emmy today?" he asks. "Or . . . what's her name?"

I sigh inwardly. "Jacquie."

"You two are looking for Jacquie?" Leah asks, smirking a little, like I knew she would. God, she's so smug and it's unbearable. I want to kiss that irritating sneer off her face. I wish we'd never seen Jacquie's car today. I wish I'd never even heard of Jacquie.

But that's not fair. Jacquie didn't make the decision to blow up my relationship. And she might be in trouble. I force myself to ignore the undertone in Leah's words.

"We saw her car," I say, looking back toward Sam. "It was sort of swerved off the road along Mesa Street on the east side, but not really parked, and the door was hanging open."

"She gave Emmy a ride home last night, or at least she was supposed to, but we don't know if either of them made it home and they're not texting us back," Logan says.

"That's weird," Sam says.

"Should we call the cops?" I ask, finally giving voice to what's been in the back of my mind since seeing the car.

"I don't think so," says Sam. "It hasn't been long enough to file a missing person report, so all they'd do is tell us to call around and ask their friends, which we can do ourselves. And I don't feel good about inviting cops to Emmy's neighborhood." Aurelia frowns but doesn't argue.

"Well, what, then?" Logan asks. "Make a flyer with their pictures and hang it on telephone poles?" Once again, I'm not sure whether that's an actual suggestion or if he just has a bone-dry sense of humor and a killer deadpan.

"We ask around ourselves, like I said," says Sam. "Emmy's roommate is Kestrel, right? Does anyone have their number? They'd know whether she made it home."

My phone buzzes. I glance down. "Oh, shit, it's from Jacquie."

I've texted her four times this morning, asking a string of questions. The last one was "Are you coming to the drag show tonight?" I don't know why I asked that—perhaps as an attempt to pretend this was a normal Pride weekend text, and not a thinly veiled panic attack. All Jacquie sent is three words that could be read as a reply to the last question, albeit a cryptic one.

See you yes

It feels weird and wrong, the same way the sign at the pharmacy rubbed me the wrong way, making the hair on my arms prickle. *Be back*. A promise or a threat?

I read it out loud to the group. Leah rolls her eyes. Aurelia and Sam look relieved. Logan scowls.

"Okay, but where *is* she? And where's Emmy?" he asks.

"Maybe they hooked up," Leah says. "Sleeping it off together."

"If they hooked up, Jacquie's a fucking asshole," Logan says sharply.

"Yeah," says Aurelia. "You didn't see Emmy when she left last night, Leah. The girl was obliterated. Nobody had any business having sex with her in that condition."

"Jacquie wouldn't do that," I say reflexively. I regret it as soon as I say the words. How do I know what Jacquie would do, really? Does getting her off a few times give me some kind of insight into her character?

"Jacquie wouldn't do that," Leah repeats, echoing my tone exactly. It sounds like she's agreeing with me, but I know she's actually mocking me.

I sigh. "Whatever. She's alive, so whatever. I'm sure it's fine. We'll see her tonight." I turn for the door, my whole body aching like I've run a marathon as the adrenaline from dodging Mike's truck drains out of my system.

"Wendy?" Logan takes a step, as if he's going to walk me to the door. And what, kiss me goodbye? There's no way.

"I'll see you all later," I say, and escape into the unforgiving sun.

I make it halfway home before I remember my other interrupted errand. It's a brief inner struggle—I really, really want to go home and sleep—but finally I convince myself to turn around. The downtown pharmacy, thankfully, is open. Even better, it's empty and dim inside compared to the blazing early afternoon, and the air conditioning is cranked to polar. I sigh with relief as I feel the sweat on my skin sublimate to ice.

The man behind the pharmacy counter is young, maybe younger than me, and white, with sandy blond hair. "Can I get some Plan B?" I ask. After only a few seconds in the store, I have goosebumps.

He arches his eyebrows at me. They're extremely well-shaped eyebrows; I hope he tips his aesthetician well. Otherwise, he offers no response.

"Plan B?" I ask again. "Uh, levo-something. The morning-after pill."

"I can't give you that," the pharmacist says.

"Excuse me?" I ask. He doesn't elaborate further. "Um, why not?" I vaguely remember hearing something on some TV show about how Plan B is less effective above a certain weight. Shouldn't he at least ask what I weigh before making that call? The idea of being deemed too fat for birth control, on sight, makes my face flush. Then I get angry at myself for being embarrassed about my weight; Lizzo would be disappointed in me. The downward spiral of negative emotional feedback sucks me down so quickly I almost don't hear the pharmacist's response.

"I don't sell the morning-after pill," he says. "It's against my religious convictions, and I have the constitutional right to refuse to offer it."

That's so far from what I was expecting that it takes me several seconds to process the words, and several more to formulate a coherent response. "What?" I mean to sound indignant but my voice comes out shaky.

"I refuse to sell Plan B," he repeats. His tone is carefully neutral, but I could swear there's a glint of a smirk at the corner of his mouth. I wonder how many times this scene has played out, how many people he's denied the medication and the peace of mind that comes with it, enjoying his power to withhold them both.

"Well, is there someone else back there I can buy it from?"

"The other pharmacist called in sick," he says, and now I have no doubt he's holding back a smile. "You're stuck with me."

Fury blooms inside me. Unfortunately, while some people are galvanized by anger, I am dissolved by it. The angrier I am, the more likely I am to cry.

"That sucks," I say, trying to keep my voice steady, already knowing I'm doomed to fail. "That's really fucked-up. That's— you're supposed to help people." I try to scrape together a cogent argument but I can feel the words melting into nothing at the back of my throat. "That's fucked-up," I say again.

"Ma'am, there's no need to be verbally abusive," he says, absolutely delighted with himself. "I have a constitutional right to not sell a product that violates my beliefs."

If I were Leah or Samantha, I'd challenge him, get up in his face and tear apart his inconsistencies and hypocrisies until he either sold me the goddamn pills or turned around and fled. If I were another, better kind of person, I'd at least ruin his day as much as he's ruining mine. I'd call the manager of the pharmacy, make a scene, file a lawsuit, end up on the news. I should do all those things. I want to.

But I'm just me, meek little nothing Wendy who runs away from her problems instead of dealing with them, so I say "Thanks a lot" with all the scorn I can muster and make it back to my car before I start crying.

By the time I get home my brain feels like it's being squeezed through a juicer by the tears, the anger, the heat. Everything above my shoulders hurts. I stumble into the shower, turning the water as cold as it will go—about the same temperature as the layer of sweat already coating my body.

Scrubbing myself with a washcloth and some agave shower gel feels like heaving a boulder uphill, and by the time I'm finished I'm too tired to wash my hair. I tell myself it's fine, that shampoo is terrible for you anyway for reasons I can't remember. Instead of toweling dry, I sprawl out still wet across my bed and let the ceiling fan's breeze on my damp skin cool me off the way the shower didn't.

I lie there for a while trying to fall asleep, but even as my body melts with exhaustion, my brain refuses to turn off. It's buzzing with anger at the pharmacist, shame at my own passivity, worry for Jacquie, frustration with Leah. I roll over, unable to get comfortable. I'm a symphony of aches: the bruise beside my nipple, the diffuse sense of impact lingering in my tailbone. My thighs are sore from riding Logan.

Despite everything I feel a tingle of excitement about seeing him again. The sex wasn't amazing, but he made me feel wanted. I forgot how intoxicating that can be. By the end, with Leah, every touch hummed with resentment and tension, and every fuck was about proving something. With Jacquie it was just sad, and wrong, and sexy in the way that sad and wrong things can be. But Logan didn't have all that emotional baggage. He was simple—or at least, sex with him was simple. Maybe next time it could even be good.

I slide a hand down between my thighs and idly consider masturbating, but I can't settle on a fantasy. The visual in my mind flickers from Logan to Leah to Buffy the Vampire Slayer without ever coming into focus.

Instead, I grab my phone and scroll through social media. Leah has shared a post from the Seabrook corporate account hyping up the drag show tonight. I scowl at the sight of the rainbow logo. For a moment, I contemplate a spiteful reply. I actually type out *If Seabrook cares so much about the queer community, why are they handing out shitty condoms that break?* but then I delete it.

I want to go home, I think. It's a familiar thought, well-worn and involuntary, like a song that gets stuck in my head sometimes. There's no image attached to the words, because there's nowhere that actually feels like home to me. I feel no nostalgia for Tucson or the Midwest or, God forbid, my parents' house, which looms in my memory like the gates of hell. Home is where, when you have to go there, they never let you escape again. I wish I had something else to yearn for.

Auburn shadows are starting to creep across my room from the west-facing window. I roll onto my side to gaze out at the sky as sunset approaches, dazzling the sky with pink and gold streaks. For a moment, I let myself be still and breathe in the simple pleasure of it. When I moved to southern Arizona, a girl raised in Michigan and distrustful of the desert, the first thing I fell in love with was the sunsets.

Somehow the day has melted away in a long, sultry swirl of worry and waiting. I haven't really rested, or accomplished anything other than lying in the heat so long I started to sweat again. It's Saturday night, and I'm supposed to be young and footloose in the never-ending summer. I have to get dressed for another party.

CHAPTER 4

LAST YEAR

"Hey, Wendy."

I snapped my head around, remembering the drinks I was supposed to be making. "Just another second," I said guiltily, but my coworker Kianna was smiling.

"No worries," she said. "It's not that busy. You could even clock out early if you just want to sit and listen."

It was open mic night at Groundhogs, the coffee shop where I'd worked for the two months I'd lived in San Lazaro. The place was as crowded as it ever got. Open mic night was great for tips, I'd discovered, but that wasn't the only reason I liked it.

Outside, the air was almost cool, a faint breeze carrying the smell of orange blossoms. The blossoming desert made me feel strange, giddy and romantic. This was my first spring in the Sonoran Desert, but I instinctively understood what a delicate thing it was, a slender borderland of a season almost immediately burned away by the heat of oncoming summer. I had been crying a lot in the last week or so, and masturbating a lot, too. The sudden onslaught of feelings was a little overwhelming, but preferable to the numbness I'd felt my first few weeks in San Lazaro. Like the town's namesake, I was ready to emerge from my tomb.

Kianna moved past me and began steaming the milk for the decaf latte I'd spaced out on. As the machine hissed, she asked in an undertone, "Is it Ashlynn?"

"What? Is who what?" My face went red, which must have confirmed Kianna's suspicion, even though it wasn't quite accurate.

"Just curious who you can't stop staring at." She flashed a sly grin, then clasped a hand over her heart and gave an exaggerated, longing sigh. "Ashlynn's a cutie, I feel you."

Ashlynn, the host of the open mic, was indeed cute, a round-faced woman with a bubbly, effusive energy. She seemed genuinely thrilled by every song or poem that was shared at her open mic, and always encouraged newcomers to sign up. I liked her a lot, although we'd never had a conversation that went deeper than her kombucha order. But I wasn't nursing a secret crush on her.

The crowd that attended the Groundhogs open mic had surprised me when I first started working there. I hadn't expected to find much in the way of LGBTQ community in the small city of San Lazaro, about which I knew nothing besides recognizing its name from Seabrook seltzer cans: BREWED WITH PRIDE IN SAN LAZARO, ARIZONA. Ashlynn's open mic, however, brought in a crowd in which visibly queer women predominated. Maybe the draw was Ashlynn herself, her long black hair shaved on one side, the T-shirt she often wore that said NOT GAY AS IN HAPPY, BUT TWO-SPIRIT AS IN FUCK COLUMBUS. Or maybe it was just the innate sapphic predilection for acoustic guitars and spoken-word poetry. Either way, if I'd wanted to become emotionally entangled with a woman, there were plenty of prospects in the room that night—but none of them were the object of my affection either.

In fact, the reason I couldn't stop staring across the room at the tiny stage—just big enough for a microphone stand and a stool—was the open mic itself. I did have an unrequited crush that spring, but it wasn't on a woman. It was on words.

I'd dropped out of the MFA program at the University of Arizona after a single semester, for the most obvious and embarrassing reason imaginable: I'd slept with one of my professors. My cohort had gone out drinking and I'd tagged along, trying desperately to appear more sociable, since in my first month of the program I'd made zero friends. Our seminar leader, Tyler "Call me Ty" Swain, dropped in as we were finishing the first round. Flirting always came easier to me than generic socializing; by the end of the night I still didn't have any friends, but I did have a Yale Younger Poets award winner in my bed, as well as a deeper understanding of why some women fake orgasms.

After that, workshops became unspeakably awkward, not because I had unresolved feelings for Ty but because he seemed to *want* me to. He kept giving me lingering, pitying looks, as though I were some virginal undergrad and not almost thirty years old. I was uncomfortable, and it showed in the work I submitted for class. When Ty eviscerated one of my poems in front of the entire cohort, demanding to know why I wouldn't "go deeper" and "get vulnerable," I sat there silent while my face flared sunburn red.

Writing poetry became a chore, then a misery. I stopped going to class, ignored emails from Ty and my advisor, and finally quit the program. Without my student loans, I couldn't afford my apartment in Tucson, which was how I ended up here. And in the two months I'd lived in San Lazaro so far, I hadn't written a word. So yes, I probably was staring at Ashlynn with yearning, just not the kind Kianna assumed.

I did, however, take her up on the offer to clock out. The stage end of the room was crowded, but I found a chair shoved slightly away from the nearest table and slipped into it as unobtrusively as possible. A woman at the table, blond and pink cheeked like a punk rock milkmaid, glanced over and smiled at me. I smiled back with my lips pressed tight together.

"All right, that was beautiful!" Ashlynn yelled as a performer left the stage. The audience cheered, caught up in her enthusiasm. "Up next, please welcome Leah!"

At the table beside me, the blond and her date, a taller woman in a jean jacket with the sleeves ripped off, whistled and hollered. "Yeah! Let's go Leah!"

The woman who stepped up to the mic was short, fat, and gorgeous, with pristine pale skin and spiky pink hair. Her voice was sweet with a little rasp to it when she announced, "This poem is dedicated to Titania Randall." Someone in the crowd booed, and Leah laughed and pointed at them. "Hell yeah! Fuck that ghoul!" I wished I knew who Titania Randall was.

Leah's poem wasn't the sort of thing I'd ordinarily read, or the sort that we discussed in my MFA program. It was strident and polemical and laced with profanity, a ferocious attack on, as far as I could tell, censorship of queer books. I remembered reading something online about a state senator trying to remove LGBTQ books from public school libraries and wondered if that was Randall. Mostly, though, I just stared at Leah, at her velvety purple lipstick and her visible cleavage. When she was done, I cheered right along with the women at the table.

"She's a powerhouse, isn't she?" the blond asked.

I blushed a little and nodded. "She's great. Do you know her?"

"You're either a hetero or you're new in town," said the taller, dark-haired woman. "Everyone knows Leah."

"New," I said quickly. Perish the thought that a hot girl's friends might think I was straight. "I just moved here from Tucson. But I haven't seen her at the open mic before."

"Yeah, she's not so much of a *listener*," the blond said with something like affectionate scorn. "She only comes when she has something to say."

I realized I was looking at Leah again without remembering when my gaze had drifted. "Seems like she has a lot to say." Despite being focused on Leah, I was aware of the two women beside me exchanging a knowing glance.

They hollered again when Leah finished her piece and made her way back toward our table, swinging her wide hips effortlessly through the crowd without bumping into anyone. She raised her eyebrows at me, and I flushed as I realized I must have stolen her chair.

"Sorry," I said quickly. "I can just—"

"Or I can sit in your lap," Leah said, causing me to forget the rest of my sentence.

The blond cackled at my bewilderment, but she didn't seem to be mocking me. "Fuck's sake, Leah," she said. "Don't harass our new friend. Just get another chair." Her more taciturn companion rolled her eyes and stood up, pushing her own chair toward Leah. Leah dragged it closer to me before she sat down, so our knees almost touched.

"Your poem was great," I said in a rush.

She smiled at me. "Thanks. You here by yourself?" Her tone wasn't suggestive, but it made me press my thighs together anyway.

"Yeah. Well, no. I mean, I work here." Under the table where she couldn't see, I dug my fingernails into my palms as hard as I hated myself.

"Thanks for clarifying," she said, still smiling. "I'm Leah, by the way. I guess you already met Samantha and Aurelia."

"I'm Wendy." At this point, I was unspeakably relieved that I didn't fuck up telling her my name.

She nodded toward the stage, where a woman a few years younger than me was somehow singing and beatboxing at the same time. "So you decided to come over and scope out the weirdos who invaded your workplace?"

"No, I'm a writer." The words—defensive, reflexive—popped out before I could reconsider them.

Leah's smile widened. "Yeah? Did you sign up to read?" She said it like she knew I hadn't. "I bet Ashlynn could squeeze you in if you go ask."

I shook my head. "I don't really, uh, in public."

Her rich violet lips pursed in exaggerated disappointment. "That's too bad. I thought you seemed like someone with an interesting perspective. Guess I'll never know."

"Maybe next week," I said, not too horny to understand that I was being baited, but definitely too horny to object. "If you have time to swing by."

Leah nodded in satisfaction and sat back in her chair, turning her attention back to the stage. As she shifted her weight, her knee touched my thigh. The tiny, soft hairs on her unshaved legs prickled against my own vulnerable skin, and I suppressed a shiver, though the room was warm with voices and bodies.

That night, I went home and wrote a poem for the first time in three months. It was much too sexy to share onstage, so I wrote another one, which was even sexier. Spring was really getting to me.

Leah didn't show up for the open mic the following week, although Samantha and Aurelia did. I steeled myself and read my poems anyway. My hands shook so hard I was afraid the paper rustling would drown out my voice. When I sat back down, breathing like I'd just run a 5K, Sam shrieked my name and hugged me. I was startled, but still leaned into her embrace. She smelled like sweat, in a nice way.

"We were gonna go dancing after this, do you want to come to the club with us?" she asked.

"There's a gay club in San Lazaro?"

There wasn't, as it turned out; we had to drive the forty-five minutes to Tucson, the two of them in my car because they'd come to the coffee shop on Aurelia's motorcycle. Samantha commandeered my aux cable and played obscure lesbian folk music, keeping the conversation moving at the same time. Her enthusiasm overcame my nerves and Aurelia's apparent natural reticence.

"How long have you two been together?" I asked, knowing that every happy couple likes to tell the story of their happiness.

"Since high school," Samantha said, twisting around to grab Aurelia's hand in the back seat.

"Wow," I said, wistful at both the answer and the intimacy of their touch. It wasn't that I wanted what they had, exactly, but that I couldn't even imagine feeling that physically comfortable with another person. "I wasn't even out in high school. That's so cool."

"Neither were we," Aurelia said. "Back then I was supposed to be a boy, so it was all very heterosexual and normal."

I hadn't realized Aurelia was trans, but I swallowed down

the impulse to say so, knowing that I *never would have guessed, you're so pretty* is only a compliment of the most backhanded sort. "Oh, wild," I said instead.

"When Aurelia finally worked up the nerve to tell me she was a girl, all afraid I was going to break up with her, I was like, oh, thank God, because I'm gay as fuck," Sam reminisced, laughing.

Aurelia picked up the thread of the story with the ease of long practice. "We didn't come out to anyone else until college, but it was so much easier when we both knew," she said.

"I wore a suit to our wedding, since Aurelia had to wear one to prom," Sam said. "Fair's fair."

I nodded, suffused with incoherent yearning. I didn't even know anyone I had gone to high school with anymore. What was it like to love someone for that long?

Later that night, after tequila shots and lots of Rihanna, Sam pushed me against the sink in the all-gender bathroom and kissed me. Then she went back out to the dance floor to find Aurelia while I locked myself in a stall and cried, unable to explain exactly why. After splashing cold water on my face, I drove them home like nothing happened. Samantha invited me into their house, but I just bit my lip and looked away until they shrugged and went inside without me.

Once I started reading my poems at the open mic, I didn't want to stop. I started carrying a notebook around with me again, the way I had in grad school. Back then the little Moleskine had felt like a weight dragging me down, fraught with the gravity of expectations, but now it was an escape. I was writing for the fun of it again. I switched my schedule around so I didn't have to work during open mic nights and could devote my full attention to the other writers and musicians, scribbling down stray words or lines from their readings like gleaning seeds for my own poems.

It was another month before I saw Leah again, not at the coffee shop this time. Samantha, deeply committed to her project of turning me into a social person, had invited me out for drinks at the intimidatingly named Hellrazors. The bar turned out to be populated by a confusing blend of older bearded dudes and younger femme queers, all apparently united by their love of motorcycles.

I spotted Leah immediately, though her hair was now platinum blond. Without giving myself a chance to hesitate, I walked straight up to her.

"Hey, I owe you a thanks," I said. Although I was irritated that she'd bailed on coming back to the open mic, I was still grateful her teasing had gotten me to start writing again.

Before I had a chance to clarify any of that, though, Leah smirked and looked me up and down. "Usually girls don't say that to me until after we've fucked."

I just stood there looking at her for some unquantifiable amount of time. I could hear myself blinking. She was just as beautiful as the first time we'd met, all soft curves in a tight black dress and combat boots. Distantly, I was aware that this would be a good time to say something charming and sexy in return, but first I needed to unplug and restart my brain.

The universe had mercy and Sam noticed me. "Wendy, you made it! You remember Leah," she added.

"Vividly," I managed to say, and Samantha gave me a quizzical look that shifted quickly into amused understanding. Leah was still smirking at me, but now I finally managed to smile back.

Aurelia bought a round of shots and Samantha piloted the conversation, but Leah and I just kept on looking at each other. I barely followed what anyone was saying all night, including myself. All that mattered was the second, silent dialogue Leah and I were having through eye contact, the excuses we kept making to touch each other. It was as though every look was an unspoken agreement, every gesture a promise.

And by the time we fell asleep, well past the smeared horizon of midnight, we had kept them all, and more.

CHAPTER 5

Downtown San Lazaro is only about three blocks by two blocks, but it gets busy enough on a Saturday night that I have to park two streets down from Hellrazors and walk. I wince inwardly when I see a handful of protesters swarming outside the bar. I try not to look at their signs—it's always the same transphobic, homophobic garbage—but I can tell they're professionally printed, not homemade. Someone is bankrolling them. The thought makes me feel powerless and ill, so I shove it aside and keep my head down, humming to block out whatever they shout at me until I make it through the door.

Hellrazors, thankfully, is always too loud, a place you go when you want to pick someone up without all the trouble of talking to them. As I walk in, Donna Summer is blasting at ear-splitting volume, and there's a drag queen on the stage in bell bottoms and a crocheted halter top. The music and aesthetic are so out of tune with the biker-dyke decor, it makes me smile.

I mouth a hello at the bouncer, a trans guy named Glen who's about five foot three and nearly as wide, every inch of it solid muscle. I haven't been here in a while, but Glen and I were friend-ly when I used to come with Leah. Tonight he stares through me, ignoring my greeting and my proffered driver's license. I try not to feel stung as I walk past him.

Behind the bar is a list of drink specials in rainbow chalk: colorful shots, cocktails named after pop stars, and of course the requisite $2 Seabrooks. I order an IPA and enjoy the little nod of appreciation I receive from the bartender, a woman with a sleek bleach-blond mullet.

Drink in hand, I look around for a place to stand where I won't be in anyone's way. I came here mostly for Logan, but of course he's backstage and I won't actually talk to him until the show is over. I see a handful of people I recognize from the party last night or from other parties in the distant past. I wonder if Mike will be here. The idea of seeing him makes my stomach twist, but at least then I'd know he isn't passed out somewhere with heatstroke or worse.

Jacquie said she'd see me tonight, so I scan the crowd, trying to find her or Emmy. If either of them is here, I don't see them.

After a minute, I do see Leah. There's a table over by the wall, next to the ATM, with a bunch of Pride merchandise: bro-chures, T-shirts, fanny packs, all of it spangled with the rainbow Seabrook logo. Leah, Sam, Aurelia, and a black-haired guy I vaguely recognize are sitting behind the table, schmoozing with whoever happens by. A blond woman in a Seabrook shirt perch-es on the edge of the table, holding a clipboard. I could join them, but I go the other way, into the anonymous crush of the crowd.

The weight of bodies and the smell of sweat and a hundred different perfumes and colognes press in on me from every side. It's both scary and comforting. I feel like no one at all, like the molecules of what I think of as Wendy could diffuse into the crowd and be absorbed by it. For a moment, I close my eyes and let the human current carry me along.

"Wendy." I feel more than hear the name, spoken close to my ear in a hot breath like an unwelcome caress. I turn and find Jacquie right beside me.

Relief pangs through me at the sight of her, but it's followed by new unease. Jacquie's eyes are wide and strange, her hair a mess. There's mascara smeared and crumbling at the corners of her eyes, her lipstick is peeling off, and I'm pretty sure she's wearing the same clothes she left Sam's in last night.

"Are you okay?" I ask. "We saw your car on the side of the road this morning."

Jacquie runs a hand over her mouth, as if trying to scrub away a bad taste. "Oh, I'm okay," she says. She smiles at me, but the smile widens and widens until it's just bared teeth. A shiver goes through me and I try to step backward, but only succeed in moving about an inch before I run into the person behind me. Jacquie pokes the tip of her tongue between her teeth, like she's mocking me. "I am. Okay."

"So what happened to your car?"

Instead of answering, Jacquie closes the tiny space I've put between us. She raises her hand to touch my hair. I can smell her body, above the throng of odors that makes up the rest of the crowd. She smells hot and sour and coppery, like blood.

"Okay," she says again, close to my face. It's her breath, I realize. Her breath smells like she's been eating raw meat. Like there's still blood congealing on her tongue.

"Jacquie, what . . ."

"I am," she says, and places two fingers across my lips. I flinch, but she stays with me, hooking her fingers into my mouth. They're feverishly hot and taste like earth. She tugs on my lower lip until I yank my head away. It's not flirtatious, the way she's touching me—not sexy or playful. It's like she's feeling around in the dark, groping for a touchstone, for some object that will save her from being utterly lost. "Stop it," I say quietly. She touches my hair again, rakes her hand through it roughly, digs her fingernails into my scalp. "Jacquie, stop," I say louder. I grab her wrist and twist out from under her grasp.

"Stop," she says back, her face falling. She steps backward, elbowing someone out of her way. The crowd parts around her, then closes again. My stomach churns. I need to get away from Jacquie, I can't stand her touching me for another minute, but I also feel like I've abandoned her. Something is clearly very wrong, and now I've sent her reeling off into the dark, loud, hot crowd, alone.

I snake between bodies until I reach the wall, where the air is cooler and less occupied. I've managed to emerge not far from the Pride committee's table. The blond woman is still there, wearing head-to-toe Seabrook paraphernalia, but I barely look at her. Leah and Sam have their heads together, giggling at a private joke, while Aurelia watches them with an air of possessive contentment. My stomach twists, some feral mix of envy and grief.

Lost in tunnel vision, I'm so startled when someone bumps into me that I almost fall over. I turn and see a short, stocky person with curly hair, staggering along with one hand on the wall to hold them up. Their eyes are mostly closed; I'm not sure they even realize they ran into me. Instead of protesting, I move away from the wall and let them pass. The curly-haired person keeps walking, dragging their hand along the wall. Something about their unsteady, somnambulant gait makes me feel queasy. It reminds me of the faraway look in Jacquie's eyes.

I look around the room again, this time not skimming for

faces I recognize but taking in the whole scene. Something is off. Throughout the audience, I see points where the organic movement of the crowd is interrupted, like sharp rocks jutting from a stream. People with vacant eyes collide and stagger, seemingly oblivious to their surroundings. It could just be drunkenness, but there's something disconcerting about it. Even if they're sloppy to the point of falling down, these people don't look *happy*. They look lost inside themselves, ricocheting off each other without connecting. They look how I feel.

"Hi! I love your outfit!"

It's the blond woman from the Pride committee table, who has gotten very close to me without my noticing. I stare at her for a long moment. "I'm Courtney," she adds. "I'm a brand ambassador for Seabrook."

She looks vaguely familiar. I'm pretty sure I've either walked her dog or tutored her children. Or maybe I just recognize her from social media, where I saw her commenting on Leah's posts about Pride events. The memory ties a little knot of jealousy in my stomach. Courtney is very pretty in a sleek, greyhound-ish sort of way. I don't really know what a brand ambassador does, but it makes sense that she is one. "Cool," I lie.

"Can I ask you a couple of questions about your favorite Seabrook beverages?" she asks brightly, holding up her phone to show me what appears to be a multiple-choice quiz on the screen.

"Oh, I'm more of a beer drinker," I tell her, holding up the bottle in my hand and trying to step around her. She angles herself so she's still in front of me.

"Well, maybe you just haven't found the right Seabrook yet," she says. "We've just introduced three new flavors. Can I offer you a free sample?"

"Wendy, hey," Leah says, sidling between us. "Courtney, this is Wendy. She's not really your target demographic."

Courtney shoots Leah a dark look that seems disproportionate to the offense of a spon-con cock block, and drifts off into the crowd.

"God, who let the straights in here?" I say as I follow Leah back to the table and drop into the empty chair beside her. I mean it as a joke to lighten the tension, but it comes out too hard and mean.

"Courtney's pretty chill," Leah says. "She's been our main point person with Seabrook. She—" Abruptly, perhaps thinking of the argument that erupted the last time we talked about Seabrook, she cuts herself off.

"Hey," Aurelia says to me, her voice gentle. "You okay?"

"I saw Jacquie," I say.

"Oh, good," says Aurelia. "That's a relief." She sees the hesitation on my face. "No?"

"She was really weird," I say slowly. I wait for Leah to make a snide comment about Jacquie, but she's silent.

"Weird how?" Sam asks. "If she drove off the road this morning, she might have gotten hurt. Did she seem like she has a concussion?"

"Maybe." I like that explanation. A concussion is real, tangible, treatable. "She was saying things . . . she wasn't making sense. Is that a symptom?"

Aurelia starts to ask another question, but the sound of feedback from the stage distracts me. Another performance has ended, and Logan—no, Dahlia DePravity—is at the microphone. She's stunning, close to seven feet tall in her platform boots, wearing black lace lingerie and a Bride of Frankenstein wig. "Thank you so much, sweethearts," she drawls, her lips shining beetle black in the spotlight. I think about catching one of those full, soft lips between my teeth.

Beside me, Leah snorts softly, a puff of air across my cheek. I glance to the side and see her knowing stare. Clenching my jaw, I stare back at her, eyebrows raised. *What*, I think loudly in her direction, *you're the only one who gets to move on?*

Not that I've moved on from Leah. Not that I ever will. But that doesn't mean I can't enjoy myself.

Dahlia is thanking some of the Pride sponsors. There's a big cheer when she mentions Seabrook. "Everyone's a fan of cheap booze," I say wryly. As I'd hoped, it makes Leah smirk.

"Can't help but notice you're here in the land of the corporate sellouts," she says. "Did you decide it was worth compromising your integrity and attending a Seabrook-sponsored event just to check out Logan's ass in heels?"

"Maybe," I say. "But at least I'm not drinking that stuff."

"Oh, God, me neither," she says. "I would do anything for Pride, but I won't do that." I laugh. Is this the first time since we broke up that Leah and I have shared a laugh? The moment feels sweet and fragile, a wisp of cotton candy that could dissolve any second. I let it melt on my tongue.

"And now, my delectable darlings," Dahlia purrs into the microphone. There's a slur in her voice beyond her usual affected drawl, and I wonder how much she's had to drink. She doesn't sound sloppy, just relaxed. I think about the taste of rum and Diet Coke and lipstick.

But as Dahlia's about to announce the next performer, a can comes flying from the audience and crashes into the brick wall behind the stage. It lands on the stage and spins in a mad circle, spraying foam. I recognize the rainbow Seabrook logo.

"What the *fuck*," Logan yelps, loud enough that I can hear him even though he's jumped back from the mic. Dahlia's boozy vampire-queen accent is gone; he's shocked out of character.

"Fuck off, Elvira," someone shouts. Disturbingly, it doesn't seem to emanate from the part of the crowd where the can originated. Closer to me, someone—after a second I recognize them as the curly-haired person who just ran into me—hollers a racial slur. There are shouts of surprise and anger throughout the crowd, but fewer than I would have expected. To my horror, I also hear several people laughing.

I look around for the bouncer. Glen's still sitting on his stool by the door. Even from here, I can see the wide, unfocused stare on his face. As I watch, he slumps forward with his hands on his knees. It looks like he's dry heaving. What is happening to everyone tonight? Is there a sickness going around? Mass hypnosis? Drugs?

Whatever the reason, Glen is not coming to help with the disruption, and it's only getting worse. Someone—maybe the can thrower, maybe not—has grabbed someone else in a headlock. People are shoving each other and yelling. The music for the next performer starts, "Q.U.E.E.N." by Janelle Monáe, bass vibrations moving through the floor, but nobody takes the stage. Logan's still up there, shouting and gesticulating, apparently trying to calm things down, but the microphone has cut out and no one can hear him.

"Jesus," Leah says, pointing. I follow her finger. Near the stage, several yards removed from the ongoing wrestling match in the center of the audience, a bunch of people are trying to drag two flailing bodies apart. They look stuck together somehow. After a moment I realize that one of them has her teeth firmly lodged in the other's cheek. When they finally separate, the taller woman's face spurts blood.

Looking around the room, I see at least half a dozen more

apparently unrelated eruptions of violence. It's as though some deep malevolence was lurking under the surface like mushroom spores, and a heavy rain brought them all bursting forth at once. Someone hits someone else with a beer bottle; unlike in a movie, it doesn't break, just bounces off their skull with a resonant thunk I feel from thirty feet away. A girl grabs her date by the hair and shakes her viciously. A kid in skinny jeans, who looks so young I'm surprised Glen let him in, shoves a woman twice his age, sending her reeling through the crowd. And everywhere, those wide, unfocused eyes are staring.

Janelle Monáe keeps playing, every beat of the drum echoed by a fist hitting a cheekbone, an elbow slamming a solar plexus. It's horrifying yet hypnotic. I stand there, not frozen exactly, because fear hasn't kicked in yet; just still and stupid, as if waiting for someone to tell me what to do.

Then Leah grabs my arm. "Wendy, look," she says, her voice knife-sharp in my ear, and I follow her gaze back to the stage. Logan's still up there, but now some people from the audience are trying to climb up too. He's kicking them, stomping on their feet, pushing them away, but there are so many of them—at first I thought four or five, but now I see that it's at least ten, maybe more—and he's all alone. The people swarming the stage are like a demented version of fangirls from old videos of Beatles concerts, reaching out with no apparent goal other than to touch, to get closer. All of them have that wide-eyed stare that seems to portend things are about to get really fucked-up. And one of them, I finally realize, is Jacquie.

"Oh, God," I whisper, feeling my stomach twist like it's turning inside out. My stasis breaks in an instant and I launch myself forward. Leah is right behind me, and I'm vaguely aware that Sam is behind her. Aurelia's probably back there somewhere too.

There's no coordination or strategy among the people attacking Logan. It seems like they've each individually decided they want to fuck someone up, and by simple chance they all chose the most visible person in the room. Logan swings the mic stand at one guy's face. The guy tries to bite it, then falls back hard, bleeding heavily from his mouth. I think Logan has knocked some of his teeth out. Meanwhile, Jacquie has gotten a grip on Logan's calf, sinking her nails into his skin, ripping his fishnet stockings.

Another drag queen scrambles up the stairs at the far side of the stage. She was interrupted halfway through getting into costume or out of it again; she's wearing a '50s A-line dress, looking like Donna Reed with more cleavage, but there's no wig over her red buzz cut and on her feet are heavy steel-toed boots. She joins Logan at the edge of the stage, kicking and stomping at the invaders.

There are still too many of them. Another can sails through the air, and this one hits Logan in the chest. He staggers backward. Leah and I are getting closer, but we're fighting through a crowd that refuses to move, and half the people in our path don't even seem to notice our presence. I glance back over my shoulder and see Sam stumble and fall. Aurelia helps her up, stooping down so Sam can sling an arm over her shoulder. Either someone finally turned the music off or the screaming around me has gotten loud enough to drown it out.

Inch by inch, I force my way between the writhing, kicking, flailing mass of bodies, making my way toward Jacquie. She's halfway on the stage now, her torso sprawled across the boards while her feet kick in the air, unable to find purchase. She grabs Logan's ankle again, but he shakes her off, then brings his foot down hard on her hand. There's no way I could possibly hear the bones in her hand splinter under the weight of his six-inch platform. But I swear I do.

Jacquie writhes, clawing at Logan with her other hand. She knocks him off-balance and he tumbles backward, landing on the stage on his ass. With a snarl of triumph, she crawl-drags herself toward him.

There's a very tall person with a half-shaved head directly between me and Jacquie, and no space to go around. Uselessly, senselessly, I yell "Excuse me!" at the top of my voice.

Against all hope and reason, the very tall person looks around, meets my eyes, and nods. They shrink backward, maneuvering their body sideways to give me just enough room to get by. I mouth *Thank you!* as I dive forward and finally, finally, grab Jacquie around the waist.

She kicks and squirms. I shout her name, but she gives no sign that she hears. Logan crab-walks backward, out of her reach. He's gasping for breath. I'm close enough now to see that his eyeliner is a mess and he's on the verge of panic.

I yank Jacquie down from the stage. She turns to face me, swinging her hand wide and slapping me full in the face with all her strength and fury. My cheek goes numb, then hot. The room reels around me.

"Jacquie, what the fuck!" I yell. "It's me!"

Nothing—nothing but the wide eyes, glazed over, like her mind is a thousand miles away. She doesn't even focus on me as I grab her arms, struggling to hold her still; not even as she whips her head back and then slams it forward, attempting to headbutt me. I pull away fast enough to take some of the sting out of it, but her forehead hits my already aching cheekbone and it *hurts*.

Now, finally, when it's too late to do a damn thing differently, I'm starting to feel truly afraid. Jacquie doesn't even seem to recognize me; she's just lashing out, trying to hurt whoever's close enough. Whatever has possessed her is both hateful and incoherent, and it's *spreading*. All through the room, people are losing their minds.

I get hold of Jacquie's wrists and try to turn her so she's looking at me. The vision in my left eye is hazy, but I stare her dead in the face, blocking out everything else.

"Jacquie, what's happening?" I say. "Don't you know me?"

For a moment, an instant, I swear her vision clears a little. Her eyes focus on me, finally, and there's something like recognition in them.

"Okay," she says, her voice very small but unmistakably hers.

Relief pulses through my body like an electric shock. "Jesus," I say, and pull her into a hug. As she crumples against me, suddenly feeling very small in my arms, I catch a glimpse of a mark on her shoulder. It's round and red and scabbed at the edges. It looks like a bite mark.

"What the hell is that?" I ask, the words falling out before I have time to consider them.

Jacquie twists her head to look where I'm looking. As she does, her whole body goes rigid. That blank, deadly look settles into her eyes again, as unmistakable as a veil falling over her face.

I have a crystal of a moment in which to think *Goddammit*. Then Jacquie roars. She grabs a fistful of my hair with one hand, while the nails of the other hand rake at my throat. There are people on all sides of me, packed in impossibly tight, absolutely nowhere to go. *Wouldn't it be fucked-up*, I think, *if this is how I die?*

"Wendy!" Leah screams. I see her over Jacquie's shoulder, her blue hair the brightest thing in my field of vision. Something glints—a knife, I realize, the one from her boot, small and sharp and mean. I'm impressed she managed to crouch down and retrieve it without being trampled. Then I'm not thinking about anything but Jacquie's teeth, bared and brutal, coming for my face.

I scarcely have room to twist my head away, but in the split second before Jacquie can bite a hole in my cheek, Leah slams the knife into the side of her neck. Blood fountains from the wound. In the hot, close air, the metallic smell is so strong it's like the blood is in my own mouth. Despite my mortal dread, my chest pangs with fear for Jacquie. What has Leah done?

Jacquie jerks her head like a horse trying to shake off a fly, but she doesn't scream and she doesn't fall. She throws her arm back, elbows Leah in the head, and then I can't see Leah anymore. There's so much blood, but Jacquie doesn't seem to care.

She gets her hands around my neck and squeezes. The pain comes from everywhere at once. I tug on her wrist, accomplishing nothing. A vast, telescoping blackness opens at the edges of my vision, and I understand that it has come to devour me.

CHAPTER 6

Then there's the loudest noise I've ever heard.

In all the confusion of having the life choked out of me, I can't identify the sound at first; all I know is that it's impossibly huge, a hot poker to my eardrums, and then, unimaginably, it gets *louder*. It wails up and down the scale like a—*siren*, that's what it is, I finally realize. An alarm. As in EMERGENCY EXIT ONLY/ALARM WILL SOUND, the sign posted on the door behind Hellrazors' stage. Someone must have opened it to escape the mayhem. I congratulate myself for figuring that out. Not bad for a dying girl with maybe ten seconds of consciousness left.

Although . . . am I dying? My neck hurts a *lot* where Jacquie is squeezing it, but I'm no longer staring down the throat of a vast cosmic python bent on swallowing the universe. Jacquie's not quite so intent on strangling me as she was a moment ago. I feel her grip faltering. Her eyes dart away from my face and back.

This might be my last chance, I realize, and I brace myself to hit her as hard as I can, to break her hold or die trying. But before I can swing, she lets me go and turns away.

I sway and stumble backward, gasping for breath. Then I look around, confused. How do I suddenly have room to stumble backward?

Because Hellrazors is emptying out, the crowd gushing through the now-open emergency door like water through a broken dam. Some people are fleeing; some are giving chase; others don't seem to know which they're doing, they just want to be *out*. Jacquie throws herself into the exodus.

Maybe I should join her, but my legs tremble under me and I don't think I have the strength to run. I make it to the edge of the stage and lean against it, breathing hard and fast.

"What the fuck was *her* problem?" Leah asks.

It hurts my throat to laugh, but I do it anyway, the sound high and breathless and very close to hysterical. Leah hops up beside me so she's sitting on the stage, her legs dangling down, the same way she sat on the counter at Sam's last night. She still holds the little knife, wet now with Jacquie's blood. *Leah tried to kill Jacquie*, I think. I don't know how to process that, or what to do with the fact that it didn't work. As I watch, Leah wipes the blade clean on her skirt. The skirt rides up enough to see plenty of round thigh, revealing the brilliant orange and gold colors of a floral tattoo that I know goes all the way up to her hip. Her skin makes me tremble, or maybe it's the blood. I look away.

"What the fuck was any of that?" I say. Throughout the suddenly deserted bar, a few groups of stragglers are pulling themselves together. The emergency alarm is still howling. I see at least three people who aren't getting up, maybe unconscious; I don't let myself think about the other possibility. One of the prone bodies is Glen, the bouncer, lying next to the smashed remains of his stool, which apparently was used to hit him over the head.

Logan is sprawled on his back on the stage, but even as my

heart lurches I see him slowly push himself up to seated. I don't see the other drag queen.

"Hey," someone says. I look around for the source of the voice. An array of speakers is stacked to the right of the stage, just before the corridor that leads to the emergency exit. From behind one of the speakers, a face peers out at me.

"Beau?" It takes me a second to recognize her. Wrinkles crisscross her handsome face, drawn tight with worry, and her silver-streaked black hair is less artfully disheveled and more actually fucked-up. "Are you okay?"

"Smashing," she says, and I realize it's not just worry on her face, but pain.

"How'd you end up back there?" Leah asks.

Beau curls an arm protectively around her side. "I opened the door. Thought I'd help people get outside, you know, your nearest exit may be behind you, but I got a little bit stampeded." She winces.

"You're injured," Leah says. "We've gotta get you to a doctor. Is everyone else okay?"

"I'm fine," I say, which is mostly true. "Logan?"

He's sitting on the stage unzipping his thigh-high boots. I see that one of his platforms has cracked in half. "That bitch ruined my fishnets," he says.

"Where's . . ." Leah glances around. "Oh, shit."

I look where she's looking. I somehow missed them on my first scan of the room, but Sam and Aurelia are crouched on the floor. There's a lot of blood on them both.

Reflexively, I move toward them, but Beau is holding my arm and she sways dangerously. Leah, unencumbered, jumps off the stage and runs to them. She kneels down, bending her head toward theirs in hushed conversation. I don't acknowledge the flicker of jealousy that tightens in my chest.

"Are they okay?" Logan says, padding barefoot to the edge of the stage. His wig is gone but his makeup still looks amazing.

After a moment, the three seem to reach an agreement. Leah and Aurelia help Sam to her feet, each of them with an arm around her waist. As soon as she's standing, I can see her face is pale, her movements unsteady. The blood that stains her and Aurelia's shirts, and now spatters Leah's, is coming from a wound just below Sam's elbow.

"What happened to you?" Beau asks as the trio makes it back to us.

"Big fucking berserker dude," Sam says, clearly trying not to sound as pained as she really is. "Fucker bit me. He came like he was going to break my nose with his face, so I . . ." She can't really demonstrate, with her arms around Leah's and Aurelia's shoulders to hold her up, but I can imagine how she must have raised her forearm to protect her head, and gotten a bite taken out of her for her trouble.

Logan looks queasy. "Wow, you're really bleeding," he says.

"I know, dude," Sam says. "I think you might be able to see the bone if you look closer." Logan literally jumps backward.

"Really?" I ask, smiling in spite of everything—or maybe sort of because of everything, because I need something to smile about very badly. "Dahlia DePravity, Empress of the Undead, is scared of a little blood?"

"Yes, and fuck you," he says.

It takes a lot of incremental shifts in position, and several pauses to catch her breath, but Beau manages to rearrange herself enough that she can retrieve her flask from her pocket and take a deep slug. She holds it out to Sam. "Want some for the pain?"

"Does it help?" Sam says skeptically.

"No," Beau says. "It just distracts you."

Sam shrugs philosophically, takes the flask, and gulps from it. "Fuck, Beau, that's horrible," she says, wiping her mouth with the back of her hand.

"What happened to Joey?" Leah asks. "I saw him up there with you a minute ago." Joey must be the other drag queen.

Logan's face falls. "Shit, I don't think he . . . I saw him pretty much get body-slammed off the stage. He's gotta be hurt bad, if . . ." Nobody wants to help Logan finish that sentence, to acknowledge that Joey being hurt would be the best-case scenario.

I look around. Joey's not on the stage, the floor in front of it, or the stairs beside it. "Where did he fall down?"

Logan gestures, and I look where he's pointing. There's a smear of blood on the concrete floor, but nothing else. "He's not here," I say. "He must have gotten out when everyone else did. Maybe someone helped him."

"Maybe he just walked it off," Leah mutters darkly. I know she's thinking of Jacquie, and it gnaws at me, too. The blood gushing from her neck, the way it barely even broke her concentration. It's all too easy to picture Joey peeling himself off the floor with half his skull flattened and staggering out the door like something from a monster movie.

"Do you hear that?" asks Beau, tilting her head.

I stop and listen. Sirens. Not the emergency alarm from the back door, but sirens outside, a low harmony to the ones blaring in the bar.

"Go," says Sam. "Go go go."

"Maybe we should stay and tell them . . ." I start. Through the big window at the front of the bar, I see red and blue lights wash over the street.

"I am not interested in telling cops anything," Sam says, her voice tight and quiet with pain.

"You can hash that out amongst yourselves," Logan says. "I'm getting out of here."

"We're right there with you," Aurelia assures him, and I don't argue anymore. As quickly as we can while supporting Sam and Beau, we make our way out the back door.

The heat of the night is more forgiving than the day, but it's still sweltering downtown, the pavement exhaling all the heat it soaked up while the sun was high. Inside of Hellrazors it looked like the aftermath of a natural disaster; out here the disaster is still happening. People are running in and out of buildings, screaming, waving each other this way and that. I see one of the protest signs lying on the pavement: STOP GROOMING CHILDREN, with a muddy footprint in the middle of the word STOP.

Two cop cars are parked in front of Hellrazors, and we try to look casual as we walk the other way. There's another cop car halfway up the street, blocking a lane of traffic. A man with long gray hair is sitting on the curb with his head in his hands, crying.

"Sam and Beau need to get to a hospital," Aurelia says. "We rode my bike here, but I don't think it's a good idea to put Sam on the back of a motorcycle right now. Whose car is closest?"

"I'm up there," Logan says, gesturing in the direction where all the police vehicles are clustered.

"My car's this way," I say, pointing to the parking lot behind the used bookstore. "There's not enough seat belts, but we can squeeze in."

"I'm not going to the hospital," says Beau. "My truck's in the alley. I'm going home."

"You need to see a doctor," Aurelia says. "Your ribs are broken."

"All they're gonna do for broken ribs is give me a painkiller," Beau says. "I have plenty of that." She pulls out her flask and takes another drink.

"You can't *drive*," Aurelia says.

"Oh, it takes more than a few sips of this stuff to knock me out, princess," Beau says. She tries to wink but it looks more like a grimace.

Aurelia does not look amused. "I mean because of your broken ribs. You live in the ass end of nowhere, and you're going to pass out from the pain before you get two blocks."

"My place isn't that far, it's just across the creek," says Beau.

"Sam needs stitches," Leah interrupts, looking at me instead of Beau. "If I drive Beau's truck back to her house, can you take Sam to the ER?"

"Yes," I say, relieved to be told what to do.

It takes some careful choreography, but Leah and I manage to trade places so she's supporting Beau and I'm holding half of Sam's weight. Leah's hand brushes my wrist as I hand off Beau. "Be safe," she says, and I don't know if she's talking to me or Sam, but I nod.

We separate, Leah and Beau walking down the alley where the truck is parked, the rest of us heading for the bookstore parking lot as quickly as we can. I try not to watch them over my shoulder, their disappearing silhouettes in the strobing light from the cop cars. Logan sticks with us instead of heading for his own vehicle, either out of a desire to help Sam or a disinclination to take off alone. I briefly consider suggesting he drive Beau home so Leah can come with me, but I can't think of a way of saying it that doesn't make me sound like a selfish asshole, which is probably because I'm being a selfish asshole.

Sam climbs into the back seat and leans against Aurelia.

Aurelia strokes her hair and whispers calming things. The smell of blood is overpowering in the close confines of the car. I hastily roll the windows down.

It's only a few minutes to the emergency room, because everything in San Lazaro is only a few minutes from everything else, but it feels like decades every time I hear Sam swallowing a wince of pain in the back seat. Beside me, Logan keeps twisting around to check on her, then sighing impatiently and drumming his hands on his thighs when he turns back around. Aurelia keeps murmuring to Sam. I wish she would speak up. I could use some reassurance too.

The patient drop-off roundabout is a nest of cars all pointing in different directions, tangled together like a pile of sleeping kittens, but not nearly so pleasant. The parking lot is closed, its mechanical arm lowered to block the entry ramp. There's nowhere to park on the street. My gut churns with dread.

This is no time to stand on ceremony. "Fuck it," I say, and drive over the curb and onto the strip of grass between sidewalk and street. Logan yelps with surprise, and Sam with pain, but I ignore them both. Aurelia and I help Sam out of the car, doing our best not to jostle her wounded arm, and make our way toward the door, Logan following.

There's a small crowd of people around the door in the bright industrial glow of the streetlight, grumbling and arguing. At first I think it's just gridlock, but as we weave our way to the front, I realize there's a security guard blocking the door. He's large and square—square shoulders, square jaw, square flattop of bristly reddish blond. He has a gun. I don't know anything about guns, but it's big and shiny and he's holding it like he wants to use it. I can't remember seeing a hospital security guard holding a gun before.

"Excuse me," I say, trying to make my voice as sweet and unassuming as possible. "Can we get inside? My friend is hurt."

Several people around us talk at once, but the guard shouts over all of them. "No one's getting inside until I get a look at them."

"What?" Sam's hand tightens nervously on my shoulder.

A Black woman with short natural hair folds her arms and glowers. "He won't let us through the door unless we take our clothes off."

"You, shut up," the guard growls. "That's not what I said. I need to see what's wrong with you or I'm not letting you in. Guy came in here an hour ago puking blood. Next thing we know he starts screaming and throwing chairs and biting people, and now all of *them* are puking blood too. We got 'em strapped to beds, but it wasn't easy, and I don't want no more of that shit tonight. So you want to show me your broken arm or your fuckin' hernia, you can come on in, but until I know you're not infected with whatever that shit was, you stay out here." There's a ring of white all the way around his eyes. He's an asshole on a power trip, that much is obvious, but he's scared, too. Really scared.

"What is this shit?" a man with a gray beard yells. "It's not your job to interrogate people! We need to see our doctors. Let us inside." He shoves forward, trying to dodge around the guard.

I have an extremely bad feeling. I want to get out of here, but there are people crowding in behind us, and Sam is leaning harder and harder on Aurelia and me as the blood loss and exhaustion catch up with her. I can't just turn and run.

"Back the fuck up," the guard yells, but people are trying to struggle past and around each other, and a stampede feels imminent. Someone slams into my right side. I stagger into Sam, trying not to drop her. From behind, Logan grabs my waist and steadies me. My heart is jackhammering, my pulse blaring like a fire alarm. This is a bad place to be.

Something goes sailing over my head. I duck, and then the night splits open with a thunderclap the size of the universe. It takes me a moment to piece together what happened, not only because my ears are ringing, but because I've never heard a gunshot outside of a movie before. One of the angry people in the crowd behind me must have thrown something at the security guard. In response, the guard pulled the trigger on his gun.

The man with the beard was standing right next to me. He's missing most of the beard now, along with the bottom right quadrant of his face.

I can't hear anything. My ears are full of bees. But I see some of the people around me leap backward in horror while others surge forward in fury. I feel the rising heat of the crowd, the urgency that throbs between us all like a shared heart. Sam isn't heavy on my shoulder anymore; I suddenly feel I could carry her for miles.

Then I realize it's not just the adrenaline. Logan is taking Sam from me, scooping her into his long arms. *Come on*, he mouths silently to me, or maybe he's screaming it. He turns to run, Sam slung over his shoulder, Aurelia right beside him, matching his stride even though his legs are so much longer than hers.

The hospital lawn is as chaotic as the Hellrazors dance floor was. People are screaming, cursing, surging into each other in waves as they overwhelm the security guard and begin rattling the locked doors behind him. I hear sounds that make me think of broken bones, broken bodies, but I don't look back.

Logan half throws Sam into the back seat, and Aurelia climbs in front with me. Instead of buckling her seat belt, she twists around so she can see Sam. "Is she okay?" Sam's face is gray and she looks barely conscious.

"She's not fucking great," Logan says.

"I heard that," Sam mumbles.

"I didn't think it was a secret," Logan says. "I assumed you were aware you're not fucking great, since you're about to pass out and you hemorrhaged all over my slip."

I turn on the car and hit the gas before I realize I don't have a plan. "Where are we going?"

Aurelia doesn't respond, still staring back at Sam. Her eyes are massive.

"Pharmacy," Logan says. "If we can't get her in to see a doctor, we're just going to have to do the best we can ourselves."

The clock on the dashboard reads a glowing 2:17 a.m. "Is anything even open?"

"Probably not," Logan says. "But I know how to get into places that are closed."

CHAPTER 7

LAST YEAR

"Seabrook?" Samantha said, her voice somewhere between laughter and irritation. "The fucking seltzer company?"

"They're launching a new line of flavors, and they like the idea of tying it to Pride," Leah said. "They want to be the title sponsor. I mean, we're talking about serious money here. We could bring in some big-name performers, really put San Lazaro's queer community on the map." Around the table in the public library meeting room, some members of the Pride planning committee made approving noises; others looked skeptical.

"Oh, sure," Sam said scornfully. "They want to be the official beverage of The Queer Community, so we'll forget the fact that they're union-busting ghouls who make huge donations to Republicans."

I stared down at my hands on the table and said nothing. This was the first I'd heard of Leah's proposal. Was that weird? Shouldn't she have wanted to discuss it with her girlfriend before bringing it to the entire committee? Or was I overreacting?

I noticed that my fingernails were short and ragged. I'd stopped biting them in high school, and couldn't remember when I'd started again.

"I mean, you're not wrong that corporate politics suck, but they'd suck either way, and this way we get an awesome Pride," said Leah. "If they've suddenly developed a conscience, why shouldn't we be the ones to benefit?"

"Please," said Sam. "They've been around in San Lazaro for twenty-five years, and this is the first time they've ever done anything for the queer community. They don't actually care about us."

"Who gives a fuck? I don't need their emotional support, I just want their money."

"When you think about it, it's a sign of how far we've come," Aurelia said. "That a big company like Seabrook even wants to be associated with a Pride festival, or with queer people in general."

"Marsha P. Johnson would be so proud," Sam snarked. Leah grinned back at her. I picked at the corner of my thumbnail until a bead of blood appeared.

Leah and I had been dating for three months now, and she'd just invited me to join the Pride committee with her and Samantha and Aurelia. San Lazaro Pride had never been the kind of occasion it was in bigger cities, but Leah had plans, a vision for what it could become in the future with the right kind of support. I never had much to contribute, but I was happy to tag along.

You know that joke about dykes and U-Hauls? It's never applied to me; my skills lie in the opposite direction, in keeping people at arm's length instead of pulling them close. I had one serious boyfriend in college, and I broke up with him after two years because of an intense flirtation with a guy in my Spanish class, with whom I subsequently went on three dates and never called again. Other than that, my romantic history is a desert, interrupted by the occasional horny oasis.

But with Leah, I didn't want to run. For once, I understood what all those other women were feeling, the architects of the stereotype, the original fools who rushed in. I knew I was falling in love with her after three dates, although I fought back the urge to say it. I wrote poems about Leah that I never dreamed of sharing at Ashlynn's open mic—awful, embarrassing, florid odes to the smell of her hair and the music of her laugh.

I wanted to carve out a space for myself inside the cup of her pelvic bone and live nestled there among her organs, surrounded by the sound of her beating blood. Leah was smart, impassioned, fascinating. And we had so much sex. Almost every night either I was at her apartment or she was at mine, fucking for hours. Sometimes she brought her laptop to Groundhogs when I was working and gave me intense looks until I followed her into the bathroom to finger her breathless against the flimsy stall door.

Leah was involved in everything, so all of a sudden I was involved in everything too. I went to protests with her, helped her write grant proposals, put together poetry readings to raise money for various queer causes. I loved that almost as much as I loved the way our bodies moved together. Being attached to Leah meant I had a purpose.

She didn't want to talk about moving in together yet, and that was disappointing, but I felt sure it was a future we were steadily progressing toward. In the meantime, I was contributing to the world by supporting her, by showing up whenever she asked me to. I made signs and handed out flyers. People recognized me. I was productive; I was useful. I had a place.

"Seabrook is the backbone of the community," Leah said. "I mean, when people hear San Lazaro, they think Seabrook. They're the biggest employer in the city. Their involvement would mean legitimacy, stability, not to mention money and media coverage."

"It's credibility laundering," Sam argued. "They want progressive clout without having to change their actual business practices."

I sat quietly and picked at my nails. It wasn't that I didn't care; rather, I sympathized so hard with both points of view that I felt crushed by the weight of my own ambivalence. Leah looked at me expectantly, her eyes asking me to jump in, to support her, but I just sat there looking back with stupid despair welling up in my throat until she moved on to someone else.

This was happening more and more often, Leah seeming disappointed in me. I knew she was waiting for me to get involved, to make my voice heard—if not on the Pride committee, then in some other way. I wondered if that was why she hadn't told me about the Seabrook proposal, why I increasingly suspected she wasn't confiding in me the way I did in her. Parts of Leah were walled off, inaccessible. I felt like a kid standing on tiptoes to get a glimpse over the fence.

One night we were walking around downtown after dinner, trying to decide whether to get a drink or just go home, when I saw a middle-aged white woman coming toward us down the sidewalk. Her body language was strange, shoulders square, heading straight for Leah like she had no intention of stepping aside. I felt the back of my neck prickle, but I squeezed over to the side of the pavement, then off it into the street, desperately hoping to avoid a confrontation.

"You," the woman said, pointing a finger at Leah. They both

stopped in their tracks, the woman's fingertip a deep breath away from Leah's collarbone.

"Hi, Marjorie," said Leah politely, as though impervious to the anger in the woman's face and voice.

Marjorie wasn't placated by Leah's calmness. If anything, it seemed to make her angrier. "You're trying to buy my goddamn house?"

Leah looked indignant, then surprised, which struck me as a strange order for those expressions to appear. "Marjorie, I—"

"I saw your fundraiser on Facebook," Marjorie spat. "Raising money to buy an empty house and turn it into, what, some kind of drag bar? That's *my house.*"

"I'm really sorry you lost your house, Marjorie," Leah said carefully. She pronounced the woman's name like a magic spell, like something that could ward off harm. I couldn't take my eyes away from Marjorie's fingertip, where it was not quite touching Leah's skin, just above the neckline of her corset top. As long as there was air between them it was probably okay, I told myself, trying to slow my breathing. Besides, we were out in public, the yellow glow of the streetlights almost as bright as day, people walking past us on both sides. Sure, pedestrians veered off the sidewalk to avoid coming near Leah and Marjorie's altercation, but someone would intervene if things got really out of hand. Wouldn't they?

"You used to be my *neighbor,*" Marjorie said, and even through her fury I could see her eyes were wet. "You fucking trick-or-treated at my house. You played in my yard."

"I know," Leah said, nodding, compassionate. "It's so hard, seeing what's happening in that neighborhood these days. People getting priced out. I thought it would be better if our group bought the house than some developer who'd just scrape it and build condos. I love that street, Marjorie. I promise we're not going to change your house."

"The fuck do I care? I don't *live* there anymore!" Spit flew from her lips and she leaned closer. Her finger jabbed into Leah's chest now, hard enough that I saw the skin around it go white, but Leah didn't take a step backward. "I lost my job and the bank took my fucking house away, and now you're trying to turn it into some—haven for perverts."

"Jesus, Marjorie," said Leah, disgust creeping in around the edges of her careful calm. "We're not starting a sex club. It's going to be an LGBTQ community health center. I know you're angry, but you don't have to be *nasty*. I didn't think you were that kind of person."

"Nasty?" Marjorie's voice grew higher and rougher, something animal trying to break through. "You're trying to steal my fucking house and you want to tell me about nasty?"

People were stopping to watch instead of circling around us now, as though they also sensed a surface tension about to break, a violence about to erupt. Still, nobody intervened. *Couldn't they see that this woman was dangerous?* I thought desperately. She had lost something irreplaceable and her anger was radiating from her skin, poisoning the air around her. Why wasn't anyone helping us?

But my hands stayed at my sides, my feet rooted in the gutter, my mouth closed. I didn't do anything to help either.

"I'm so sorry you lost your house, but *it is not my fault*," Leah said, her voice getting quieter as if to balance out Marjorie's volume. "There's nothing I can do to get it back for you, so should I just let it sit there until some asshole from Phoenix buys up the whole block? At least this way it will *help* people."

"You could have helped *me*," Marjorie shouted. "That money

you're raising to turn my home into some kind of freak show, you could have raised it for *me*."

"I didn't know you were behind on your mortgage," Leah said, still so quiet, and there was significance to the way she kept her voice down—like she, at least, had the courtesy not to shout Marjorie's financial struggles all over the street, even if Marjorie herself wasn't so polite. "How was I supposed to help you if you never told me you needed it? And if you're just going to stand here and insult me—"

"No wonder your parents like to pretend they never had a daughter," Marjorie snarled. "I'd be ashamed of you, too, if you were mine, you heartless . . . cunt . . . *dyke*." She hesitated over the last two words, as though she wasn't used to saying them, but they came out loud and laced with ferocity.

Leah's face went pale under the golden sheen of the streetlights, and finally she slapped Marjorie's hand away from her chest.

"Don't touch me," she said, so quiet I could barely hear her.

Marjorie reared back, snorting like an affronted horse, and I couldn't tell if she was about to scream more slurs or punch Leah in the face, but before she could do either Leah ducked past her, grabbed my arm, and hurried me down the sidewalk. My legs had a good six inches on hers but I was still almost running to keep up.

"Hey! Hey! I'm talking to you, goddammit!"

I looked back over my shoulder and was relieved to see Marjorie shouting after us but not moving from where she stood, a circle of empty sidewalk around her like a spotlight. Now that I found myself in motion again through no actual choice of my own, my brain belatedly leapt into crisis mode.

"Holy shit, Leah," I said, gasping harder than could be

explained by how fast we were walking. "What was that?"

"She's been emailing me for a few weeks," Leah said, her voice still low and tightly controlled. "I just wasn't expecting to run into her."

"What, like—harassing you?" I looked over my shoulder again to make sure Marjorie wasn't following us.

Leah shook her head impatiently. "No. It's no big deal. She's harmless, she's just upset."

She didn't seem harmless to me. And upset people can do a lot of things they swear under calmer circumstances they never would. "If she gets in your face like that again, I'm going to call the cops." Actually, I was embarrassed I hadn't done so already. In retrospect it seemed like the obvious response to Marjorie's behavior.

Leah came to a stop so suddenly that I jumped and almost stumbled again. "Jesus, Wendy," she said. Her eyes were big and cold, her mouth a dry chasm in the earth. "No. Why would you say that?"

I bit hard on the inside of my cheek to keep tears from flooding my eyes. I felt shaky and hot with adrenaline, confused, slightly queasy. "I'm sorry," I said, not sure exactly what I was apologizing for, but certain it was necessary.

She shook her head, then reached out and squeezed my hand. "Calling the cops only ever escalates things," she said. "It wouldn't help. And I mean, whose side do you think they'd be on, anyway, between me and the nice middle-class white lady?" That was a strange comparison, I thought, since Leah was also white, and Marjorie couldn't be that well-off if she'd lost her house. I slipped my sweaty hand out of Leah's and stuck it in my pocket. Leah started walking again, and I followed her.

"Anyway," she said after a few seconds of silence, "I'm not

afraid of Marjorie. I'm just sad."

"It is sad," I agreed. As much as Marjorie had scared me, I could imagine how heartbreaking it must have been to lose her home.

"Like, I've literally known her since I can remember. I would never have expected her to say bigoted shit like that to me."

I nodded slowly. I wasn't sure that was the saddest part of the interaction, but I didn't want to argue with Leah. That sick churning in my stomach was getting worse. It must be the heat combined with the residual nerves from the confrontation with Marjorie. And maybe a bit of embarrassment for how I'd handled myself—how I'd stayed to one side, frozen, hoping someone else would come to the rescue.

Leah didn't hear from Marjorie again after that, or if she did, she didn't mention it to me. The money to buy Marjorie's old house came through, with a lot of help from Seabrook. Despite Samantha's very vocal qualms (and my own unexpressed ones), the Pride sponsorship moved forward smoothly. Summer softened at the edges without ever becoming something I recognized as autumn. Leah was busy and satisfied, and I was happily along for the ride.

So it came as a shock when Leah sat me down and said, "You need to see someone about your depression."

I protested. I wasn't depressed. I was an active and engaged member of the community. I went out with her friends, I attended her protests—

"Exactly," she said. "You've attached yourself to everything I do, but you don't have anything of your own. You're not passionate about any of this. You're just going through the motions."

"What do you want me to do?" I asked.

"What do *you* want to do?" she countered. "What do you

want out of your life? What do you imagine when you think about the future? Because I'm worried that you're going to wake up one day and realize that you never pursued your dreams, and you're going to blame me for it."

It didn't feel like a good time to say that what I saw in the future was the two of us, together. That nothing else in my life felt as urgent or necessary. Suddenly, it seemed extremely risky to let Leah know she was the only good and important thing in my life, the source of all momentum and meaning.

"I don't know," I said instead.

"Do you want to keep serving coffee forever?" she pushed. When I shook my head, she said, "What, then? Do you want to be a poet?"

"No," I said. If I'd learned nothing else in grad school, I'd learned that. Poetry, for me, was meant to be a hobby, not a career. Trying to do it full-time killed my joy.

"Well, what, then?" she said impatiently. As though it were that easy, as though everyone had a bright clear North Star dream lighting their path.

"I don't *know*," I said again, frustrated now, feeling tears sting my eyes. All I knew I wanted was to stop talking about this. "I don't have a plan. I'm making enough to live on right now. Why isn't that good enough for you?"

"It's not good enough for *you*," Leah said. "You're not going to be happy like this forever. You're just treading water." She reached across the table and squeezed my hand, preventing me from surreptitiously wiping the corners of my eyes the way I needed to. "I'm not criticizing you, Wendy, I promise. I'm just concerned about you. I care about you." She didn't say "I love you," and I thought about that a lot in the days that followed.

Okay, so I needed to get my life together, if not from any inner sense of urgency, then to be the partner Leah wanted and deserved. Of course someone with her drive and ambition wouldn't be satisfied dating a barista who wrote poetry in her spare time. Of course that wasn't good enough for her. Now that I thought about it, this was probably why she didn't want to move in with me yet—she didn't want to get stuck with some deadweight girlfriend dragging her down.

But knowing all that didn't motivate me, it terrified me. For a while I'd felt safe and secure with Leah, wanted, accepted. Now I realized I'd been coasting, taking her for granted the whole time while making no attempt to better myself. I felt like I was standing at the top of a landslide. The ground under my feet wasn't stable, but I couldn't see a safe path to move forward, either. What could I be? Who could I become? What sort of dream would make my life worthwhile?

One afternoon, when I'd just finished my coffeehouse shift, my phone rang with a call from Leah. For a moment, I considered letting it go to voice mail; I could claim later that I'd been napping, as I often did after work. But I shoved the impulse away—I wasn't avoiding talking to my girlfriend; that would be nonsensical—and answered.

"Can I come pick you up?" she said. "I have a surprise for you."

A surprise date! Leah must have sensed the cracks in our relationship and was seeking to fix them, to pull us back together with a romantic gesture. She wouldn't give me any more details, so I just showered as fast as I could and put on a sundress. I looked, I hoped, cute but not like I was trying too hard.

Leah seemed nervous when she pulled up in front of my building, which I found endearing. "Where are we going?" I asked, imagining a picnic in the park, maybe mini golf, something a little overdone but still sweet, something where we could roll our eyes at the obvious romantic cliche and enjoy it at the same time. Leah smiled at me with her lips pressed tight together. My stomach twisted, and I tried to tell myself it was from excitement.

Leah pulled into a parking lot in front of an office building, and even then I tried to hold on to my optimism, to hope this was some kind of weird mystery date. "Leah?" I asked, hating the high, desperate note in my own voice. "What are we doing here?"

"I made you an appointment," she said. Another tight smile, showing no teeth. "Dr. Ryley Glenn—that's Ryley with two y's. She's on the third floor. It's sliding scale, but they already have my credit card on file, so don't worry about paying for it. I've got you covered." She patted the back of my hand. I didn't pull away, but it was only because I was too stunned and angry to move.

"A therapist?" I said. "That was your surprise? You made me a therapist appointment without even telling me?"

"She has great reviews," Leah said, as though that was my concern with this situation. I couldn't even articulate what my concern was; all I knew was that my stomach felt full of rocks, and my throat felt full of acid. "She's trained in a bunch of different modalities, and she's queer, so, like . . ." She held her hands out toward me, palms up, as though offering me a gift. She was, I realized—or at least she thought she was. She meant to. I was supposed to be grateful now, to cry and hug her and thank her for giving me what I was afraid to admit I needed.

"Take me home," I said.

"Wendy," Leah said in a gentle tone of voice I had never heard before and hated immediately, "I'm just trying to help. I know you've been struggling lately." Scalding, humiliating tears pooled behind my eyes, and I turned my head to stare out the window. "This is just an intake appointment, so you can get to know the doctor. Then if you don't like her, we can look into other options."

"And will we get ice cream afterward?" I said. I wanted the words to come out bitter and scornful, but instead I sounded weak, on the verge of tears.

"We can if you want to," Leah said, apparently not even realizing I was being sarcastic.

"Jesus, Leah," I said, still scowling out the window at the bleak sunbaked parking lot. "No. I don't want ice cream. I want you to drive me back to my apartment."

"You have an appointment," she said, her voice going steely. "It's too late to cancel."

That finally made me turn to stare at her. "An appointment you made without consulting me? You think you can just make plans, and I'm obligated to fulfill them? You're in charge of my life now?"

"Of course not." The sweet, placating voice was back. "I'm just trying to get you the support you need to get out of this stuck patch."

I shook my head hard, not because I had nothing else to say, but because if I opened my mouth again I would cry.

"Do you want me to go in with you?" she said. I looked down at my hands in my lap, resting on the skirt of that sundress— dark blue with a sunflower print. Bitten nails, ragged flesh. Underneath, my freshly shaved legs were sweating, a tiny razor slip scabbing at the back of my knee. For a moment I thought about suggesting that we leave and go play mini golf. That we try to salvage something from the ruins of this day.

Instead, I just shook my head again. Leah drew in breath to

speak, but let it out without words. We sat there for a few more minutes, until it was clear that I had missed the opportunity to check in for my appointment, and then she drove me home.

CHAPTER 8

We tear through the neighborhood, screeching around corners and swerving to avoid a full-blown fistfight in the middle of a crosswalk. I've never driven this recklessly in my life. It should be terrifying, but somehow it's actually calming me down: focusing on nothing but the road in front of me, the fastest possible route to our destination.

There's a quiet sound like humming. For a moment I assume it's my ears ringing from the gunshot, but then I realize it's Aurelia speaking Spanish, very fast and under her breath. I make out the words *madre de Dios* and I think she's praying. I didn't know Aurelia prayed.

I park next to the east side drugstore, just as empty now as it was this morning. "Sam, why don't you wait in the car," Logan says, swinging his door open before the car is fully stopped. Sam groans an assent.

"I'll stay here with her," Aurelia says, the first time in at least ten minutes I've heard her speak at full volume.

The brightly lit windows are practically daylight. That

handwritten sign, BE BACK, is still taped to the door. I look nervously up and down the empty street. "So what's your plan for getting inside?" I ask Logan. When he said he could get into places that are closed, I'd assumed he meant, like, picking locks or hacking security alarms—something skillful and impressive. I briefly imagine Logan as a character in a heist movie, meticulously carrying out his part of an elaborate plan to take down a giant, evil organization. He already wears all black; it's not hard to picture.

He surveys the landscape. "Hmm. I might have to . . . oh, wait." There's a baby ironwood tree growing on the edge of the sidewalk, braced upright with wires. Surrounding its base are smooth white stones the size of my fist. Logan picks one up, hefts it from one hand to the other, and hurls it through the window of the drugstore, shattering the glass into a million mirror-bright fragments.

"Impressive," I say.

Logan, impervious to sarcasm, flashes me a wisp of a smile and says "Thanks."

He steps up into the display window, carefully avoiding the broken glass with his bare feet, then reaches back through to offer me his hand. We climb down into the drugstore together. Beyond the bright window lights, it's dark inside, except for the pulse of one piercing blue light that must be connected to the security alarm.

"That's probably calling the cops," I point out.

"Yeah, but I figure it's not at the top of their priority list tonight," says Logan. "They're probably busy dealing with . . ." I'm relieved when he trails off instead of finishing that sentence. I don't want to hear how he'd describe everything we've seen tonight.

"So what do we need? Bandages, antiseptic . . ."

"More booze," Logan suggests. I'm not sure if he's joking.

He heads for the first-aid aisle. Remembering our first foray here this morning, it occurs to me to look for Plan B, but there's none on the shelf. Sold out. I'm sure there's more in the back, but of course the pharmacy area is behind a rolled-down steel door, inaccessible as the moon.

Then I hear Logan calling my name. I think he's already said it once, but his voice is so quiet it didn't breach my attention until now.

I walk in his direction and see what I could vaguely make out through the window earlier: the first-aid aisle is in shambles. A shelf is toppled over, its contents poured out in a heap. One of the refrigerated compartments along the wall is hanging open, alcoholic beverages knocked askew as though someone swiped a furious hand along the whole shelf. Several have spewed their contents on the floor in a sticky, poisonous-smelling puddle.

And there's blood. Lots of blood. That's the stain I saw earlier, that I thought from a distance might have been cough syrup. Up close, the iron tang is unmistakable. Pooled on the carpet, still wet in the middle, dried in streaks dripping down the glass refrigerator door, spattered like a Jackson Pollock painting across the contents of the adjacent shelves. Bloody footprints lead away from the mess to the locked front door, and now I see that on the back side of the BE BACK sign is a deep red smear.

I can't imagine how someone could lose this much blood and live.

"What the hell happened here?" I ask.

"Something bad," says Logan. I shudder in agreement. Logan's arms are overflowing with rolls and rolls of bandages.

"Sam's not dead," I say. "I think it's a little premature to mummify her."

"It's for her arm," he says earnestly. Eventually I'm sure I'll learn to stop using sarcasm on Logan.

"Are those Cheetos?" I ask.

"Yeah, those are for me."

We walk carefully to avoid stepping in any of the blood. Logan tosses our loot onto the sidewalk, then helps me through the window.

Aurelia is standing on the sidewalk, alone. Her arms are folded tightly over her chest. My heart drops—the feeling of falling when you're almost asleep, that snaps you awake gasping.

"What happened?" I ask.

"Sam," Aurelia says. "She was . . . she tried to . . ." She shakes her head hard, like she's trying to dislodge the words from her throat. I remember Jacquie's strange, empty eyes, and I feel like I'm sinking. Not Sam, too.

"Oh, fuck," Logan says. "Did she hurt you?"

"No. I got out." Her eyes are so huge and dark, glittering like the broken glass in the drugstore window. I can't imagine Sam hurting Aurelia. Their mutual tenderness is as much a part of them as Sam's sharp voice or Aurelia's dark hair. It's fundamental to who they are, inseparable and entwined like two trees that grew around each other, sharing earth and light.

But here's Aurelia standing on the sidewalk, hugging herself like she's cold, looking smaller and more afraid than I've ever seen her, and Sam is in the car alone.

I step toward the car and look in the back window. Sam is still stretched out on the back seat with her arm cradled to her chest, just like the last time I saw her. Now, though, there's a stain of bloody vomit on her shirt, and more smeared on her chin. She's gazing into space, but her eyes focus on me as I peer inside.

"Hey, Wendy," she says.

"Motherfucker!" I leap backward and look around wildly at Logan and Aurelia. "She—that's Sam," I say. "She's her." I know I sound stupid, but I can't articulate what I mean any better. She hasn't gone away from herself and left the lights on, like Jacquie. Aurelia was wrong, Sam is okay, there's still time to help. I reach for the door handle.

Aurelia grabs my wrist. "No," she says, as if the word hurts her mouth. "Wait. Watch."

Reeling with confusion, I turn back to Sam. I can barely hear her, but I see her lips moving. "I'm sorry," she says. "Aurelia? I'm sorry, baby. I didn't know. My arm hurts. Can we go home now?" She pauses, coughs, spits out a little more blood. "Aurelia? Wendy? What time is it? What's—oh, you fucking bitch, do you think you can just shove me down the well?" Her voice rises quickly, stumbling over the incoherent words until she's screaming, tendons standing out in her neck. "The light, Aurelia, I'm gonna eat that fucking bird, get *away* from me!" She grabs her own face, digging her fingernails into her cheeks and leaving angry red scratches.

It's like what happened to Jacquie, but worse. I can still see the real Sam, but she's obviously not in control anymore. She writhes on the seat, cursing and pleading, lucid one moment and feral the next.

"Holy shit," says Logan.

"Baby," Sam whimpers, her voice unnaturally high. "Get in the car. It's time to go." Then she presses her face against the window, like a little kid making silly faces. Except this isn't funny; it's hideous. Bloody bile from her lips smears the glass, and she drags her flattened, distorted nose through it.

Aurelia takes a step back. "Please stop," she says quietly.

Sam looks at her, eyes full of tenderness and grief. Then she slams her head against the window with all her force. I wrench myself backward, almost falling on my ass. There's a terrible splintering sound, but the glass doesn't crack, and a moment later I realize what broke was Sam's nose. It sits on her face wrong, twisted and already swelling.

"I'm scared," Aurelia says in that same small voice.

"If we can get her to a doctor," I start to say, but Logan interrupts me.

"No way. I'm sorry, guys, but that's exactly what people say in zombie movies right before they get their fucking faces eaten. There's no cure, okay? There's never a cure, and trying to find one is just a way to waste time and get killed."

"This isn't a movie, Logan." The rage in Aurelia's voice is cold and quiet, the diametric opposite of Sam's hysteria, which continues unabated in the background. It's not terribly different from Aurelia's usual calm, quiet voice, except that it's a universe apart. "I don't give a single tiny fuck what happens in the shitty horror movies you like to watch, because that is my *wife* in that car."

"Fine," Logan says. "Climb back in there and drive her back to the hospital."

Sam screams, an ugly, dry sound, and we all flinch. Staring at us, she lifts her injured forearm to her mouth and bites into the wound. Blood flows down her wrist, and she chases it with her tongue.

"Please," Aurelia says, turning to me. "We have to help her."

I bite my lip. "Fuck. Okay." I don't feel a lot more optimistic than Logan does, but what's the alternative? We can't just leave Sam here. I dig in my purse until I find my phone. It rings for what feels like a ridiculously long time before a harried voice says

"911, what's your emergency?"

"My friend," I say, and suddenly my voice is quavering. Trying to put into words what's happening to Sam lets me feel the awfulness of it in a new way. "She's throwing up and not making sense, and she tried to . . ."

"Where are you?" the operator interrupts.

"Um, corner of Third and Nopal, by the drugstore." I glance at the smashed window and wonder if we should have moved to a different location before calling, but there was no practical way to do that and it's too late now anyway. "She needs a doctor, but we—"

"Someone will be there soon." There's chatter in the background followed by an exasperated sigh, and the person on the other end says, "Well, eventually." Then I'm disconnected.

"Fuck," says Logan. "Do you think they're going to send cops?"

"Sam hates cops," Aurelia frets.

"She can kick my ass for it after she doesn't die," I say, but there's no fire in my voice. I don't like it either, but what other option do we have? "Maybe they'll just send an ambulance."

But of course what shows up is a squad car, flashing red and blue lights as they cross the street to park on the wrong side, front bumper almost kissing mine. "God fuckin' dammit, Wendy," Logan breathes. Two officers get out and survey the scene. They don't seem fazed by the sight of Sam in the car, fingerpainting on the windows in her own blood, and I wonder how many calls like this they've already answered tonight.

"You do this?" one of the officers asks, pointing to the smashed window. She's a stocky woman in her mid-forties with a strong jawline and asymmetrically cropped hair. I want to trust her, because she's obviously a lesbian, but her beady eyes give me almost the same creepy feeling as seeing Samantha chew on her own hand.

"It was like that when we got here," says Logan. It's a total bald-faced lie and he doesn't even bother to make it sound convincing. There's a pile of drugstore loot at his feet. But the police have more important things to worry about.

"She's the one," the other cop says, this one a wiry man with acne scars on his light brown skin. He points to Sam inside the car. She bares her teeth and laughs.

"When was she infected?" the lesbian cop asks.

"I don't know," I stammer. "She just started acting—"

"Was she bitten?" I nod. "Around what time?"

"Maybe an hour ago," I say.

"She bite anyone else?" asks the guy. He glares suspiciously at each of us, but we all shake our heads. He looks at his partner as if to confirm that she believes us. She shrugs and nods. "Okay," he says. "We got this."

For a moment, I feel a whole-body wave of relief. It's under control. It's all going to be okay.

Then the male officer pulls out his gun and fires three times into the back seat of my car.

SAMANTHA

Her arm doesn't feel like part of her anymore. It's a separate, swollen, ugly thing, only stitched into her nervous system with hot threads of pain. She can't look at it, but it's red at the edges of her vision.

She's stuck in a car that's going nowhere, but she still feels motion sick, still feels the miles rolling by under her wheels, blank and dark, feels herself plunging into a thick hot darkness that smells like the inside of a mouth. She's speeding with the headlights off, even though she's sitting still. Inside the car is hot and sweaty: plastic sweat, metal sweat. Everything is slippery except her teeth, which are too dry. She tries and fails to bring spit to her tongue. Her mouth is made of sand.

Something bad is coming for her, and she knows she should run away, or drive away, but where is Aurelia? She can't leave without Aurelia. She is deep inside a dark bad place, deep inside a dark mouth, deep inside her own teeth, and she needs Aurelia to come and pull her out.

Samantha's brain has always been full of wild animals, hungry, vicious things. Aurelia is the one who gives them names, teaches them to eat from the palm of her hand. Now Aurelia isn't here and teeth are digging into Sam's meat from the inside.

A voice comes from very far away, muffled, like it's on the other side of glass. For what feels like a very long time Sam can't track it, until her head hits something hard and cool, or at least cooler than her skin. Oh, the voice *is* coming through glass. Sam is inside, a spider in a terrarium, a captured crawling thing.

It's Aurelia. Aurelia is outside, speaking to her in that sweet soothing voice she loves so much, that voice that Aurelia was so self-conscious about for so long. Aurelia has always been a more taciturn person than Samantha, but for a long time she was so quiet, so careful not to use her voice unless she knew she was safe. It took a long time for Aurelia to square the sound of her own voice with the person she knew herself to be, with the way she wanted to be seen and heard.

Samantha never had any difficulty with that. She always knew who Aurelia was, saw her as herself from the very first moment she looked up through the velvet shadow of her eyelashes and said, "Would you call me Aurelia?" It was a perfect moment, the pins of the universe tumbling into place. Samantha looked into Aurelia's face and recognized the woman she loved. She has always heard that woman in Aurelia's voice. She loves Aurelia's voice more than any other sound. She yearns toward it now, stretching her neck until her forehead hits the glass again.

A fucking window. She remembers now—she's not a spider, she's stuck inside a car with no driver. A passenger hitchhiking to nowhere. Why is Aurelia outside? Wherever Sam is going, Aurelia should be there too. She tries to push on the door but it won't open. Pulling doesn't work either. There's a trick to this, but the secret is hidden somewhere in the muscle memory of her fingers, which are far away at the end of this useless arm. She can't think about her arm. She can't think about anything except her arm. She holds it up in front of her face and sees black threads curling under the skin.

"Just hang on a few more minutes," Aurelia says through the glass. Sam looks around. She's in a car, for some reason. A few more minutes to what? Where is she going? Are they almost there? She remembers asking her mother that question as a child. Is her mother driving? No, there's no one in the front seat. Except if she turns her head, she can almost see someone sitting there. Someone red and ugly and indistinct. Samantha doesn't trust that person. That's not her mother.

"You're not my mother," she says loudly, but the red shape doesn't flinch. Aurelia flinches on the other side of the window. Sam loves Aurelia and never wants her to be afraid, but somehow her fear is also very, very funny. Sam laughs. The sound of her own laughter makes her teeth hurt.

Sweat drips into Sam's eyes, making her vision sting and blur. Wiping with the heel of her hand doesn't help. The shape of Aurelia in the window swims, doubles, triples. No, someone else is there now. Maybe they'll let her out. She tries to knock on the door politely, but her hands won't do what she tells them to, so she knocks with her head instead.

Why do her teeth hurt so much? It's like the way they hurt when she was twelve and had braces, before she even knew Aurelia, when her bones were being dragged around in her skull. The ache goes deep, almost as deep as the terrible heat from her arm, from the place she can't look at.

Suddenly, the heat is an itch she wants to scratch. She digs into it with the fingernails of her opposite hand, and it hurts, but it's also such a fucking *relief*. The white flare of pain obliterates the itch, obliterates the heat, obliterates the toothache, wipes everything out in its own incandescence, but only for a moment. Then she's back where she started, feeling the scum of salt drying on her skin. The itch is everywhere: her scalp, her neck, her thighs. Her cheeks burn, and she tries to scratch them, to peel the feeling away like sunburned skin, but that clean bright relief doesn't come.

"Please stop," someone says. Pretty voice. The words wander around in Samantha's head. They don't mean much to her, but she tries them out for the way they feel on her tongue.

"Please, please, please," she says, and laughs again. Her voice isn't as pretty. She doesn't like the way that laughter sounds, but it keeps pouring out. Trying to stifle it would be like trying to close the mouth of a wound, to keep blood inside by sheer force of will. "Stop, stop, stop."

Sam presses her tongue against her aching teeth and feels them shift. She thinks of sand again, about how it spills into footprints left behind in the desert, fills in holes until you can't tell anything was there. She imagines her teeth falling out and sand pouring into the holes in her gums. Bloody, gritty, raw and red. Somehow the desert has made its way inside her. Somehow she has become the sandy horizon, punctuated by growing things with thorns. Creatures are burrowing under her skin. Snakes, scorpions. She can see the hole in her arm where something dug inside of her and built a nest. It's moving down there, inside her veins, parallel to her bones. The sky is so dark, even though the sand is still hot. Desert creatures come out to hunt at night.

Samantha lets out a low moan that doesn't even sound like her own voice as she sees something squirming inside the half-scabbed flesh of her wounded arm. Whatever that is, she needs to stop it before it emerges. She doesn't want to see its face.

For one heartbroken moment, Sam wishes Aurelia was here. Aurelia would keep her safe.

Sam digs her aching teeth into her arm. She feels the pain, but it's on the other side of the glass. In here, there's only heat. A greenhouse where nothing is green. She bites harder, savoring the pressure on her sore jaws, feeling something rip. Finally, finally, something hot and wet pours into her mouth. Are the monsoons here? She gulps and gulps, she's *so* goddamn thirsty, but this water is all wrong. It's salty and stagnant and clotted with something foul. Beyond the glass, someone is shouting. *Are we there yet*, thinks Sam, and then the glass breaks.

CHAPTER 9

Aurelia screams.

My mouth drops open but I cover it with my hand. I don't make a sound. The echo of the three gunshots lasts forever. Aurelia keeps screaming.

The officer's gun isn't as loud as the security guard's at the hospital. My ears are ringing, but not enough to drown out the rest of the world.

"What the fuck," says Logan in an almost conversational voice. "Oh, man. What the fuck."

Aurelia does not stop screaming.

"Can you get her to shut up?" the male cop asks his partner. The white lesbian cop—God, I was right not to trust her—swings around on Aurelia with her shoulder squared for a fight. Aurelia is six inches taller, but she's willowy everywhere the cop is solid. And the cop has a gun. The cop has a gun exactly like the one that fired the shots still reverberating in my bones.

I wonder, again, how many calls like this they've already answered tonight.

"Ma'am," says the lesbian cop. "Ma'am, are you going to calm down? Am I going to have to restrain you?"

Aurelia abruptly stops screaming, her mouth snapping shut. She shakes her head. I can see white all the way around the brown irises of her eyes.

"Ma'am, I need a verbal response."

I could vomit at the cruel apathy in the woman's voice, but Aurelia just says, very quietly, "No, I do not need to be restrained."

Logan manages to summon the courage I can't. "Fuck you guys," he says. His voice is low and shaky, but the words are perfectly clear.

"Don't do anything stupid, son," the male officer says.

Logan holds his hands up, palms out, empty. The universal signal for *I am not a threat.* Then he says "Fuck you" again, even quieter this time, almost reluctantly. Through my shock and rage, I'm terrified for him, but the cops don't respond. Apparently they're too busy shooting defenseless women in cars to be bothered by a Black drag queen cursing them out.

The officers get back in their car and drive away. They leave us there, standing on the sidewalk, the throb of gunfire still fresh in our ears.

They leave us there with Sam.

I don't look. I can't. But Logan, as the squad car rounds a corner and disappears, sucks in a deep breath, crosses his arms over his chest, and walks to the hatchback. He looks in the back window, bits of glass still circling the gaping hole at its center like the remaining teeth in a moldering skull. He stands there, very still, for a long time.

Aurelia makes a tiny sound beside me, like a sigh, or a tuneless hum. After a moment I realize it's the same scream as before, with the volume turned all the way down. I'm not sure she even knows she's doing it.

At last, as though he's reached some kind of conclusion, Logan turns away from the car, rubs his jaw thoughtfully, and bursts into tears.

As soon as I see him crying, I'm no longer frozen. I throw my arms around Aurelia and hold on to her hard. The quiet hum of Aurelia's muted scream sinks so deep into my skin I can feel its vibrations in my own vocal cords.

"Fuck," I whisper. "Goddammit." I wish I could tell her it will be all right, but I've never been good at lying.

"What are we going to do?" asks Logan.

I could spend a thousand years thinking and still not come up with a good answer to that question, but someone has to say something and it's obviously not going to be Aurelia. Sam is dead and we're in danger. "We've gotta get inside somewhere," I say. "We can't just stand around on the sidewalk. Not with . . . everything."

"Where do we go?" Aurelia asks, and I hear the deep chasm of despair open under her words. I hear, because I feel it too, the fear that wherever she goes, she will never fully leave this place, this moment. The concrete under my own boots feels like quicksand, like I could get sucked down by the weight of tonight's horrors and never take another step.

But I shake it off, because this is Aurelia's tragedy, not mine, and that means it's my job to keep her moving so she doesn't melt into the pavement. "We can go back to my apartment," I say. We have to get indoors, find a place to regroup, and I don't want to suggest Aurelia's house, where traces of Sam will claw at her fresh wounds.

"How?" Logan asks.

At that, finally, the reality of our predicament—the exquisite depth to which we are fucked—becomes clear to me. I stare at my car, at its broken window, at the slight curve of shadow I can see in the back seat, hinting at something unthinkable. There is, of course, no way we can get back into this car and drive it home.

What am I supposed to do with it? I wonder, my mind skidding like it's hit an unexpected patch of black ice, all friction gone, pure momentum without direction. Am I expected to clean out the back seat? Dispose of the . . . of Sam? Surely there are official protocols in place, people whose job it is to deal with this kind of thing. Is my car a crime scene now? And who would I call to report it? The officers who shot my friend in the face? Their friends and colleagues? No one in my life, to my recollection, has ever explained to me how to respond when someone gets murdered in the back seat of my car.

I walk to the edge of the sidewalk and crouch down, my hands on my knees, bracing myself as best I can while I vomit what feels like my entire body mass into the street. After the first heave, Logan is behind me, rubbing my back gently. His hand is too hot and only makes me feel worse, but I don't push him away.

At last, I straighten up and rub the back of my mouth with my hand. I gesture to the pharmacy, its neon sign gleaming cheerfully through the darkness, impassive to the horrors it illuminates. "Can we hole up here?" I ask, trying not to sound like I've just puked my guts out and failing. "There's plenty of room, at least." I don't want to go back into the drugstore, I don't want to see that puddle of blood again, but I don't have any better ideas.

"I don't like it," says Logan. "Too exposed. With the broken window, there's no way to keep anyone else from getting in." I have a spiteful flash of an urge to ask why he didn't think of that before breaking the window, but of course if he hadn't done that, we wouldn't be able to get inside either.

Okay. We're stranded on the outskirts of San Lazaro with no car in the middle of the night. There's one bus line in town, but it won't start running again until six in the morning. What do we do? "We could call an Uber," I suggest.

Logan bites his lip. Most of his lipstick is gone by now, but there's still a ring of black outlining his mouth. "I feel weird about getting in a car with someone we don't know," he says. "We can't be sure . . ."

He's right, of course. I remember Emmy vomiting blood, Jacquie's wide eyes pointing slightly different directions. "It's spreading, isn't it?"

He shrugs helplessly.

"It's like rabies," Aurelia says. It's the first thing she's uttered in several minutes, and it catches me off-guard. "The guy at the bar had it, and he bit Sam, and . . ."

"Jacquie had a bite mark too," I remember. "She left with Emmy last night, and Emmy was acting weird. Emmy must have bitten her and passed it on."

"And Joey got body-slammed off the stage and then got up and walked away," Logan says.

I shudder. I don't want to think about that; I don't want to think about Jacquie bleeding from her neck and not even noticing. I don't want to think about the blood soaking into the carpet of the pharmacy, who all that blood came from and where they are now. I can't think about that. It isn't my problem.

But whose problem is it, then? If some kind of plague is spreading through San Lazaro, turning everyone it infects into mindless violent beasts, who's going to stop it? The cops aren't doing anything but firing their guns and leaving the mess behind. Is anyone going to show up and clean it?

"Well, I don't think Sam is getting up and walking away," Aurelia says. I see her eyes swimming, but she keeps it together. I glance toward the car again, thinking about what Sam deserves—an investigation of her death, a proper burial, not simply being abandoned here on the side of the road, lying in broken glass and her own blood—but I just can't make myself move toward the body. I can't be Sam's chauffeur on her last ride across town. When I try to take a step in that direction, my legs and lungs seize up, threaten mutiny.

"But we have to," I say, as gently as possible. "Can you walk?"

Aurelia nods. I look at Logan, barefoot in his fishnet stockings and slip dress. He looks exhausted, dark circles under his eyes that I know aren't just smudged mascara, tired down to the bone, but what else can we do?

"I'm golden," he says. "Are we still heading to your place?"

An idea rattles in my worn-out brain. I remember Beau saying she lives "just across the creek," and we're not far from the creek that marks the eastern boundary of the town. "What about Beau's house?" Instead of trudging back into town, where who knows what threats await us, we could walk out into the desert. All that black empty sand sounds a lot safer than being surrounded by people right now.

"Great idea," Logan says with a tired but sincere smile. "Do you know how to get there?"

"I don't have Beau's number, but I can call Leah and ask for directions," I suggest. Even amidst the terror and exhaustion, the possibility of reconvening with Leah, seeing her and knowing she's safe, sparkles like a mirage in my mind.

"I've been there," Aurelia says. Her voice sounds like it's coming from a long way away. "I came over to help when her bike wouldn't start. I don't remember the address, but I can get us there."

As she speaks, Logan tenses up. Aurelia sees him and goes rigid too, listening. I cock my head and hear what they hear: sirens, climbing up the scale as they move in our direction.

"Let's go," Logan says. Without further discussion, we cross the street and start walking east, clustering together as though we're just wandering home from a party, holding each other up in drunkenness instead of horror and grief. I feel the carnage pulling at me, like a beckoning finger at the back of my neck, urging me to look back at the car, at Sam, but I resist and look straight ahead. Logan and Aurelia do the same.

Nevertheless, I hear the ambulance as it pulls up behind my car and cuts its engine, as paramedics jump out and shout instructions at each other. They're much too late to do anything for Sam, but I hope they'll at least take her somewhere quieter, where she can have some privacy and dignity. I find Aurelia's hand by my side and squeeze it hard. Then we turn down an alley, ducking out of the orange streetlight glare.

We walk without speaking for several blocks, zigzagging down empty streets at random, heading north and east. This far from downtown, in the dark blue hours when it's no longer yesterday but not yet today, the streets are quiet. The loudest sound is the cicadas in the trees. The streets are wide and well-lit, golden pools of streetlight overlapping each other in the hot, sticky night. The monsoons aren't here yet, but I can feel their humid breath as they get closer.

Ahead of us, a black city-issued trash bin blocks the sidewalk. Wordlessly, Logan steps into the street to walk around it, and Aurelia and I follow. My mind is wandering a little, hazy from exhaustion, from the heat, from the surreal quality of everything that's happened tonight.

The thin sheen of daydream shatters when the trash bin tips over and something enormous rolls out of it, directly into our path. It takes a moment for my eyes to focus enough to see that it's a person down on all fours, crouching in the street like a dog defending its territory. The person's face is smeared with blood, so that it's not immediately possible to ascertain race or gender. But then I see the brown beard, streaked with spit and blood but still painfully familiar.

I thought my heart was as heavy as it could get, but it sinks lower. "It's Mike," I say quietly.

Mike grimaces as he rises to his feet. His shirt is ripped, most of the right sleeve gone, and there's broken glass in his hair. For some reason, I pretend I don't know how this is about to go down.

"Mike, are you okay?" I ask. "Can we call someone to . . ."

Before I'm finished, he lunges at me, raking out with his fingers hooked as if to claw my face. I scream and jump back, dodging so the fallen trash bin is between the two of us.

While Mike's attention is on me, Logan grabs him from behind, trapping Mike's arms under his own. Logan is taller, but Mike is heavier and more muscular; plus, he has the advantage of apparently not giving a shit what happens to anyone, including himself. He slams his head backward into Logan's face, then squirms out of his grasp and dives toward me again.

I kick the sideways trash can into his knees, and he falls into the street. The asphalt opens up a long, bloody scrape on his bare arm, but Mike doesn't even flinch. He crawls toward me with horrifying speed. Aurelia is screaming for help, but there's only silence up and down the street. Not even a porch light comes on.

Mike, on hands and knees, grabs my ankle. I flail and kick his hand away. He gnashes his teeth at me, and I think of the bite marks on Jacquie, on Sam. If he gets hold of me with his teeth, I'm as good as dead. Logan kicks Mike in the ribs, knocking him back several inches, but Mike crawls toward us again, undeterred. I'm so scared and furious it feels like I'm rising out of my body, watching everything unfold from a distance. A bright light shines in my eyes. For a moment I'm sure I'm dying.

Then Aurelia grabs my arm and yanks me out of the way, and a car plows into Mike's chest.

Into and *through* his chest. Somehow, iron spikes like fence posts have been affixed to the hood of the car. Two of them impale Mike's torso and emerge from his back. He falls forward across the hood, pinned in place, his legs flailing in the air. The car comes to a stop with its front wheels on the sidewalk and its rear wheels still in the street.

Apparently I have a certain number of screams per twenty-four-hour period and they haven't yet regenerated, because all that comes out of my mouth is a gasp. Mike only grunts, as if annoyed at the interruption. "Oh shit, oh shit," Aurelia murmurs beside me.

Mike slams his fists on the hood of the car, trying to squirm free of the tines piercing his chest, but all he does is shove himself backward and forward, dragging the spikes back and forth in the wounds and making him bleed more. The hood is smeared with blood—not just fresh blood, either, I realize. Under the slick red spill is a dry, rusty stain. Mike isn't the first to bleed out on those iron teeth. The layers of blood are so thick it's almost, but not quite, impossible to make out the Pizzapocalypse logo underneath.

The door swings open and a driver steps out. It's Sunshine, who delivered our pizza last night; the long, middle-parted blond hair and the broad shoulders in their oversized polo shirt are familiar. Last night, though, I'm pretty sure they weren't wearing roller-derby-style elbow pads and wrist guards. And I definitely would have noticed if they'd been carrying a machete.

Sunshine raises the machete overhead with both hands. They take a slow practice stroke to check their aim. Mike whips his head back and forth, trying to follow what Sunshine is doing, but there's no understanding in his face. Sunshine takes aim again, exhales slowly, and brings the blade down in a lightning flash.

The sound of metal on metal is horrible. Mike's head rolls on the pavement.

My stomach twists, but after throwing up by the car earlier, there's nothing left for it to reject. Aurelia clings to my arm, as though any second she might turn and run, dragging me behind her.

Mike's headless body squirms a final time, blood spouting from the stump of his neck, then goes limp. On the sidewalk, his head comes to a stop almost face down, like a child burying his face in his pillow. He was trying to kill us, but before that, he was someone I knew, someone I drank with, part of the landscape of my life. I don't know how to feel in this moment. In an instant of almost complete disconnect from reality, I note that Sunshine looks really fucking good swinging a machete.

"Y'all okay?" Sunshine asks, looking around at the three of us. Logan manages a nod, which I'm comfortable cosigning as our official group statement.

"What are you doing?" Aurelia says, her voice hoarse.

Sunshine is getting a plastic poncho, already stained with blood, from the back of the delivery car and putting it over their polo shirt. The poncho bears the same Pizzapocalypse logo as the shirt and car. I'm a little surprised not to see it on the machete.

Now somewhat splatter-proofed, Sunshine climbs up on the hood of their car and plants a checkered Vans sneaker in the center of Mike's chest. Fresh blood pulses from the slashes in his torso, and I wonder queasily how much he had inside him to begin with. Surely he ought to be running on empty by now.

Even without the bloodstains it would be clear that Sunshine has done this before, probably several times. They use their foot to shove Mike's body off the spikes with no apparent hesitation or difficulty. The noise his chest makes sliding free of the last few inches of wet steel is, even after everything that's happened tonight, one of the worst sounds I've ever heard. The thud when he hits the sidewalk should be ghastly but in fact comes as a relief.

Sunshine hops off the hood of the car, sticking their landing right in front of Aurelia and me. They've mostly avoided Mike's blood spatter, and now they shrug off the poncho and fold it carelessly into a small squarish shape. Belatedly answering Aurelia's question, they grin at us and say, "I'm delivering pizzas."

"The fuck you are," says Logan from the other side of the car.

"Just dropped off the last one," Sunshine says. "I'm about to head back to the store. My boss said to take the long way and make sure everyone sees the sign." They point to the side of the car, where a freshly painted YES WE ARE OPEN!!! RIGHT NOW!!! drips lemon yellow onto the pavement.

"Fuck. Fuck." I look at Aurelia and realize she's gray and glassy-eyed. "What the fuck? You just killed him."

"He was trying to kill your girl here," Sunshine says with a shrug in my direction. I wince at their choice of words, and see it hit Aurelia too.

"He was a person," she says roughly. "That was Mike. He was at my *house* yesterday."

"And he tried to kill us then too," Logan points out, his tone much gentler than Sunshine's. He puts a hand on Aurelia's arm. "Listen, I know . . ."

"You don't know shit," she says very quietly.

"I know," Logan says again, and pulls Aurelia into a hug she doesn't return. One of them is shaking, and the tremors move through both of their bodies. I feel like I could shiver myself into pieces, too. Sunshine just saved my life, but they also just killed a human being, hardly any different from the cops who shot Sam. I don't know whether I'm grateful or disgusted, and the combination—and the exhaustion—makes me dizzy.

"I'm sorry about your friend," Sunshine says, and for a moment I wonder how they know about Sam before I realize they're talking about Mike. "But I've seen a lot of scary shit tonight. If I hadn't put him down, he was going to kill you, and not as fast as I killed him."

"I know," I say. I wish I could tell them it's okay.

Logan rubs Aurelia's back once more, then lets her go. She looks around at us and does something with her face, which I eventually realize is supposed to be a reassuring smile.

"You know what, I could go for pizza," Logan says.

"You want to hitch a ride back to the store with me? We sell by the slice," Sunshine says.

Logan pats his hips like he's feeling for his wallet, but there's nothing under his slinky black dress but fishnet stockings. (Not even padding; I've been close enough to tell the difference at several points this evening. Those shapely thighs are completely his own.) "That would be dope, but—"

"But actually," I say in a flash of inspiration, "can we place an order for delivery?"

CHAPTER 10

It's well past midnight when Sunshine drops me, Aurelia, Logan, and three large pizzas on Beau's front porch. I've texted Leah several times in the last hour, to no avail, but I'm hoping the fact that we bear food will garner us forgiveness for showing up at this ungodly hour. I paid with my credit card at Pizzapocalypse, making sure to write in a ridiculous gratuity for Sunshine, but Aurelia still fishes a crumpled bill out of her wallet and hands it to them as we clamber out into the night.

"Thanks, folks," Sunshine says with a little salute. "Hang in there."

"Are you done after this?" I ask.

"Whenever people are hungry, Pizzapocalypse is there to answer the call," they say, grinning like a pirate. "There is no rest for the righteous."

Beau's house is a half mile of driveway from the main road, surrounded by a gravel lot and, farther out, by towering saguaros. A big garage stands separate from the house, its door open. Inside it I can see the silhouettes of some motorcycles and what looks like a friendly copper robot—that must be Beau's moonshine still.

The night is huge and dark this far from town, and profoundly quiet; I don't even hear cicadas. The air is still hot and thick with the unrequited desire for rain, but it's fresher and cleaner here, with a tang like woodsmoke and creosote. A single naked bulb on Beau's porch spills yellow light into the silver-edged blackness.

Sitting in Sunshine's car, drifting in the smell of pot smoke and garlicky tomato sauce, the exhaustion of the night settled like lead into my veins. Now I can barely walk up the front path. If no one answers the door, I think, I'll just curl up on one of the concrete porch steps, rest my head on a pizza box, and fall asleep.

But before Logan even raises his fist to knock, the door swings open. "Oh, fucking Christ," Leah says, exploding out of the door and hugging Logan, then Aurelia, and finally me. "I've been freaking the fuck out. I'm so glad you're okay." The last part is delivered directly to me, although that's probably just because I'm the direction she happens to be facing. The sight of her, eyeliner smudged and blue hair ratted, unfolds something tight and sore inside me. I'm glad we came here.

We follow Leah inside. "I tried to text you," I said. "I thought you were asleep when you didn't reply."

"No, I think my phone got fucked up back at the bar when—you know. We haven't slept yet." Inside, all the lights are on and Beau is perched on the couch in a nest of pillows.

"Did you know it fucking hurts to have broken ribs?" is what she greets us with.

"Her brilliant plan is to drink moonshine until she passes out," Leah explains. "Unfortunately—"

"Unfortunately," Beau interrupts, barely slurring, "I have the alcohol tolerance of a Greek god. And ass."

"You have the alcohol tolerance of ass?" Logan says, dropping onto the couch opposite Beau.

"Fuck you," she says fondly. "If I wasn't so fucking tired I'd throw these pillows at you."

Leah sits down next to Logan. "I'm gonna die of sheer exhaustion before she gets smashed enough to close her eyes. Anyway, hi." She scans the three of us, finally realizing our number has depleted. "Did you leave Sam at the hospital?"

Fuck, I wish I'd put the pizza down before she asked that question. "No," I say quietly.

"Oh." Leah looks from my face to Logan's and back, and I can actually see her steeling herself. Finally, she meets Aurelia's eyes. I can't imagine what she sees there, and I don't want to. "Oh, Aurelia," Leah breathes, and reaches out as if to embrace her.

"I can't," Aurelia says, and backs out of the room.

There's a long, heavy silence, and finally Beau says, "What happened?"

We tell her an abridged version of the story. I hurry past the part where I called the cops, where Sam's death is at least somewhat my fault, but Leah's eyes find mine and I know she hasn't missed it. I look down. I'm still holding the pizzas.

"And then Mike tried to eat us, but Sunshine the hot pizza driver cut his head off, and then we ordered pizza delivery so they'd drive us out here," Logan concludes. There's a terrible swirling silence.

"Man, that's fucked-up," Beau finally says. "Not the pizza. Thanks for the pizza. You want to grab plates?" she asks me, and I nod gratefully.

Beau's kitchen is on the other side of the entry hall. I glance out the window in the front door and see Aurelia sitting on the concrete steps, glowing artificial gold in the porch light. Her head is down, maybe resting in her hands. Her back is to me, and if she's crying, she's doing it without moving a visible muscle.

I put slices on plates and balance them, two in each hand, my college years as a waitress manifesting in my smooth stride back to the living room. "Who wants veggie and who wants meat?"

"Meat, please," says Beau. Logan claims a veggie plate. Without asking, I pass the remaining sausage and pepperoni to Leah. She quirks the corner of her mouth at me; I haven't forgotten that she's a vegetarian, but I also know that she makes exceptions in stressful situations. This definitely qualifies.

"Should we . . ." Logan gestures toward the door.

Leah shakes her head. "She knows it's in here. She'll get some when she wants it." I know Logan wasn't talking about pizza, and I know Leah knows it too.

For a while, we're all silent, except for the sounds of chewing. I want to say something—about Sam, about Mike, about Jacquie and Joey and all the horrific things that have happened tonight, about what in the world we're going to do next—but I can't find a way to get started. Beau clears her throat and looks around at all of us, then looks back down. Leah scrubs at her eyes in between bites, coming away with streaks of eyeliner on the heel of her hand. Logan goes back for seconds and brings some for Beau as well. He doesn't meet anyone's eyes on the way out of or back into the room.

When she's done with her pizza, Beau pulls out her flask and takes a long gulp, then passes it to Logan. He swigs, grimaces, and hands it to Leah. She drinks in solemn silence, hands it to me for my turn, and then we start again.

Aurelia comes back inside during the flask's second lap and joins us without speaking. There's no sign on her face that she's been crying. In fact, there's no sign on her face of anything whatsoever. She takes long, hard pulls from the flask without appearing to taste it. I've never seen Aurelia drink like this, but if ever she deserves to, it's this night.

Finally, Beau upends the flask and licks the last drops of moonshine from the neck. That, apparently, is the signal that the night is over. Still not speaking, Logan helps Beau rearrange herself into a supine position among her throne of pillows. Leah gestures down the hall, and I follow her.

Beau's guest room has a queen bed covered in a blue-and-green quilt that looks older than me. Leah opens the window, turns the blanket back and climbs in, fully clothed. I kick my shoes off and follow her lead.

In the dark, I hear her shifting, trying to get comfortable. My own body aches, but I know that will be the case no matter what position I'm in. As soon as I'm horizontal, I feel too heavy to move again, possibly ever.

Leah catches her breath and then lets it out slowly, as though preparing to say something and then deciding against it. Muscle memory urges me to ask what's bothering her. It was one of our longstanding rituals when we were together: her pretending she didn't want to talk about something, me cajoling it out of her, both of us already exhausted and resentful by the time we started discussing the actual issue. I want to take what she's offering—I'm grateful for the invitation to something that feels familiar, even if it stings—but tonight I just can't. It feels physically impossible, the way I couldn't get back in the car with Sam's body.

I stay where I am, still and silent. Leah inhales another prelude to speech, but again I let it pass without comment. After a long moment, she rolls onto her side, her back toward me.

No matter what, I think, no matter how strange and devastating this night has been, no matter that I'm tired and more than a little drunk—there is no way I can fall asleep with Leah's body this close to mine. She radiates warmth in the already hot room; she smells like sweat and earth and orange blossoms. I want to burrow into the softness of her, to listen to her pulse and taste her skin. The few inches of bed between us are as vast and unforgiving as the desert outside, and as I'm imagining dragging myself across that parched landscape to throw my broken body at her feet, I stumble into sleep and fall for hours or years.

CHAPTER 11

I wake from a dream of drowning in a swamp, dragged down by bony fingers around my ankle as I gasp and strain for air. Flailing awake in a strange bed, I still feel swamp sludge clinging to my skin. Then I realize it's just my clothes from last night, heavy and stuck to my body with July sweat. The sun is barely up on the other side of the blinds. Leah's still asleep, as far from me as possible on the opposite edge of the bed. I can smell the familiar humidity of her body, and despite everything, desire rings through me like a bell. I want to lick the sweat from behind her ear.

Instead, I roll out of bed, landing with an awkward thump that somehow doesn't disturb Leah. After sniffing myself, I strip off my sweaty crop top and leave it on the foot of the bed.

In the bathroom at the end of the hall, I find a stack of faded blue washcloths in the linen closet, and use one to wash my face and under my arms with cool water. This is the second morning in a row I've had to half-ass morning ablutions in someone else's bathroom; at least that part of Pride is living up to my hopes.

Slightly cleaner, wearing my mermaid leggings and black lace bra from last night, I walk down the hall and find Beau in the kitchen.

"Looking good," she says, but there's no lechery in it.

I look down at my sweaty cleavage and can't summon the energy to feel embarrassed. "Sorry for the indecency, but I sweated through my shirt in the night."

"Is that why you're up so early?"

"I guess so. Just got too hot to sleep anymore. You too, huh?"

"Turns out broken ribs are very stimulating," she says with a grimace. "Wish I'd known about this in my twenties. Coffee?" She points to a full pot on the counter. "There are mugs on that shelf. Can you get one for me?"

I don't normally drink hot coffee in the summer, but if I'm going to be awake I need all the help I can get. I grab two mugs and fill them, then, at Beau's direction, find the carton of half-and-half in the refrigerator and a bag of sugar in the pantry. I go through the motions of fixing both of our coffees in silence, a small peaceful ritual in the buttery morning sunlight.

Beau takes a long drink and savors it with her eyes closed. I follow her lead, letting the coffee sit on my tongue, just shy of scalding. It feels good as it burns a path down my throat, like being cleansed inside.

After a minute or two of quiet, Beau says, "So what are we going to do?" It sounds like the continuation of an ongoing conversation, maybe one she's been having with herself.

"Do about what?" I ask. I know what she means, but I'm stalling because I have no idea how to answer her question.

"About people going fucking crazy," she says. "Trying to eat each other and shit."

"What can we do about it?" I say, feeling defensive. "I'm not a doctor. I don't know how to fix this. What are we supposed to do except stay inside and try not to get killed until it's over?"

Beau looks unimpressed by my lack of bravery, and I can't say I blame her. This is exactly the kind of thing Leah used to get mad at me for, when we were together. "How do you know it's ever gonna be over?" she says. "You think someone else is gonna swoop in and fix this? We're in the middle of something really fucked-up. I've seen some things, but what went down at the bar last night was a new one on me. And then what you all saw at the hospital . . . this is bigger than just a bar fight."

I think about Mike, writhing on the hood of Sunshine's car with metal sticking out of his chest. The raw-meat smell of Jacquie's breath. Samantha's last, incoherent words. "I know it is," I say. "It's really bad."

"Yeah, and people are gonna be scared and pissed off when they figure out how bad it is, which will only make it worse. So we have to look for ways to help."

She makes it sound simple. "Like what?"

"Man, I don't know." Beau lifts a hand as if to rake it through her hair, then winces and lowers her arm slowly. "Maybe we start by figuring out what the fuck even happened last night. What are they saying on the news?"

I dig my phone out of my pocket. The battery is low, but not critical, and I pull up a local news site.

The first headline I see says VIOLENT ATTACK AT DRAG SHOW MEETS QUEER RESISTANCE. Below that, LGBT SAN LAZARANS SAY PRIDE MUST GO ON.

"That's not right," I say out loud.

"What's up?" Beau asks.

I read the article out loud, watching her frown deepen with every word.

"An unknown group of assailants disrupted a Pride weekend

drag show at Hellrazors Bar last night, throwing bottles, shouting homophobic slurs, and assaulting community members. Hellrazors employee Glen Cohen was hospitalized following the altercation and is in stable condition."

"Shit," says Beau. "I know Glen."

"He seemed weird before the show," I remember. "Kind of out of it, like Jacquie was acting before she tried to kill me. I wonder if he's got whatever it is."

She nods, knuckles white around her coffee cup. "Keep reading."

"No arrests have been made, and it is unknown whether further attacks are planned as the city's Gay Pride festivities continue on Sunday. However, organizers say the San Lazaro Pride Parade will take place as scheduled. 'This community will not be intimidated,' said Courtney Moire, spokesperson for parade sponsor Seabrook Beverages."

"This community?" Beau scowls. "Who's this Courtney person?"

"She was at the bar last night before everything went to shit," I say. "She's like Seabrook's liaison on the Pride committee, or something. Leah knows her. I don't even think she's queer." I can't remember seeing Courtney leave last night, but she must have been gone before things got scary.

"That's all there is," I say. "They're calling Hellrazors a hate crime. No mention of people taking bites out of each other. They're talking like it was organized, but that's—I mean, you were there. It wasn't like that at all."

"It's a cover-up," Beau says, her face sharp and worried. "Why?"

"To keep people from panicking?"

"I don't like it." She drums on the counter with her good

hand. "I can't believe they're not canceling Pride. People who weren't out last night have no idea. They're gonna walk right into a slaughterhouse. If they're trying to stop a panic, it's gonna backfire."

I hit the BACK button and scroll through more headlines, then open social media. Beau pulls out her own phone.

Seabrook has seized the opportunity to brand themselves the official alcoholic beverage of the resistance. "A portion of every sale of Seabrook Hard Seltzer this weekend, nationwide, will go directly to building a new health center to support the queer community of San Lazaro," their press release says. The health center has been in the works for months, but they're making it sound like it's a new project somehow related to last night's madness. I have to admit it's quick thinking, if painfully opportunistic.

There's even a new hashtag: #SanLazaroStrong. People around the country are using it to express their encouragement. When the hashtag appears on Twitter, it automatically generates a little emoji of a bottle, rainbow bubbles foaming from its neck. It's redundant, since most of the people who use the hashtag include pictures of themselves drinking Seabrook.

"There's some other stuff about violent incidents last night. All unrelated, of course. Oh, here's something about the hospital, but it just says an unidentified man attacked a security guard and was shot." I look up at Beau like she'll have an answer that makes sense of this. "There must have been thirty people at the door when that happened, but no statements from any of them. What the hell is that about?"

She shakes her head, presses her lips together. I keep scrolling. "The SLPD chief says violence always increases during the hottest part of the summer. Thanks, that's helpful. Oh, fuck." The ambient anxiety I've felt all morning, like a sweaty hand resting on the back of my neck, tightens into a claw as I see the picture below the headline INTRUDER KILLED IN ALTERCATION WITH HOMEOWNER.

The woman in the photo is my age or a bit younger, her shaved head emphasizing her big eyes and high cheekbones. Last time I saw her, Jacquie was half carrying her out the door of Sam and Aurelia's house. The article calls her Emilia Vasquez, but everyone I know has called her Emmy.

"What's up?" Beau notices my silence, my stricken face.

"This girl." I show her the phone. "She was at the party Friday night. She was acting weird, and everyone thought she was just drunk, so my . . . so someone drove her home. Except I don't think they ever made it home." The image of Jacquie's car, abandoned in the road, rises up like bile in my throat. I take the phone back and keep reading. "This says she broke into a house on the north side. She smashed a window and . . . fuck, she attacked a little kid."

"Jesus," Beau groans.

"The dad shot her. It says the kid was scared but not injured." I squeeze my eyes shut, remembering the wound on Jacquie's shoulder. It looked like a bite mark. Had Emmy tried to bite the child, too? What had she been thinking, in those last few moments? Did she hear the screams, the glass breaking? Was she afraid?

I feel nothing but contempt for the cops who killed Sam, but Emmy's death is more confusing. I remember the terror when Mike ran at me last night, and it's easy to imagine how the father must have felt, seeing this strange, wild-eyed person attacking his child. Was Emmy a monster or a victim? What about Mike, or for that matter Sunshine? What about Leah, plunging a knife into Jacquie's neck? I don't know how to sort it out in my mind.

"They don't say anything about her being . . . sick, or on drugs, or whatever," I say, reaching the end of the article, which is only a couple of paragraphs. "Nothing to connect it to Hellrazors, but I swear whatever was wrong with Emmy on Friday night, it's the same thing that fucked up all those people at the bar."

"So what is it?" Beau asks.

"What's what?" Leah is standing in the doorway, looking blearily gorgeous with her hair tangled around her head in a blue cloud. She's wearing a T-shirt I don't recognize, which must have been scrounged from Beau's drawers. Beau gives her an appraising glance, then looks away without answering.

"We're trying to figure out what's making everyone act so crazy," I say, feeling obscurely embarrassed, as though Leah walked in on Beau and me talking behind her back.

"Drugs?" suggests Beau. "Maybe there's a bad batch of something making the rounds."

"I don't think so," Leah says sharply. "Sam certainly didn't use anything. Ask Aurelia."

I take a step toward her and hold out my hand. "Hey," I say, trying to make my voice sound soothing. I've never been very good at comforting people, much less comforting the woman I'm still in love with about the death of someone she was fucking. "Whatever happened, if it was drugs or whatever, that wouldn't make it Sam's fault. No one's blaming her. It's no one's fault," I repeat. Leah doesn't meet my eyes, and my heart aches.

"It could be a drug," Beau repeats. Then she adds, "If it's mostly queer people getting it, maybe it's sexually transmitted."

"It can't be, or—" I cut myself off without finishing the thought. If Samantha had some sort of sexually transmitted madness, she would have gotten it from—or given it to—Leah or Aurelia, who both seem fine. But talking about Sam is painful to Leah; I can tell by the way she's folding in on herself, as though she can physically avoid the words. I don't want to make it worse.

"It's not," Leah agrees, still refusing to look at me.

Beau glances at Leah, then back at me, and rolls her eyes. "Not that I don't sympathize, ladies, but figuring out what's happening is more important than your dyke drama at the moment."

Finally, Leah looks up. "We are not—"

"Sam said that guy bit her," I say quickly, not wanting to hear what Leah will say: that we couldn't possibly have drama, because her feelings for me are dead and buried, irrelevant in the extreme. "And Jacquie had something that looked like a bite mark. I think that's how it spreads."

Beau nods. "Yeah, I can see that. Like rabies or something."

"Or zombies," says Logan, slipping past Leah into the kitchen. He's still wearing his slip dress from last night. "Oh my God, coffee." He picks up the pot and takes a drink directly from the spout, which is deeply gross but also, for some reason, kind of hot.

"They're not fucking zombies," Leah says, still hunched in the doorway like she's trying to disappear. "This is real life."

"Denying what's right in front of your face is the number one cause of death in unprecedented situations," says Logan. He reaches over my head to grab a mug from the cabinet. I could move out of his way, but I don't, and his hip presses into my side.

"I think you made that up," Beau says. "But you're right that we shouldn't be ruling out possibilities just because they're unlikely."

"Whatever," mutters Leah. "I have to pee." She disappears back down the hall.

"How'd you sleep?" I ask Logan, whose hip is still lightly touching mine. I lock my legs and try to hold perfectly still, so I don't either lean into the contact or break it.

"I mean, pretty bad." He nods to Beau. "Not that your couch isn't comfy, but, like, it's still a couch." To me, he adds, "Where did you sleep?"

"Leah and I slept in the spare bedroom," I say without thinking. Then I realize how it sounds and my face gets hot.

"Oh," Logan says, his perfect eyebrows rising almost imperceptibly. "Oh, word. I bet y'all were more comfortable in there, huh?"

Instead of answering, I take a gulp of my coffee, now lukewarm. Beau is watching me with obvious amusement, and I wish I'd stayed in bed.

"So what happens next?" she asks.

"There's so much fucked-up shit happening," Logan says. "I think we all need to lay low and stay safe until—"

"No, what happens next with the people who go crazy?" says Beau. "Do they get better? Because rabies is fatal if you don't get a shot right away. What happens to these people if they don't get killed, like Sam and that Emmy girl?"

I shake my head frantically at Beau, but it's too late. Beside me, I feel Logan freeze. "Emmy?" he says very quietly.

"Ah, shit," says Beau.

"I'm so sorry, Logan," I say. "We found a news story. Emmy broke into a house and . . ." I can't bring myself to say the words.

Logan's face twists, and he turns his back on both of us. I'm at eye level with his shoulders, and I can see them trembling. He takes a few shaky breaths, sniffles, and runs a hand over his face. Then he turns back around.

"I knew she wasn't okay," he says, his voice thick with tears.

"I knew it last night, when all those people freaked the fuck out, I knew the same thing must have happened to Emmy but I didn't want to think about it."

It seems to take an inordinately long time to reach across the few inches between us and put my hand on Logan's arm. As soon as I touch him, he slumps against me. His skin feels hot and dry, and he isn't shaking anymore but I can feel the effort it's costing him.

"I'm so sorry," I say again, uselessly.

"This is all so fucked," Logan says. "And it just keeps going."

I know what he means. Sam, Mike, Emmy . . . the deaths are piling up. There's no time to process them before the next crisis hits. Even this, now, in Beau's quiet kitchen with sun scorching through the blinds, feels like a pause instead of a respite, a quick-caught breath in the middle of a scream that hasn't stopped.

"And they're lying about it," Beau says. Her voice is soft but unwavering. "The story they're telling in the news, it's not real."

"Why?" asks Logan, a raw red wound of a syllable. I feel the vibration as he gulps down a sob.

"Absolutely fucked if I know," she says. "But that's why we have to figure out what's going on and how to stop it, because I don't believe for a second that anyone else is coming to help."

When Logan has calmed down and is sitting at the table with a second cup of coffee, I make my way down the hall, looking for Leah. There's a closed door across from the room where we spent the night; I listen and don't hear any movement inside. It must be Beau's room, where Aurelia slept. I move away from the door quietly. Sleep is a threadbare mercy, but it's the only one I can offer her right now.

The guest room where Leah and I slept is empty, except for the thick hot human smell in the air. I see her backpack slung over a chair beside the dresser, and it triggers a flash of urgency that's been buried for most of the last twelve hours under much greater crises. Leah usually carries a stash of supplies for various kinds of emergencies. While there's nothing in that backpack to shore up the crumbling world outside, she might at least have a solution to the worry that's been gnawing my brainstem since Logan told me the condom broke.

Still moving as quietly as I can, I crouch beside the chair and unzip the backpack. A paperback book, a couple of spiral notebooks, wallet, makeup pouch. Underneath all that are some of the supplies Leah keeps on hand for her reproductive health work: pads, tampons, condoms, latex gloves. There's a couple of unlabeled prefilled syringes, and a box of pregnancy tests, but no Plan B.

"Can I help you?" Leah says sharply, and I jerk my head around so fast I nearly fall over.

"Hey. Hi. Good morning," I say, trying to sound nonchalant but coming off extremely chalant.

"Why are you in my bag?" she asks. She's not angry, but she's prepared to get angry if I give her a reason.

"Uh, looking for a tampon," I say stupidly.

Leah frowns. "Since when do you use tampons?" Of course she hasn't forgotten her months-long campaign to get me to switch to a reusable menstrual cup. I'm not a good liar.

"Well, I don't, really, but I don't have my cup because I didn't think I was going to get my period today, but with all the stress and, you know, violence and everything, I guess my hormones are a little . . ."

"Whatever," she says. "Help yourself."

"No, wait. That was a lie," I say.

Leah stares at me, then gestures *go ahead.*

"I was checking to see if you had, um, emergency contraception." My face goes red and I have to look away from her.

Her voice is measured when she says, "Why?"

"Because I like to take some with my coffee to start the day off right," I snap. The rancor in my tone is unnecessary, but I can't seem to dial it back. "Why do you think?"

Even without looking at her directly, I know exactly what expression she has on her face. "You and Logan didn't use a condom?"

"Actually, if you want the specifics, we used one of those rainbow condoms from your besties at Seabrook, and it fucking broke," I say, feeling furious and spiteful. The specter of Seabrook has haunted every awful moment of this weekend, they're actively profiting off the deaths of our friends, and I'm still angry at Leah for defending them—for inviting them into Pride in the first place.

My rage bounces off her. "Well, I don't have any Plan B in there," she says. "Sorry. There's some at my place, though. Do you want to come with me to pick it up?" I hear the effort in her voice, and I appreciate it. This is an olive branch, and not one I can afford to turn down.

"Is it, like, safe? How would we get there?"

"I can't promise it's safe," she says. "But at least we'll be together."

I follow Leah back into the kitchen, where Beau is still nursing her coffee. She looks up as she walks in, and I see bad news in the cant of her eyebrows.

"What happened?" I say, wishing I didn't have to ask, not wanting to know.

"I called Dorian," Beau says slowly. "Glen's husband," she adds at my blank look. "I told you, Glen and I go way back. We were dykes together in the '90s."

"Okay," I say. "What did Dorian say?" I glance at Logan, but he's looking down at the table.

"Glen has brain damage," she says.

"I'm so sorry," I say, but she shakes her head.

"Not from the fight," she says. "He got hit at some point last night, but the doctors said it doesn't explain a fraction of the damage they saw. He woke up this morning screaming horrible shit, puking blood, tried to bite a nurse—they sedated him and did the scan, but then he didn't wake up. He's still out. Dorian said they don't know if he'll ever wake up, or who he'll be if he does."

"Oh my God," Leah murmurs. I feel her sway, and without thinking I wrap my arm around her waist, steadying her.

"He's not the only one, either," Beau says. "Obviously the doctors aren't saying anything, but Dorian's been talking to some other families at the hospital and there's at least three other people there with unexplained brain damage."

"Great," says Logan. "So whatever this shit is going around, it turns people into zombies and then destroys their brains."

"Why isn't there some kind of public health alert?" Beau says. "If people knew what was happening—"

"We need to go to my place," Leah says abruptly. "Can I borrow your truck? Or one of your bikes?"

Beau looks up in surprise. "What for?"

I hear the effort it costs Leah to soften her tone. "I just need to grab a few things," she says. "Wendy's going to come with me. I've had street medic training and I want to grab some supplies."

"You're coming back though, right?" Logan asks me, stretching and cracking his back. I can't help staring at his arms just a little.

"Yeah, we'll come right back," Leah answers for me. Beau nods in satisfaction, and I'm grateful. Coming here last night was a panicked last resort, but now I find I don't want to be separated from Beau and Logan and Aurelia any longer than I have to. It feels like we're all in this together, a feeling I haven't had in a long time. And Beau's house is the safest place I can think of to wait out the apocalypse.

The bike Beau lets Leah borrow is beautiful. I don't know motorcycles at all, but it's low and dark and shiny, chrome and black leather and candy-apple green. The purr of its engine is loud and deep.

It's been a long time since I've climbed onto the back of a motorcycle driven by Leah. It feels comfortable, but nostalgic—like putting on an outfit that fits perfectly but isn't really my style anymore. I slide my arms around her waist. Her belly is soft, just like I remember, warm through the thin jersey of her T-shirt. I'm wearing my leggings from last night and a shirt I borrowed from Beau, the leather of the motorcycle seat already hot between my legs. It's intimate, riding two up with someone, and not just because your whole bodies have to fit together: chest to back, thigh to thigh. It's the way the rider has to move with the driver, following their weight, keeping their spines parallel so they move as one. I wasn't always good at listening to Leah, but I'm good at listening to her body. We still fit seamlessly like this.

In Beau's borrowed helmet, I'm alone with the roar of the bike and the quiet of my thoughts. I hold on to the curve of Leah's waist harder than I really need to. She's in her own helmet, her own separate space, although our bodies are closer than they've been in months. I can feel from the tension in her shoulders and the way she rolls the throttle that she's not happy with me. She doesn't want us to be stuck together like this. She'd rather be snarling off into the sunset alone.

Leah takes side streets to get across town to her apartment, and we don't see many other people. The sun is high and hot, though it's only midmorning. There's a stoplight out, several cars slowed to a crawl with no traffic cops to direct them through the intersection, but Leah just eases us onto the shoulder and turns right, veering around the tangle of impatient cars. I see smashed glass and what might be blood on the sidewalk in front of a gas station, and there's a food truck lying on its side at the entrance to Jackalope Park.

At Leah's apartment, I lounge uneasily in the doorway. It feels strange to be in her space again after all this time. The coffee table is in a different place, and there's a vintage *Thelma and Louise* poster on the wall that wasn't there before. But I recognize the rose quartz candleholder I gave her on the bookshelf; I still remember kneeling on the floor in front of that ratty thrift-store couch with Leah's thighs clenching around my head. Most of the places I visit in my daily life have had their associations with Leah scoured off through repetition in the months since we broke up, but I've never been in this room before and not been Leah's girlfriend.

She shoots me a glance. "Are you stuck there waiting for an invitation? I can't deal with zombies and vampires on the same day."

"No," I say with an awkward laugh, and take an awkward step inside. Leah grabs a stepstool from the kitchen and carries it into the living room to reach the top of her bookshelf. If we were still together, I'd make a joke about her being short, and she'd feign offense and make me get the high-up thing for her, and then I'd hold it out of her reach until she tickled me and we collapsed on the couch, laughing and kissing. I don't do any of that now, but I do check out her ass while she's turned away from me. She's wearing tight jeans and I'm only human.

"Catch," she says, turning and tossing something underhand. I don't react quickly enough because I'm still staring at the air where her butt used to be, and the little cardboard box bounces off my chest and lands on the floor.

"Sorry," I mumble, crouching to pick it up. Leah looks at me with her mouth pursed, as though considering exactly how sorry I am. Looking at her from this angle, standing over me like an idol, does things to my brain.

"So what the fuck, anyway, Wendy?" The question comes abruptly, as though she's been holding it back for a while. "What were you thinking?"

"Um," I say incisively. "What?"

"What were you thinking with Logan?" She puts her hands on her hips. I feel small and helpless gazing up at her like this. I could stand up and then she'd be the one looking up at me, but I don't.

"Who says I was thinking?" I say. "I was at a party, a hot guy offered to show me his room, it's really not a complicated story. And it's none of your business, anyway."

Leah scowls. "Kind of made it my business, don't you think?"

"The way you made it my business when you started climbing all over Aurelia right in front of me?"

"Uh, *no*," she says, eyes widening. "I meant when you asked me to get you birth control, but thanks for letting me know you're up in your feelings about that."

"I'm not in my feelings! I fucked someone else, you fucked someone else. We're even."

"You're still keeping score in a relationship that ended six months ago," Leah says angrily.

"I'm not," I say. "I already lost. I'm over it."

"How did you lose when I'm the one who got cheated on? How is this *your* pity party?"

"You were leaving me anyway!" I shout as I finally break. I've been holding this inside for six months and I'm exhausted and the world might be ending and, honestly, just fuck it. "You were about to dump me. You were all closed off and distant and canceling plans and ignoring my calls. Your mind was a million miles away and I knew you were just trying to find a good reason, so I fucking gave you one. You're welcome."

She stares at me, mouth gaping. For once I've actually left her without a quick response.

"Yeah," I say, feeling satisfied and hollow all at once. "So feel free to keep blaming me for everything that went wrong, but I made your life easier at the end and we both know it. Don't pretend everything would still be sunshine and orgasms if I hadn't fucked it up. You were on your way out, so don't be pissed at me for opening the door."

"No," she says. "You don't get to do that. You don't get to hold a grudge against me for what you imagined I might do and use that as an excuse for the shit you actually did. I *didn't* leave you, Wendy. Maybe we were having problems, maybe I'm not the greatest at intimacy, but we could have worked on that shit if you hadn't decided to burn it all down. I would have worked on it." Suddenly, she runs out of steam and looks away. She finishes in a quieter voice. "I thought you were worth working on it."

I deflate too. Not knowing what else to say, I ask, "You did?" My voice sounds too loud suddenly.

"Yeah." She shrugs. "But it wasn't worth it to you."

How can I explain that that's not it at all—that I didn't ruin things with Leah because I didn't care, but because I cared so *much*, because I felt it prickling inside me like I'd swallowed a thousand pins, shredding my guts every minute of the day? How can I explain that I never stopped thinking about her, that even when I was with Jacquie it was love letters to Leah I was writing on the insides of her thighs?

I can't. It's stupid and it doesn't make any sense. *Baby, I only cheated because I loved you too much?* She'd throw me out onto the street if I said that, apocalypse be damned, and I wouldn't blame her.

So I don't say anything. I stand up and walk the three steps to the kitchen, peeling the pill out of its foil wrapper as I go. It's small enough to dry-swallow, but I need the excuse to get out of Leah's line of sight, to bend over the kitchen sink and cup my hand under the copper-tasting water from the faucet and gulp it down while excess runs down my chin and neck. I stand there for another beat, listening to my own breathing, before I gather myself enough to go back into the main room. Leah is standing exactly where I left her, like she hasn't moved at all.

"There," I say quietly. "It never happened."

She opens her mouth as if to say something, but then stops, bites her lip, and sighs. "We should go," she says.

I get to the door just before she does, and I'm reaching for the doorknob before I realize she's doing the same thing. Her hand closes over mine, and we both freeze. I hear her catch her breath behind me. The apartment is sweltering. I can smell her sweat, her breath. I'm trapped between her body and the door.

"I'm so fucking sorry," I say without turning to face her. I've never said that to Leah before, not really, not for the things that matter. The hand covering mine on the doorknob tightens just perceptibly.

"You're sorry?" There's tension in her voice and thrumming

through the lines of her body, but I can't quite tell what it means.

"I'm sorry I ruined everything," I say. And I have just enough room to turn around, my back pressing against the door, looking down into Leah's face when I say, "I wish I could take it back."

She stares up at me, her eyes huge, velvety brown, the pupils infinite lakes covered in black ice. I could freeze or drown there, but I don't flinch. I want to dive in. "You can't," she says. "You can't fucking take it back." Then she kisses me.

CHAPTER 12

It's not a sweet kiss. It tastes like salt and all the different ways we've hurt each other. I can feel her teeth, and I kiss her back with all of mine. Her hands are on my hips, pinning me to the door, and even though she's shorter than me she makes me feel small. My hands are still at my sides, unsure if I'm allowed to touch her, unsure if I deserve it.

Leah pulls back, keeping my lower lip caught between her teeth until I whimper, then lets go and kisses down my neck. She knows exactly where to touch me, where even the warmth of her breath leaves me helpless. "Please," I say, and I don't know quite what I'm asking for but I know it's too much. Instead of responding in words, she slides her hands under my borrowed shirt and up to my waist, fingers hot against my bare skin.

That's when I give in and grab her, take her chin in my hand and tip it up to kiss her again. It's slower and softer this time, but it still hurts. It feels more like a last kiss than a first kiss. Her thigh is between my legs, and I can't help but grind against it, just a little bit. I think I might cry.

"Come on," she says, and takes me by the wrists. Leah pulls me to the couch and I kneel in front of it, half muscle memory, half genuine reverence. She sits facing me, her legs apart, but I don't move to open her jeans. I have a sense that I haven't yet been given permission.

Mimicking my gesture from a moment earlier, Leah cups my chin in her hand and tilts my head back. I stare into her eyes as she traces my mouth with the tip of her thumb. My lips part and her thumb eases between them. I hear her sharp inhalation as I gently close my teeth.

"Wendy," she says softly, and I surge up to kiss her again, crashing into her like a shipwreck survivor clinging to a rock. Her tongue is fierce and hot, her gasp sucking the air out of my lungs. God, she tastes so good, so sweet and perfectly *Leah*, but I'm already cracking inside with the knowledge that this isn't real, it can't last. It's like walking into a beloved home that I know has already burned to the ground, because I lit the match myself.

I'm still wearing the T-shirt I borrowed from Beau, but I might as well be wearing nothing, the way Leah's hands are everywhere, all over my body. I can't get enough of her. My hands slide over her skin as though I could devour her with my fingers, but as I grab the hem of her shirt to pull it over her head, she stops me. I pull back just far enough to see the dark fire in her eyes as, with her hands on my shoulders, she pushes me back down to my knees.

This time I don't hesitate to unzip her jeans. She helps me, wiggling out of them before the fly is even all the way open, stripping off her underwear too. Then she leans back, parts her thighs, and just lets me stare.

"You are so goddamn beautiful," I say. "I missed this so

much."

"So fucking do something about it," she replies, closing her eyes and tipping her head back.

I wrap my hands around her thighs, enjoying the way the soft dark hairs feel under my palms. Leah moans and arches her back under me. The taste of her is fucking perfect, ocean-brine with a hint of sweetness, wet like she's melting on my tongue. I'm wet too, my hips rocking in vain against nothing, keeping time with the frantic rhythm of my lips and tongue.

Leah tangles a hand in my hair and pulls me in, grinding into my face, using me. I groan, but my voice is swallowed up by the hurricane roar building in Leah's body. My tongue follows her wetness back to its source, circling and then dipping inside of her. Leah whimpers. I know what that means, so I slide two fingers into her, curling them where I can feel the swelling of her clit from the inside.

"Yeah, yeah, fuck yeah," Leah groans, her thighs tightening around my head. I can barely breathe, but I barely care. She's always quiet during sex until she's close enough to lose control. Suddenly it feels like a race: how deep inside her can I get, how much of her can I taste, before she falls apart? With my free hand, I dig my fingernails into her thigh, determined to leave her with a reminder when this is over.

"More," she says breathlessly, and I give her more. I give her everything I have, pour it all into her until she can't take anymore and she comes with a sob.

I don't stop until she pushes me away, and then only reluctantly. She's sprawled on the couch, glowing with sweat, hair a mess and still wearing her shirt. For a long moment, only because her eyes are still closed, I let myself look at her the way I want to, my eyes lingering the way my mouth did a moment ago. Her lips are soft and open, her cheeks flushed. Leah is so beautiful. I understand in an instant, natural as the blink of an eye, that I'm still in love with her and I probably always will be.

Her eyelids flutter open and I have to pretend I wasn't staring. "Damn," she says, catching her breath. "You stayed sharp." For some reason the compliment makes me feel like crying.

"I just have a good memory," I say.

"What about you?" she says, her mouth quirking up at the corner. "I know how much you like giving head. You must be dripping by now." Her voice is light, like it's nothing, like it doesn't matter that she knows things about me no one else has ever bothered to learn, and it makes my thighs tremble.

"Yeah," I say, my voice nothing, barely more than a sigh.

"Get the fuck up here, then," she says.

I climb into her lap, straddling her soft thighs. She looks up at me, her smirk gone, her brown eyes deep and serious. One of her hands holds my waist, and the other slides down into my leggings, her thumb pressing against me through my underwear.

"You want this?" she asks. "You want me?"

If I answer that question, my voice will give everything away. Instead, I reach between my legs to guide her hand where I need it. Pushing thin wet cotton aside, she fucks me slowly with two fingers, then three. It's perfect. She's perfect. I rock in her lap, gripping her shoulders for leverage. I'm so close.

"Wait," Leah breathes, hot on my neck. "Let me just—"

Before either of us can finish, someone bangs on the door.

Leah's hand stops moving, and she stares at me with huge, baffled eyes. I know I'm staring back, equally frozen, unable to fathom moving from this moment into the next one.

"Help," yells a voice from the breezeway outside. "Someone help—oh, no!" The voice moves away, and I hear pounding that must come from the next door down.

I see the calculation in Leah's eyes. There's somebody out there in trouble, which could mean they're being chased, or they might already be infected. Staying in here with the door locked is our safest option.

But Leah could never do that, and we both know it. So instead of waiting for her to tell me, I climb out of her lap, pull my leggings back into place, and go to the door.

Leah's apartment door opens inward. I have to turn the knob, pull it back toward me, and step past it into the doorway so that I can see down the hall. That's how long it takes me to realize I've made a horrible mistake.

IRIS

Iris Delgado is not superstitious. She doesn't believe in psychics, tarot readers, or Bigfoot. Her son Quentin loves those ghost-hunting shows, and anything to do with aliens, but Iris finds it all silly and even a little embarrassing, though she'd never tell Quentin that. She was raised Catholic by her Mexican mamá and abuela, but she doesn't buy into God and Jesus either. Iris believes in what she can see with her own two eyes.

So it's not a premonition that shudders through her when her phone rings at ten o'clock on Saturday night. Her mind simply jumps to the assumption of bad news because it's been a hot, strange day and she's a little on edge. The grocery store was understaffed, full of stressed, impatient people in long lines, and the pharmacy was closed. Then she ordered delivery from the only Vietnamese restaurant in town, but the driver never showed up with her pho. It's no wonder Iris is in a bad mood and assumes the worst.

The feeling of dread intensifies when she sees Quentin's name on the caller ID.

"Hi, baby," Iris says instead of what she really wants to say, which is *What's wrong?*

"Mamá, I don't want you to freak out," he says in the extra-calm voice he only uses when he's freaking out, "but I'm in the ER."

She's on her feet instantly, reaching for her purse. "Are you okay? You need a ride? Oh, I knew it was a bad idea, you going to that show." Ever since what happened in Miami, Iris hates it when Quentin goes to clubs. She tries to keep it to herself, because it doesn't do any good to beg her son to stay home, but there are crazies out there, and putting a bunch of gay people in one place with a big neon sign is just asking for trouble.

"I'm fine. I'm just getting stitches—"

"I'm on my way."

Quentin tries to dissuade her, but Iris is already out the door and in her car. "Mamá, you don't need to do that. Caleb drove me here, he can drive me home." The fist of anxiety squeezing in her gut relaxes infinitesimally. She trusts Caleb, Quentin's boyfriend. She knows he'll do whatever he can to take care of her boy. But he's still not Quentin's *mother*. Iris needs to see her baby with her own eyes and be sure he's really safe.

"What happened?" Iris says, driving too fast, swerving around two cars locked in the aftermath of a crash. The drivers are nowhere to be seen; no cops or traffic cones either. That's disconcerting, but Iris has no energy to spare for wondering what's going on.

Slowly, reluctantly, Quentin says, "This girl—"

"A *girl* attacked you? Was Caleb there?" Her boy is still a skinny thing at the age of twenty-five, but Caleb is tall and imposing. It's part of why she likes him; his physical presence assuages her anxieties about Quentin getting harassed for being, well, *obvious*.

"Yeah, but—there was nothing he could do, Mamá," Quentin says defensively. "She just came *flying* at us. We didn't even make it into the bar, it was right as we were walking up. I think she was high on something. I had my wallet out in my hand, and she . . ." He takes a deep breath, steadying himself, and Iris squeezes the steering wheel until her knuckles ache. "She *bit* my hand and grabbed my wallet. It was the weirdest thing," he finishes, too lightly.

"Baby," Iris says, fighting the urge to scream. "The human mouth is full of germs. You need a shot for rabies and who knows what else."

"I know, Mamá," he reassures her. "I'll make sure they take care of it. We're going to be out of here before you even get here. You should just go home."

But they're not out of there by the time Iris arrives at the ER. The waiting room is absolute chaos, every chair taken up, people standing against the walls while the more seriously ill or injured slump on the floor. Someone is crying in a low, monotonous drone that echoes inside Iris's chest.

She sees Caleb first, standing with his muscular arms crossed, looking tense. Behind him, separated by Caleb's body from the rest of the room, is her son. His arm is wrapped in something plaid—a flannel shirt that must have come from Caleb, who's wearing nothing but a white undershirt with his jeans now. Quentin is pale, hunched over with his wounded hand clasped to his chest. Iris's stomach twists when she sees him. This looks much worse than just a cut on his hand. Is he in shock?

When Caleb sees her making her way apologetically through the crowded room, his relief is so obvious it scares her a little.

Caleb isn't the kind of boy whose emotions usually show on his face. "Mrs. Delgado," he says, and when she opens her arms he crumples into her hug, even though he's an entire foot taller than her.

"It's so crazy here," Caleb says into her shoulder. "I guess there have been, like, a ton of car accidents tonight?" She thinks of the abandoned wreck she passed on the way, wondering if those drivers are here now.

"Is he okay?" Iris whispers to Caleb. She should ask Quentin himself, but somehow she doesn't want to, is afraid of what he'll say, or won't. His gaze hasn't flickered from where it rests on the floor. Iris is not sure whether he knows she's here.

"I can't tell if it's still bleeding," Caleb says. "He won't let me unwrap his hand to check." That wasn't really an answer to her question, Iris thinks.

She crouches down next to Quentin's chair, ignoring the creak of her knees. "Baby, I'm here," she says. "How are you feeling?"

"Mamá?" Her son's eyes track from side to side dizzily before focusing on her. That can't be a good sign. His pupils are so huge she can barely see the warm brown of his eyes. He stinks of sweat. "It's hot in here," Quentin says. He sounds eerily young, shocked back into his child self. "Can you get me some water?"

"Of course, baby." Relieved to have a task, Iris pushes herself to standing on the arm of Quentin's chair and looks around for a fountain. She sees a vending machine on the other side of the room. "Excuse me," she mutters as she tries to weave through the crowd without touching anyone. There are so many *bodies* in this room, and Quentin's right, it's far too hot.

There's a panic at the back of Iris's throat she keeps swallowing down. Her boy, her *baby*, is hurt. God, she hates this. She worries so much, all the time. Those people on the news, that awful Randall woman and her compatriots, they're always talking about how men like Quentin are dirty and disgraceful and want to hurt children. And people believe them. Everyone wants something to be scared of, something to rally against. Even people at Iris's office talk about the threat, the perversion, the need to reaffirm good old-fashioned values that would have seen her sweet, sensitive child locked up or beaten or worse.

Iris remembers seeing on the news what they did to that boy in Wyoming. Quentin was five then, and Iris had no reason to believe there was anything different about him, but she still clutched him to her chest until he squirmed, trying to sob quietly into his hair, so he wouldn't know anything was wrong. How could any parent live through something like that?

She worries so much about all these awful people stoking all this fear, and what it might do to Quentin and Caleb and their friends. She thinks about the girl who bit him. Belatedly it occurs to her to wonder whether someone called the police on Quentin's attacker, but they must have, she thinks. Although whether anyone responded, given the level of chaos she's seen tonight, is a separate question entirely. That girl could still be out on the street, and even if she's not, there are hateful people like her everywhere, with brains full of poison and mouths full of teeth.

Quentin has explained to her over and over why Pride is so important to him, why he and Caleb need to connect with their community, to let people know they're not ashamed. And she gets it. She does. But if this is the kind of thing that happens, is it really worth it? The bite on his hand is already bad enough, but what if it gets infected? What if he gets some kind of horrible illness—rabies, or worse? Is that a price worth paying just to go to a drag show?

Iris only realizes she's been standing in front of the vending machine, staring vacantly into space, when someone slams into her from behind. She staggers forward and catches herself on the glass front of the machine, the bright colors of soda bottles and shiny candy wrappers swimming in her vision. Ready to unload all the night's frustration and fear in one cathartic shout at the person who knocked her down, Iris spins around—only to see that the confusion of the waiting room has spiraled into something even worse.

It looks like a circle of hell. Like a painting she saw once, she can't remember the title or the artist, just the awful feeling that everywhere she looked was another terrible detail. A woman has her hands around the neck of a nurse in scrubs and is squeezing, choking her. A man is punching another man in the face, over and over, blood splattering from his nose with every swing. A child is curled up, trying to hide under a chair, hiccupping through tears. And so much more. Too much more.

Reflexively, Iris squeezes her eyes shut against the horror. When she opens them again, she sees a chair—a heavy one, made of solid wood—sailing toward her head. Iris closes her eyes again in the moment before impact, but she can't block out the piercing crunch, or the glass shards that fly in all directions. The chair has missed her and hit the vending machine. Heat speckles her face, her arms, as though she's been sprayed with hot water, but those points of contact get hotter and hotter until her nerves are screaming with pain. Iris raises her hands to her cheeks and brings them away streaked with blood.

Someone crashes into her, shoulder to sternum, and Iris stumbles backward. Her feet leave the floor but she doesn't fall; instead she's carried by the force of the crowd stampeding away from the maelstrom of violence. Pain lights up her right arm, then her collarbone, as people collide and grab for any handhold they can reach. Fingernails rip one of the scratches on her cheek open wider. Iris bangs her head on the doorframe and then she's shoved outside, into the night air.

The crowd thins out, bodies pouring in all directions, and Iris staggers and lands on her hands and knees on the sidewalk. Blood spatters her hands and clothing, along with several splinters of broken glass, throwing fragmented streetlight into her eyes. Her right upper arm throbs. Looking closer, she realizes it's not just from the glass shrapnel. A ring of deeper wounds pierces through the fabric of her sleeve, oozes blood just below her shoulder. In all the turmoil, she didn't even notice that someone *bit* her.

Iris hears retching and tries to flinch away, but she's too weak and dizzy. Just beside her, someone—she can't see them, only their shadow—bends over and vomits. Horrible black stuff pours onto the pavement, smelling not just bile-sour but somehow worse, chemical and acrid. In a burst of disgusted adrenaline, Iris shoves herself to her feet and runs.

Her heart screams at her to go back, to help Quentin, but she can't turn around, can't even slow down. She's too afraid, too in pain, to wade back into that nightmare. She'll go—somewhere else, she doesn't know where yet, but she'll find someone to bring back to help her son. Her vision grows stormy and red. She wipes sweat out of her eyes but only succeeds in smearing blood and that horrible black stuff onto her face. She keeps running. She'll find help.

She pretends she didn't see what she knows she saw, just before she closed her eyes—pretends maybe she was mistaken or confused, or that she missed it in the onslaught of violence and dread all around her. She tries to forget that she saw her son, her Quentin, grabbing his beloved Caleb by the hair and ripping a huge, bloody bite out of his cheek.

CHAPTER 13

The woman is probably my parents' age. She's very thin and possibly white, although it's difficult to discern skin color or facial features under the filth that covers her. She's wearing what used to be a conservative floral dress, but most of the skirt has been ripped off somehow, leaving her legs bare except for shredded and bloody pantyhose. There's a bald patch on the right side of her head where the hair has been torn out. Her right shoulder is a mess of lacerations, blood and tattered fabric and flesh.

I see all this in a flash, not processing the individual details so much as the overall impression of *danger*. What stands out to me in the moment I look at her, in the moment she looks back at me, is her eyes. They're as huge and deep and empty as Jacquie's or Mike's last night. I can't imagine how this woman managed to shout intelligible words a few seconds ago, when it's perfectly clear no facet of her thinking mind remains intact.

I curse reflexively and go to slam the door again, but I have to step out of its way to close it, and before I can succeed the woman is *there*. She slams into the door with her shoulder, and even though she can't weigh more than a hundred pounds, the force of it sends me reeling backward. I fall back into Leah's apartment, screaming. No other doors open along the breezeway. Either we're the only uninfected people left in the building, or everyone else has learned from my mistake.

"Mrs. Delgado?" I hear Leah say, her voice small and confused, and then she groans "Motherfucker" as Mrs. Delgado bares her teeth and snarls at both of us. There are *things* stuck between some of her teeth, things I can't stand to look at or think about.

I lunge toward Leah's bedroom, no real plan in my head except to try again to put a door between myself and the ghoul that used to be Leah's neighbor. The scrawny woman grabs me around the waist and tries to drag me back. I flail at her wildly, ineffectually, like trying to fling away a spider crawling across my hand. Mrs. Delgado is more tenacious than a spider. Her jaws snap as I try to push her away. Thank God for the oversized shirt that Beau lent me, which gets caught in Mrs. Delgado's mouth as she tries to take a bite out of my rib cage.

I punch her in the side of the head. It would be a terrible angle even if I knew how to throw a punch, which I absolutely don't. Mrs. Delgado doesn't even seem to register the blow. Like all the infected people I've seen, she's apparently beyond feeling pain. Anything shy of total bodily dismemberment is barely an inconvenience.

"Hey! *Hey!*" Leah is screaming, I dimly realize, trying to get her neighbor's attention away from me. I'm grateful, though I don't expect her to succeed. Mrs. Delgado wrenches her head back, taking part of Beau's shirt with her. I have nowhere to go. She spits out a mouthful of faded blue cotton and bares her teeth at me again. Her next bite will take a chunk out of me, and leave me with some kind of brain-destroying plague in exchange.

"—off her, you cunt!" There's a crash, and the sinewy vise grip around my waist loosens. The pain I'm braced for, teeth tearing through flesh, never comes. Leah stands there holding the tea kettle she's just slammed into Mrs. Delgado's head, looking almost as shocked as the older woman whose nose is now broken and bleeding.

I squirm free of Mrs. Delgado's arms. The bedroom is too far away; I run for the kitchen. Mrs. Delgado, after just a second's pause to get her bearings, throws herself at Leah. A scream rips the air, so agonized I barely even recognize the voice as Leah's.

Fuck. I need a weapon. Leah's knife block is on the other side of the sink from where I remember, but it's close enough. I grab the biggest handle and pivot back toward the living room.

Leah has her hands around Mrs. Delgado's neck and is using all her strength to keep the older woman at arm's length. "Stop, fucking stop," Leah pleads. I hear the tears in her voice. I don't know how to fight. I certainly don't know how to kill someone. But I don't let that stop me.

I plunge the eight-inch chef's knife into Mrs. Delgado's back. The infected woman twitches and makes a surprised noise, but she doesn't stop straining to grab Leah. I pull the knife out and slam it home again. This time it meets more resistance, but I just push harder. There's a sound like tearing open a plastic bag of chips. Mrs. Delgado squirms in Leah's grip, trying to turn around to see who's stabbing her. I pull the knife out, thrust it back in. Yank. Stab. Slick. Spurt. Crunch. Scream.

By the time I stop, her upper back looks like pulled pork, and she's hanging limp. Leah holds her up by the neck with the rest of her body dangling. I must have utterly macerated her spine.

Blood spatters my arms up to the elbows. Suddenly disgusted,

I take a step back, releasing the knife and leaving it sticking out from between Mrs. Delgado's shoulder blades. But her back no longer has the structural integrity to hold it in place, and it slowly slides out and clatters to the floor.

Leah still stands there as if frozen. She's breathing hard and there are tears on her face.

"Hey," I say. "Hey, it's okay. It's okay now."

Leah makes a panicked wheezing sound. Mrs. Delgado's corpse trembles in her grasp, and I realize it's because Leah is shaking all over.

As much as it repulses me to touch Mrs. Delgado, I swallow the bile in my throat and grab her under the arms. "I've got her," I say to Leah, trying to keep my voice soothing. "You can let go now."

Leah releases Mrs. Delgado's neck, hugging her own arms to her chest in a belated gesture of self-protection. I lower the dead woman to the floor, trying not to get any more blood on me than I already have. As gentle as I try to be, her skull still hits the hardwood with an awful thud.

When I stand up, Leah hasn't moved or stopped shaking. I think she's in shock. What are you supposed to do for someone in shock? She cradles her left hand in her right, tucked up protectively almost under her chin.

"Are you all right?" I ask her, already knowing it's a stupid question, but then I see the blood trickling down her left wrist.

"Oh," I whisper. "Leah." Images flash in my mind: Jacquie's eyes in the club, my car window shattering, Mike pinned to the hood of Sunshine's car like a beetle to cardboard. *God, no*, I think, *not Leah. Anyone but Leah.* A wave of despair looms over me. I try to gulp air before it breaks, but I know it won't be enough to get me through to the other side.

Tears burn in my eyes and I try to blink them back. Whatever I'm feeling in this moment, however terrible the realization clawing its way through my guts, it's worse for Leah. She needs me to be strong right now. I reach out to touch her shoulder, knowing that it isn't enough, nothing could ever be enough, but needing to try to comfort her anyway.

But she isn't there anymore. Sometime in the last two seconds, while universes were collapsing into black holes within my chest, she's jolted into motion. Belatedly, I track her to the other side of the room, where she's scooping her backpack up from the floor.

She dumps the whole bag onto the carpet and rummages frantically through the spilled contents. I drop to my knees beside her, feeling helpless, knowing whatever she's searching for is futile. "Leah, I think . . ."

"There it is," she gasps, and sits back on her heels. She's holding one of the prefilled syringes I saw earlier, unlabeled, wrapped in plain white paper. Awkwardly, trying not to use her left hand, she holds the wrapping between her teeth and tears it open with her right hand. The liquid inside the cylinder is clear with a greenish cast. She pops the lid off the syringe and I see the short, sharp needle gleaming.

"What the fuck?" I say, but she doesn't respond and I wonder whether I even asked the question out loud. I'm soaked in sweat but suddenly the apartment feels cold.

Leah takes a few fast, deep breaths, like a kid psyching herself up to go off the high dive. She holds her left hand out in front of her, palm up. For the first time I see the bite clearly. It's deep in the meat of her palm, a whole chunk of flesh cratered away, blasting a hole through lifeline, heartline, all her pasts and futures.

She sticks the needle right into the red, raw center of the

wound and thumbs the plunger down. A groan of anguish drags itself from between her teeth, and another tear runs down her face, but her hands remain perfectly steady until the syringe is empty. Then she stands up, walks to the kitchen, and disposes of the syringe and its wrapping in the trash can under the sink.

I'm still crouched on the floor, several steps behind, my brain working furiously to catch up. I hear Leah open her refrigerator, an aluminum can cracking open with a hiss, and then a long silence during which I can picture Leah with her head thrown back, swallowing and swallowing the beer without coming up for air.

"Fuck!" she screams without warning, and I hear the can crash into the wall. That brings me to my feet without consciously thinking about it, and I'm in the kitchen to catch her in my arms just as she collapses into sobs.

"Leah," I say, my lips brushing against her midnight-blue hair while she buries her face in my chest. A day ago, an hour ago, I'd have given anything to hold her like this one last time. Now I feel like I'm going to throw up again. Before the world started ending, I never knew I had such a delicate stomach.

She doesn't respond to me saying her name. She just keeps crying, a pool of hot tears spreading across my borrowed shirt. I want to kiss the top of her head, or rub her back in soothing circles, but I don't. I just wait it out, thinking about how much my back and my feet and my heart all hurt.

"Leah, what was that?" I finally ask.

She snuffles into my collarbone and says nothing.

"Leah," I say again. I want it to sound firm, like a demand, but it comes out soft and pleading.

"It was nothing," she says, her voice very quiet. Her arms tighten around my waist. "It's okay, Wendy. We're okay." I stiffen my spine, refusing to melt into her touch.

"Why is it okay?" I know the answer, but maybe I'm wrong. Maybe there's a different explanation for what I just saw, one that won't shatter what's left of my world and send me spinning through empty space, alone. I want her to tell me what just happened, and I want her to make me believe her.

Leah finally looks up at me. Her eyes are wet, the remains of last night's mascara smeared from crying. Her cheeks are red. I want to kiss her so hard it turns back time. If only I hadn't let Mrs. Delgado into the apartment, I wouldn't have to know what I'm about to find out.

She doesn't lie to me, and I don't know whether I'm furious or grateful for that. "Because I just gave myself the antidote."

I take a step back, and Leah's arms fall to her sides. "The antidote." My mouth is dry.

"Right."

The dots are laid out in front of me, but I don't want to connect them. "There's an antidote. And you have it."

Leah nods.

"So you knew this was going to happen."

"Wendy, I . . ."

I hold up a hand, and her voice dies. I can't look at Leah, so I look at my hand, dividing the space between our bodies, gesturing *stop*. I notice that it's shaking. "And you didn't give it to Sam?" I ask.

"I didn't know," she says quietly. "I didn't know you could get it from being bitten. They said—" Abruptly, but too late, she cuts herself off.

"Who's they?" She just looks at the floor. "Who the fuck is *they*, Leah? Was someone handing out zombie pamphlets with the rainbow condoms?" Leah flinches. Her flinch is articulate.

Then she tries to steel her face, but I've already seen enough.

The rainbow condoms. The logo T-shirts. The social media hashtags. The corporate sponsors of the fucking apocalypse. "Seabrook. It's everywhere. They've been pouring it down our throats all weekend. And it's . . ." I have to swallow hard before I can keep talking. "And that's where it comes from? The rabies or whatever it is. It's in the goddamn hard seltzer?"

"The new formula," Leah says in a small voice.

"They knew about this? *You* knew about this? And you all just thought, fuck everyone, letting them all die is cheaper than doing a recall?"

She's quiet again, and again her silence is an open book I wish I couldn't read.

"It's not an accident." I say the words slowly, like each one hurts on its way out, because it does. "They planned this whole thing. You helped."

Leah tips her chin up in defiance, but her eyes look shattered. "I didn't know it was going to be this bad."

"Jesus, Leah. What the fuck." I have a thousand questions I should ask her, but the words escape me. Except for one. "Sam?"

She shakes her head helplessly. "She never drank Seabrook! No one ever said anything about biting. I had no idea it could spread that way."

"Then why do you have a fucking *antidote* in your bag?"

"They said—like Narcan, kind of. If someone partied too much."

"Partied too much?" I rake my hands through my hair because I need something to do with them that isn't punching walls. "This isn't a fucking party drug, Leah!"

"Well, I know that now!"

I force myself to take a deep breath. "What did they *tell* you it would do?"

She twists her hands together. "It was supposed to be like . . . guerrilla marketing. They said it would make people aggressive, and there would be fights, and it would get us media attention. It would help raise money for the health center."

My head feels like a thunderstorm. It's so unbearably hot in Leah's apartment, and the smell of blood is so heavy. "So this was always the plan. The whole savior angle, the hashtags and everything. It's all just so they can sell more fucking seltzers? They're killing us for brand loyalty?"

"No one was supposed to die," Leah says, and I can hear her struggling to keep her voice low, fighting the urge to shout. "They didn't say people would die. They just said—nothing brings people together like feeling attacked."

"Yeah, well, I feel fucking attacked," I say. It's all there when I close my eyes: the broken car window, Aurelia screaming, the ache of the gunshot in my ears.

There's a long silence.

"What about me?" I finally ask.

Without looking, I can see the expression on Leah's face perfectly. "You're not infected," she says.

"I could have been. Mrs. Delgado could have bitten me instead of you. Would we be having this same conversation if that had happened?"

Leah doesn't say anything. I suppose I should be grateful she's not lying to me, but the horror and sadness drown out all my other emotions. If I had been bitten, Leah would at this very moment be stroking my hair and whispering empty words of comfort, watching me face my own slow death and never mentioning the cure only a few feet away.

"Leah, what were you thinking?" Even through the fury and

the hurt, it's a genuine question. I want to understand. I want an explanation that will quell the disgust roiling in my stomach, the hurt in my idiot heart that still loves her just as much as it did an hour ago. I want to reach across the chasm that separates me from Leah and touch her hand.

"I don't know!" It bursts out of her, loud, defensive, a tone I'm very familiar with in her voice. "It was supposed to bring in donations for the health center. Media attention, too. They said people would notice San Lazaro, that we'd be iconic for fighting back." And I know Leah well enough to hear what's underneath her words: that *she'd* be iconic. A queer hero, rising from blood and dust to rebuild her community. A Sylvia Rivera for a new generation. I know that's what Leah truly wants, more than money, more than sex. She does the work she does because she believes in it, but she also wants people to remember her name.

"Some of us might be iconic, but a lot of us are dead," I say.

"I didn't know it would be this bad," she repeats.

"But you didn't do anything to stop it, either," I reply, and she doesn't say anything else for a long time, until I finally understand that she isn't going to, until the gap between us is so vast I can't see the other side anymore, until the door to her apartment clicks shut behind me.

CHAPTER 14

So here I am, alone outside Leah's apartment building with no car, no weapons, and no backup, heartbroken, bloody, exhausted, and wearing someone else's shirt, which has a giant hole in it. This isn't exactly how I hoped my Pride would turn out.

All I've been thinking about all weekend is Leah: who she's with, what she's doing, how to get her back. I was so scared for her when I saw the bite mark on her hand. My chest still aches from that spike of adrenaline. I would have thrown my body between Leah and Mrs. Delgado—or Mike, or Jacquie—and all this time Leah was conspiring with the people who turned our friends into monsters, for the sake of drink sales and social media clout.

I stand at the bottom of the concrete steps, the late morning sun scouring my face. The street is enveloped in the languor of high summer, any living people hidden inside with shades drawn ineffectually against the heat. I hear a high buzzing sound in my ears and wonder if I'm having a panic attack, but it's just cicadas in a scrawny ironwood tree.

At first I thought maybe Leah would chase after me, pleading for forgiveness, offering some kind of explanation, but her door stays silently closed. I try to convince myself it's for the best, that nothing she could say would make it right anyway. It doesn't matter that it's true. All that matters is that I walked away, and Leah let me go. Again.

What can I do now?

Sam and Emmy are dead, and Mike, and probably Jacquie too, and who knows how many others. Leah is a traitor. I can't picture crawling back to Beau and Logan and Aurelia, let alone explaining to them why Leah isn't with me. And I have no way of knowing Leah's not calling them right now, giving them some twisted version of the story, telling them not to trust me. Why should they take my word over hers? It's not like they know me all that well, or have any particular reason to trust me. They're her friends first.

I want to go home, I think again, still not knowing where that is or how I could get there.

On a wild impulse, I pull my phone out of my pocket, ignore the low battery warning and all my notifications, and type in a number I blocked years ago but still know by heart. It will be fine, I tell myself, holding my shaking finger over the CALL button. Just a quick check-in, just to let her know I'm okay. I'm so scared and so confused and I want to hear my mother's voice.

Instead of pushing the button, I drop the phone again. My mother doesn't even know what city I live in, and it's better that way. I can't call and tell her I'm okay, because to her, it wouldn't be true. To her, *okay* would mean "renouncing my sinful ways and coming home to beg forgiveness." It would erase me just as surely as the plague, or whatever it is, erased the humanity from Mike and Jacquie and Sam. I have a horrible, visceral memory of fluttering into consciousness in a bath turning cold, tendrils of my own vomit floating on the surface, of the thick gray despair that choked me when I realized *it didn't work*. I can't go back to that. Staying here might kill me too, but I'd rather go out fighting than numbly hoping for it to be over. If I have to die, I don't want it to be by my own hand.

When I exit the phone app, I notice I have three missed calls and a string of texts. They're all from Aurelia's number, which I'm surprised I even have saved. I open the text conversation first.

Bitch are u alive???

I scroll up and see that she's been sending frantic variations on the same theme for the last half hour. Above them is the first text she sent me, only a few minutes after Leah and I left Beau's house.

as soon as u see this make an excuse and get away from lea. Shes in on all this. Ur not safe w her

"Oh, God," I say out loud. How did they figure it out? Then I remember coming across the syringe of antidote in Leah's backpack while looking for emergency contraception. She didn't do a very thorough job covering her tracks. Maybe, on some level, she wanted to be found out. Or maybe—the thought shoves its way into my mind uninvited, like Mrs. Delgado through the apartment door—maybe she didn't think any of us would live long enough to discover her secret.

I have to call Aurelia back. She's trying to save my life; the least I can do is reassure her I haven't died yet. As I hit the CALL BACK button, however, my phone's last sliver of battery flickers into oblivion, and the screen goes dead in my hand.

"Fuck," I mumble, wiping sweat from my forehead. The air is growing stickier by the moment, and now I notice that it smells foul. Could I be smelling Mrs. Delgado's corpse, all the way up on the second floor? I glance up from my phone.

A face hovers only inches away, staring at me with one gray-blue eye, the other a mess of bloody pulp. Reeking breath floods my face as the mouth opens in a growl.

I scream and jump backward. The man reaches out as if to grab me by the neck, but only succeeds in knocking my dead phone out of my hand. Glass shatters on the sidewalk.

Why did I drop the knife I used to kill Mrs. Delgado? Why am I standing out here with absolutely no plan to defend myself? Maybe if I can get up the stairs Leah will let me back inside, but even as I formulate the thought, the man's bony hand is around my wrist and holding on hard.

Self-defense classes teach you to aim for an attacker's soft spots in the hope that a sudden burst of pain will shock them into letting go, buy you a few seconds to escape. But whatever Seabrook put in those drinks seems to shut down any reaction to pain. The infected don't get distracted. They keep going until their bodies can't anymore. And that means you can't stop them without tearing them to pieces.

I didn't think about the moral ramifications before I shredded Mrs. Delgado's back, but I'm thinking now. This person grabbing my arm, digging in hard enough that his nails draw blood, is a human being, or at least he was yesterday. I killed Mrs. Delgado in the heat of the moment, because it was the only way to save Leah. If I kill someone else, will I be able to live with myself?

The man snarls and drags me closer, snapping his jaws in anticipation, and I remember that in order to live with myself I have to avoid getting eaten. I twist my arm out of his grasp. He's—it's between me and the stairs, so I run the other way, toward the street.

Beau's motorcycle is parked at the curb where Leah left it,

with the helmet balanced on the seat. *Better than nothing*, I think. I grab the helmet by its strap and spin around, swinging it straight out so the fiberglass crown smashes into the infected man's face.

The impact reverberates up my arm and into my shoulder. I stagger back and bump into Beau's bike. The man reels a little, but keeps coming, despite the fact that his cheek looks dented.

I swing the helmet again. My arm sings with pain as it slams into the half-dead thing's temple. Skin peels back from his forehead with a wet sound. The man staggers sideways, then stops, weaving his head from side to side as if trying to remember where I am.

In that split second of a grace period, I run, dodging around the motorcycle and into the street. When I look back, the man has adjusted his trajectory and is moving toward me again. I can keep hitting this thing with the helmet, but it won't stop coming at me, and I'm afraid the helmet will crumble into pulp before the guy's skull does. The other option is to run: straight down this wide, sunlit street with closed doors along every side, screaming for help that isn't going to come.

The man's mouth yawns open, showing stained teeth as he lumbers toward me. I think of the killers in slasher movies, how they never move quickly enough to get out of breath, but they still run a dozen coeds into the ground. No distractions, no obstacles. Only meat.

I know I have to run. I don't have any other choice. My legs feel heavy, my hands numb, but it's time to run for my life again. Yet I stand still for another second, looking at what used to be a thinking, hoping, dreaming person—someone I might have liked or hated—now reduced to nothing but rage and destruction.

The man walks straight into Beau's bike and stops.

It only takes a moment for him to straighten out his confusion, identify the obstacle and reorient himself, but that's all the time I need to leap forward and shove the motorcycle with all my strength. I'm on the left side of the bike, where the kickstand is. It takes a monstrous heave to shift it from its resting place, but then the kickstand leaves the ground and the huge machine wobbles. It leans back toward me, almost slumps over to the left again. I brace my feet, thighs and back burning, and give another push. The effort tears out of me in a scream.

Beau's motorcycle, all eight hundred pounds of it, topples over to the right. It crashes into the man, who loses his balance and tips over too, like a domino. The bike hits the sidewalk with a grating, scraping crash, and just as I'd hoped, the man's legs are trapped underneath it.

I stand there panting and sweating, excess adrenaline zinging through my veins. "Fuck!" I shout. Then, "Fuck *you*!"

The man snarls, not at me, but at the motorcycle, his captor and tormentor. He squirms under the weight of all that tangled steel. I hear an awful ripping sound and realize that the infected man, feeling no pain, is struggling hard enough to tear his own flesh under the pressure of the bike.

That shakes my aimless energy back into focus. This is barely a human being in front of me; it's just a thing that won't hesitate to disassemble its own body to escape its predicament. I haven't defeated it, only inconvenienced it. I look at the helmet in my hand. How long would it take to beat someone to death with it? Can I really stomach that? Briefly I consider knocking on Leah's door and asking to borrow the knife I used on Mrs. Delgado.

Or I could simply run. Get out of town. Disappear into the desert and be untraceable by the time this hideous thing claws what's left of its mangled near-corpse to freedom. Escape from the plague, from Leah, from Seabrook, from my own embarrassment of a life. Let Wendy Fitzgerald be missing, presumed dead, in the wave of violence that subsumed San Lazaro. Start fresh.

The cicadas are screaming in the trees, making my ears ring so that I don't hear the motor at first, but as it gets closer and rises in pitch, it crosses the threshold of my consciousness. I hurry to the sidewalk to make way for the car, a mundane action almost rendered catastrophic when the man under the motorcycle stretches to grab my leg.

I can't help but notice that the fingernails clawing through my leggings are resplendent with lavender glitter polish. I imagine the lips now peeled back in a grimace pursed in concentration, painting with small careful strokes, looking forward to a glamorous, transformative Pride weekend. Heart aching, pulse hammering, I kick his hand away.

Instead of blowing past, the approaching car pulls up to the curb in front of me and stops. It's a big, rusty pickup truck with Beau at the wheel. Aurelia leans out the passenger window.

"Are you infected?" she asks abruptly.

I stare for a long moment, unable to process what I'm seeing. Why are they here? Did they come for me? To save me? It never crossed my mind to hope they'd do something like that. "No," I say.

"What the fuck did you do to my bike?" Beau shouts across Aurelia.

My face, already red with the heat and the exertion, burns brighter. Shame clenches in my belly. Beau came all this way to rescue me from Leah, and I repaid her by trashing her motorcycle. "I'm so sorry, Beau," I start, the words feeling huge and blocky in my mouth, but she cuts me off with a laugh.

"I'm joking. I don't fucking care," she says. "I'm just glad you're alive." She smiles at me, uncharacteristically earnest.

"It's not too bad," Aurelia says, eyeing the downed bike carefully. "I can fix it up. We don't have time to load it into the truck right now, but we can come back for it later." I don't ask when she means because I suspect this is wishful thinking. Whatever is currently happening in San Lazaro, it's going to be a long time before anyone has a chance to tend to its vehicular casualties.

Still, I nod and say, "I'll pay for the repairs."

Beau reaches behind her and bangs on the glass separating the cab from the bed of the truck. "Cleanup on aisle three," she yells.

Logan climbs out of the back, his long limbs unfurling like a butterfly from a cocoon. He's dressed in cutoff shorts and a Guns 'n' Roses T-shirt, the whole outfit clearly borrowed from Beau since none of it's black, and he holds a baseball bat.

"Hey, Wendy," he says. "Leah didn't kill you?"

I shake my head. "How did you guys figure it out about her?"

"Exposition later," Beau says. "Zombie-killing now." Apparently we've all adopted Logan's horror-movie language. It does feel appropriate. The man lying trapped under Beau's bike, still hissing and snapping his jaws at us, could easily be a reanimated corpse driven by nothing but hunger for flesh. Whatever he has left can barely be described as a life.

"I hate this," Logan says to her. "You know I don't even kill spiders, right? I'm into peaceful coexistence."

"Okay," says Beau, "but this bitch wants to coexist his teeth into your spleen. You can't catch him in a cup and take him outside."

"I don't even know what a spleen is," Logan grouses. This feels like a rehash of an argument they've already had. "And why can't you do it if you're so unbothered?"

"Because you're the one who logged all the hours at the

gym building those pretty, pretty shoulder muscles," Beau says, batting her eyelashes at him. "With great triceps comes great responsibility. Also, my ribs are broken."

Logan gives me a pleading look, and I shrug. "She has a point," I say. "Plus, I already stabbed a woman to death, like, half an hour ago. It's someone else's turn."

"I'm sorry, Wendy," Aurelia says very quietly. I give her a grateful nod.

Logan rubs his forehead with the hand not holding the baseball bat, turns away from me, and yells "Goddammit!" at the indifferent, sun-bleached sky. Then he turns back around, takes three deliberate steps, and brings his bat down with a crack that splits the air.

He hits the infected man squarely on the bridge of the nose, and the man's face seems to collapse inward, like a jack-o'-lantern on November 10. Blood spatters the sidewalk and the chrome of Beau's motorcycle. I can smell it cooking on the metal, gleaming murderously hot in the sun. But the creature still scrabbles at the pavement with broken-off pale-purple fingernails.

Logan brings the bat down again. The infected man's ravaged body shudders, and this time he goes still. Pooling blood obliterates most of the damage Logan has done to his face, for which I'm grateful.

Logan stands there breathing hard for a long moment. Blood smears his baseball bat and freckles his face and arms. I think of reaching out to him, but I don't do it. I can imagine only too well how he feels.

Finally, without a word to me, he turns and walks back toward the bed of the truck. Beau taps the horn once, just a quick, bright blip, to get his attention. When he looks over his shoulder, she nods at him solemnly.

"Thank you," she says. Logan closes his eyes, and when he opens them again, some of the strain is gone from his shoulders.

"You want to hop in back with him, Wendy?" Aurelia asks. I nod gratefully. There's nothing I want more than to get the fuck out of here, and that goes for pretty much any definition of the word *here*.

The bed of the truck is searing hot from the sun, stinging my legs through the thin material of my mermaid leggings. Beau starts the truck and we rattle down the road. Every bump and crack in the pavement feels magnified back here, with nothing to soften the never-ending impacts. Rusty tools slide around and threaten to maul our toes.

After a minute, Logan reaches over and takes my hand, lacing his sweaty fingers through mine. I stare down at a dot of blood on his thumbnail. "I'm sorry about Leah," he says.

"Shit, I'm sorry too," I say. "If I'd figured out what she was up to sooner I could have saved us all a lot of grief."

"Still," he says. "I know that must have been hard for you. All this violence is a fucking nightmare, but having to kill someone you love—"

"Wait, what?" I turn to stare at him. "Jesus, Logan. I didn't kill Leah."

"Oh." He looks confused, then relieved. "Well, who did you kill, then?"

I sigh and give him a brief synopsis of what happened with Mrs. Delgado, skipping over the part where Leah and I fucked. I tell him about the antidote, about realizing that Leah was conspiring with Seabrook.

"And then what did you do?" he asks. His hand is still in mine, squeezing so hard my wrist is starting to hurt.

"I just walked out," I say.

"She didn't try to stop you?" Logan asks. I wish I could explain why it was that simple. I know Leah's secret and she just let me leave. Does that mean something, that she feels something about me? Or is it just that she was willing to let other people die for her cause, but couldn't bring herself to get her own hands dirty?

Instead of answering him, I redirect. "How did you guys figure it out about Leah?"

"She posted on Facebook," he says. "A selfie of her and that Courtney chick setting up for the parade."

I stare at him. "She wasn't setting up for the parade," I say. "She was at her apartment with me. I only left a few minutes ago, and she was still there."

"Which is why we were pretty sure it was a plant," he says. "She must have made the posts in advance and scheduled them to run all weekend. There was one from last night, too, around the time we were scraping ourselves off the floor at Hellrazors. 'Having so much fun at Pride drinking Seabrook™!'" He says "TM" out loud.

"Leah doesn't drink Seabrook," I say.

"It was fake," he says impatiently. "She set it up to post happy Pride selfies while everyone was getting eaten by zombies. And it wasn't just her. There's a bunch of accounts doing it, pushing that fake story where everything was golden until some Republicans showed up."

"Fuck," I say, letting it sink in. All of this was planned, every minute of it, and Leah was in on it the whole time.

"We started putting the pieces together just like you did. All the free Seabrook and people going batshit. Aurelia remembered that Leah was the one who pitched the sponsorship in the first place. And that was when we started worrying that you weren't safe with Leah."

"Well, shit." I lean my head back against the side of the truck, but it bumps and shakes so bad I immediately sit back up. "Thank you for coming and getting me."

He looks surprised. "Of course." Then he looks around, and I realize we're slowing to a stop. "We're here."

"Where?" I thought we were going back to Beau's house, but we haven't been driving nearly long enough for that.

Instead of answering me, Logan stands up and climbs out of the truck. I follow him. The fierce sunlight goes through my skull like an ice pick. It takes a moment before the spots in my eyes clear and I realize where we're standing.

We are in the gravel semicircle of Sam and Aurelia's driveway, almost the exact spot where Mike tried to run over us with his car yesterday. I can still see the hollows his tires left when they spun and sprayed gravel. I remember hurrying, shaken, for the door of the house, finding Sam and Aurelia and Leah in the kitchen.

Now Sam is dead, and Leah is—better not to think about it. I realize Aurelia is still in the passenger seat with her door closed, looking straight ahead as though taking in her surroundings could shatter her. Beau walks around the cab to open Aurelia's door, holding out her arm for Aurelia to take. Aurelia is a full head taller than Beau, but she clings to her gratefully.

"Why are we here?" I ask Logan under my breath.

Aurelia hears me and replies. "It's the closest safe place," she says, her voice tight. "I didn't want to take the time going all the way back to Beau's. We have shit to deal with right now."

Feeling chastised, I lower my head and follow her to the front door. A shudder rolls through me at the sight of a dark smear on the concrete porch, broken bits of carapace still glittering in the muck: the remains of the palo verde beetle I crushed on Friday night.

Aurelia stops at the threshold, but I don't see her take a deep breath or straighten her spine; she just goes still in midstep, like a paused film, then keeps walking into the house.

I can't help pausing and taking a look around. I was here less than twenty-four hours ago, but it feels like returning as an adult to a place I loved in childhood, like I'm taller now and seeing familiar things from a strange angle. The house has been cleared of bottles and cans and other detritus, but the party funk still lingers in the air, sweat and musk and a cacophony of booze odors, the noxious sweetness of Seabrook prominent.

We cluster just inside the doorway, hesitant to move further into the house as though we risk disturbing a crime scene, though as far as I know nothing horrific took place here. "Okay," Aurelia says, slapping her hands on her thighs decisively. "What the fuck do we do?"

"What do we know?" counters Beau.

I run quickly through what Leah said about Seabrook's plan: incite violence, position themselves as saviors, profit. Beau postures detached cynicism, but Aurelia and Logan are horrified.

"I can't believe she was in on this the whole time," Aurelia says. "I mean, this took so much planning. They've got people on the other side of the world drinking their booze and thinking it's doing us a favor. Us. The people they're poisoning and killing."

"It makes sense," Logan says. "Look at what happened in the '80s, the way the government ignored the AIDS epidemic. You can totally use the LGBTQ population as guinea pigs and no one looks twice."

Beau shakes her head. "Nah," she says. "You kids weren't there in the '80s. This isn't the same play. They're not leaving us to die, they're fucking with us so they can swoop in and be the saviors. This is all a big exercise in branding. That's how they get us now, turn us into consumers with brand loyalties instead of community ties."

"They've been pushing those drinks so hard," says Aurelia. "There were—I don't even know how many cases at our house. We—*gave* people that stuff." Her voice wavers.

"You didn't know," I start to say, but Beau cuts me off.

"We do not have time to dick around with feeling guilty for shit none of us had any control over," she says, her voice clean and bright as a knife. "They lied to you and tricked you into helping them. You have to put it aside and move on. We know who's responsible for this, and it's not you, Aurelia, okay? So get it together."

If Beau lit into me like that, I'd cry, but Aurelia nods and rolls her shoulders, her eyes clearing. "Thanks," she says.

"That bitch sold us all out," says Logan. "If we're blaming anyone, blame her."

I have to physically swallow the impulse to defend Leah, and it burns going down my throat. Logan is right. Leah betrayed us, betrayed the community she claims to love, no matter how much she insists that she was only thinking of the greater good.

"But now we know there's an antidote," I say, trying to shift focus. "If we can get the word out, find a way to put pressure on Seabrook . . ."

"And then what? Make them give out the antidote?" Beau shakes her head. "They'll never admit they have it, because then the whole thing would come out."

"The whole thing is going to come out anyway," I say. "It has to." Aurelia and Logan look skeptical, and Beau folds her arms over her chest.

"How?" she asks.

I open my mouth and then realize I have absolutely no idea what to say. How do we get people to believe what we know? All I have to go on is Leah's word, except . . .

"The drinks," I say. "If we get a can of Seabrook to . . . a lab, or something, they can test it and figure out what's in it. There's physical evidence."

"Maybe," says Beau. "If we can find a facility where they can do that, and convince them we're not just nutjobs wasting their time."

"Um, I hate to interrupt," says Logan, "but I really think there's a higher priority here. Everything we've seen so far this weekend is just the preshow."

Realization washes over me, and with it comes new horror. I can't believe I forgot. "Pride," says Aurelia, looking stricken. "Of course. Seabrook has four drink tents. Plus they'll have people circulating in the crowd handing out free samples."

"It's going to be a bloodbath," Beau says grimly.

"Don't you think a lot of people will stay home after what happened last night?" I say, already knowing it's a futile hope.

"Maybe some of them," says Aurelia. "But a lot of people don't come to the other events, just the festival. That's the big draw. And without any kind of coherent public safety message . . ."

"It's not just that no one's saying to stay home," Logan adds. "The message Seabrook is pushing is, go to Pride or the terrorists win. It's the hashtag resistance."

I remember Leah's fake posts from Pride, and the still-fresh wound of her betrayal pulses. "We have to tell people," I say. "Call everyone, put it on social media."

"I've been trying to post on social media since this morning,"

Aurelia says. "First time, they flagged my post for misinformation. When I tried again I got locked out of my account."

"They were ready," Beau says. "They had a lot of time to plan this."

"So we call people," says Logan. "Everyone we know. Tell them to call everyone they know."

There's a low buzz, and we all reach to check our phones. My hand goes into my pocket and comes out empty; I briefly forgot that my phone smashed on the pavement outside Leah's apartment complex. Beau's phone is the one ringing, and she steps away from the rest of us, covering her free ear while she answers.

"Even if all of us call everyone we've ever met, that won't be enough to stop the festival," Aurelia says.

"Also, my phone is dead," I say.

"Then what do we do?" Logan asks.

Aurelia twists a lock of hair around her finger, a nervous tic I've never seen from her before. "I'm thinking," she says. "Maybe if we can call someone in city government we could get the parade permit canceled?"

The click of Beau ending her call is somehow very loud. We all look at her as she turns slowly back to us. "That was Dorian," she says. "Glen died."

Silence billows in the wake of her words. We stand there in a circle, staring at Beau, everyone waiting for someone else to say something. I think of Glen's easy smile every time I spoke to him before last night, the way he'd always ask me if I'd read any good books lately. I don't know him well enough to grieve, exactly, but I still feel an appalled sense of loss, as though a beloved landmark burned to the ground. For the thousandth time in the last two days, I can't think of anything useful to say.

"Well, shit," Logan finally says.

Beau bursts out laughing. "Shit," she agrees through convulsive chuckles. "Fuck. Motherfucker!"

"Son of a bitch," Aurelia adds, starting to giggle. Logan joins in too.

"Fuck *this*," I say, and without meaning to I realize I'm laughing too. It feels strange and not entirely good, spasming through my body, but the sound of all our laughter together is comforting. I gasp for breath, and Logan reaches out and squeezes my hand.

Beau laughs louder and longer than anyone, the pitch climbing higher until it verges on frightening, and I'm convinced she's about to shift into full-blown sobs. But instead she calms down, catches her breath, and rubs her dry eyes with her fists.

"So it's fatal," she says matter-of-factly. "Glen had a seizure and died without ever waking up. That fucking drink kills people."

"We can't be sure it's fatal in every case," Aurelia says carefully. "You did say he had a head injury."

Beau shakes her head. "Save the nuance. Seabrook killed my friend. They killed your wife, too, even if someone else pulled the trigger." Aurelia presses her lips into a thin white line and says nothing.

"So we need to stop them," Logan says, sounding less like a laser-focused action hero than a kindergarten teacher reminding his class to stay on topic. "How do we get the message out?"

"In the next, like, twenty minutes," I add, glancing at the clock on Sam and Aurelia's (no, I correct myself internally, just Aurelia's) microwave. "People are probably already getting to the park."

"What about local news?" Logan says. "Can we call someone at the *San Lazaro Sunrise*?"

"That's not urgent enough," says Beau. "We need to reach people *now*, not when tomorrow's paper comes out."

"I have an idea that everyone will hate," says Aurelia.

Logan gives her a sliver of a smile. "Let's hear it."

"We call the cops."

I take a reflexive step backward. "No. No way. No fucking chance."

Aurelia raises her eyebrows at me, still painfully calm, but I see heat behind her eyes. "Wendy, trust me, I am not feeling any better disposed toward the police than you are right now. But I don't know what kind of choice we have. The festival is already set up, and people are on their way or already there. I promise you Seabrook is already there, handing out frosty beverages. I can call the other organizers and ask them to tear it all down with their bare hands, but even if they listen to me, that doesn't clear out the park as fast as we need to keep people safe. Right?"

I hate it, but I agree with her. "Right."

"The only people who have the capacity to shut everything down immediately are the—" She makes a show of choosing her words carefully, emphasizing each syllable for maximum sardonic impact. "The fine upstanding members of the San Lazaro Police Department."

"So you're gonna call the cops and tell them to shut down Pride," says Logan.

"On the anniversary of the Stonewall riots," Beau adds.

"Yes, thank you, that's the pitch," Aurelia says. "I hate it just as much as you do. Please tell me now if you have a better idea."

"It's not the *actual* anniversary date," I say. "It's just Stonewall-adjacent."

"Okay," Beau says. "Let's get this bullshit over with."

One minute later, Aurelia is holding out her phone in front of her, eyes wide with dismay. "They called me a psycho and hung up on me," she says.

"Telling them what's actually happening was probably a mistake," Logan says. "You should have called in a bomb threat."

My stomach twists with dismay as well as the terrible satisfaction of being right. Even after what happened to Sam, I still shared a little of Aurelia's hope that someone in authority could come in and fix everything. But of course they won't; of course they were never going to.

"Well, we tried dishonoring our forebears and everything our community stands for, and that didn't work," says Beau. "Any other suggestions?"

"Social media is fucked, calling people takes too long, the news doesn't reach enough people—" Logan ticks off the unworkable options on his fingers.

I look from Logan to Beau to Aurelia, waiting for one of them to say what's becoming uncomfortably apparent. I don't want to do it. I'm not brave like Beau or strong like Logan. I don't have a shred of heroism in me. But we can't let hundreds or thousands of people die at what's supposed to be a celebration of our community, and we're out of workable options.

"Guys," I say, but nobody hears me.

"If we could get Leah to blow the whistle on Seabrook," says Logan.

Beau counters, "That still doesn't help us unless we can get the word out."

"Guys!" I say, louder this time. Finally, they all turn and look at me, and I wish they hadn't.

"Okay." I spread my hands out in front of me. My guts clench, and I wish I could take a quick break to pee before saying my piece, but it's too late now. "We have to go to Pride and tell people ourselves."

"No," says Logan immediately. "No, seriously, I'm not walking back into a crowd of zombies."

"For the last time, Logan, they are not fucking zombies," Aurelia snaps, but no one responds to her.

"You're organizers, right?" I gesture to Logan and Aurelia. "You can get on a microphone and tell people to clear out. Tell them Seabrook isn't safe."

"You think they're going to believe us when the cops didn't?" Logan asks.

"I do, actually," Beau says. "At least some of them. Queer folks who know anything about history won't have trouble believing there's bad shit going on behind the scenes." She grins at me, and I smile back in relief.

"That's true," Aurelia says slowly. "And if we can get some people to clear out, others will start to follow."

"If nothing else, we can kill the vibe so bad no one's having fun anymore," Logan says reluctantly.

"Yes! That's the spirit," I tell him. On a flash of impulse, I wrap my arms around his waist and hug. He hugs me back, resting his chin on the crown of my head, enveloping me in the warm comfortable smell of his body.

"Oh, we can do more than fuck up the vibe," Aurelia says. "Come with me."

She leads us out the side door in the kitchen. Prickly, scrubby weeds decorate the lawn with the yellow-brown-gray color palette of summer in southern Arizona. They scratch at my ankles as Logan, Beau, and I follow Aurelia.

She throws open the door and shows us the inside of the garage. There's Aurelia's motorcycle, hulking black and red, bigger and heavier by far than either Beau's or Leah's. Behind it, hanging from the wall and spread out across benches and shelves, are an assortment of tools I assume are for fixing motorcycles. I see wrenches, screwdrivers, something that might be a tire pressure gauge. But interspersed between the mundane hardware are stranger items, and I remember that Aurelia isn't just a mechanic, she's a sword lesbian.

She walks to her wall-mounted array of sharp objects and hoists a long-handled ax, testing its weight in her hands. "We go to the festival," she says. "We tell people not to drink Seabrook, and we try to get them to leave."

"And if they don't?" I ask, already knowing the answer but happy to play my role as straight woman.

Aurelia gestures to the wall display like she's presenting the prize on a game show. "Allow me to introduce the backup plan."

COURTNEY

Courtney sprawls across her bed in yoga pants and a sports bra, scrolling through Leah's social media profiles. It's not like her to procrastinate this way, but today the number of crises demanding her attention is simply too overwhelming, and she needs to tune them out for a little while. If anyone asks, she's meditating.

The photo of her and Leah at what's supposed to be the Pride festival—the one they actually took at Salt River Park last week—looks good, she thinks. Her cheeks are pink like she's been out in the sun, and Leah is laughing, her mouth open a little too wide to be attractive. The awkwardness is good, makes the picture look less staged. They're toasting with open cans of Seabrook: Melon Splash for Leah, Cucumber Mint for Courtney. Of course, neither of them drank a drop.

Courtney has already reposted the shot to her own profile and the Seabrook page, but she keeps coming back to it. They look like they're having fun. They were having fun. Sort of. Maybe.

Courtney is never quite sure *how* she feels about Leah, except while they're fucking. She remembers the look on Leah's face when Courtney explained—in carefully curtailed language—how the new formula would affect those who drank it, and how Seabrook and the health center would benefit. She'd timed it perfectly; just as Leah's brow started to crease, just as she was about to voice her disapproval, Courtney said, "And we think you're the right person to make those connections between the health center and the community." Leah's forehead smoothed. Her eyes lit up. Courtney smiled to herself at a job well done.

It's easy to understand Leah because they're so deeply alike, but Leah isn't willing to admit it. Her refusal to acknowledge her own hunger makes it an incredibly effective lever to use on her. Deep down in Leah is a survival drive that Courtney recognizes, a hard kernel on which you could break a tooth if you weren't expecting it.

Courtney scrolls down a few pictures and sees one of Leah and Aurelia at the bar before the drag show. They're sticking out their tongues between their fingers. As Courtney wrinkles her nose—why don't these people have the slightest sense of decorum?—the phone buzzes in her hands.

Before she even checks caller ID, she knows it's Titania Randall. Courtney desperately wants to let the crone go to voice mail—or even better, answer and tell her to fuck off—but she didn't get where she is today by giving in to every impulse that crosses her mind. Instead she picks up and gives her most cheerful "This is Courtney."

"Have you seen the videos?" says the senator. Her voice is lovely and smooth, practiced from years of public speaking, but it still makes Courtney flinch like nails on a chalkboard.

"Yes, ma'am," Courtney says, allowing herself the small outlet of an eye roll. Seabrook's agreement with the local news channels has kept the most disturbing images out of the public eye, but some of the raw footage is being shared internally.

"This is not what we agreed upon," says Randall. *Upon*, like she's some upper-crust British dowager instead of a real estate agent from Scottsdale. "For heaven's sake, they're throwing around words like *bioterrorism*. Those people looked like something out of a horror movie."

"I know," Courtney says. "We're still trying to identify why the effects are so dramatic. This didn't happen in the trials, but of course those were rushed and limited in scope. It could be that the heat is exacerbating the neurological—"

"I'm not asking you why it's happening, I'm asking you how you're going to *fix* it," says Randall.

Courtney clenches her jaw and wonders how she's supposed to fix a problem without first identifying *what the fuck went wrong*, but of course she can't say that out loud to Titania Randall. Her mother used to tell her to count to ten when she felt herself getting angry. To save time, Courtney counts by fives. Five. Ten. It doesn't help very much.

"I know this is a departure from the scenario we envisioned, but I still think it accomplishes our goals," she says. "People are frightened and confused. The right wing"—Courtney almost lets the word *fanatics* slip out, but she stops herself—"is blaming drag queens. The gays are trying to circle the wagons, but they don't have a clear enemy to rally against. It's chaos out there."

"Chaos wasn't the goal," says Randall.

"No," says Courtney. "The goal was fear, and we've generated plenty of that. Everyone is scared, and scared people are easy to turn against each other."

In truth, Courtney is nervous. Violent outbursts were always the endgame, but they were intended to be read by the public as a further escalation of the ongoing clashes between the queer community and its opponents. It was supposed to seem inevitable, the natural next step in the rising tensions of the last few years.

But what's happening in San Lazaro does not look natural or inevitable. It looks, although Courtney would never say this out loud, fucking terrifying. She left Hellrazors last night as soon as the first can was thrown, but she's seen the footage of a young woman stumbling out of that bar with a visible wound in her neck, blood soaking through the whole right side of her shirt, not a hint of fear or pain in her eyes. From the chin up she might have been any mildly tipsy twentysomething, until the blood loss finally caught up with her and she dropped flat on her face.

The dulled inhibitions Seabrook's scientists induced in lab animals, allowing them to act on their worst impulses without hesitation, had translated in humans to a frightening level of indifference or simple numbness. People under the influence of Seabrook do not notice anything that happens to their bodies until it actually kills them.

"Are you at the festival yet?" Randall asks. "What's going on there?"

Lying doesn't seem worth the effort. "I'm not going," she says. "It's too risky." The original plan was for her to be seen at Salt River Park today, with a Seabrook security detail ready to whisk her to safety after she'd been publicly and photogenically harrowed. But this morning, drinking her green smoothie and scrolling through last night's news and the #SanLazaroStrong hashtags on social media, she decided *fuck that.*

There's been speculation about a possible mutant strain of rabies, because people in San Lazaro keep biting each other. No one at Seabrook was prepared for the biting. Whatever they're saying on the news, Seabrook isn't in the bioterrorism business.

The new formula isn't a virus. It shouldn't be contagious. It's insane, like those horror stories that went around about fentanyl a few years back—that you could overdose just from touching a fentanyl patch, or from the sweat of someone who used it. Fearmongering madness, which Courtney supposes is adjacent to the business she's gotten herself into, but that doesn't make any of it real.

Does it?

She doesn't like all these variables. The situation is unpredictable and therefore difficult to control. She has no doubt that Seabrook and Randall will find a way to profit from the mess; Courtney will help them find it, because that's what she does. But she'll do it from indoors, where it's air-conditioned and no one is trying to eat her.

"Well, I want you to get out there and take control of the situation," Randall says. "At the very least, you need to *look* like you have it under control."

"What did you have in mind?"

"Hold a press conference," says the senator. "Reassure people that the violent incidents will stop now that the . . . gathering is over." Courtney has noticed that Randall never refers to the Pride festival by name. It's as though the very concept of gay pride bothers her too much to speak it aloud. She's the same way about the LGBTQ community; she usually refers to them as *those people*, except when she uses much more colorful language in her speeches.

Courtney isn't at all sure that's true, but of course she doesn't get paid to tell the truth, either. "I can put that together this week," she says.

"Do it *today*," Randall insists.

Five, ten, Courtney counts. "All right," she says out loud.

"Anything else?"

"Make sure you do it before five p.m., so it doesn't conflict with my own conference," says the senator. "I'm taking the opportunity to push for a ban on sexually explicit performances in public places. I've also been on the phone with folks in New Mexico and Kansas talking about what happened here and how they can keep displays like this out of their hometowns." Randall pauses, as if waiting for Courtney to congratulate her, but Courtney is silent. She doesn't care about any of that. It's not about the ideology for her. Titania Randall—and whoever else she's working with that doesn't want to be identified—is paying Seabrook a lot of money to provide them the ammunition they need, or at least believe they need, to scrape queer people off the face of public life. Courtney doesn't need to agree with them to cash her checks.

"Have the press conference at the brewery," Randall adds. "It's a recognizable landmark, so people will know that it's safe to stay in San Lazaro."

So much for staying indoors. Courtney sighs, careful that her phone doesn't pick up the sound. "Great idea," she agrees. "By the way, are you here in town?"

"No," Randall says sharply, and hangs up. Courtney groans, then goes to her closet to choose a press conference outfit.

When Courtney's phone buzzes again, she shrieks in frustration and throws the shoe she's holding at the wall. It startles her; she's more wound up than she realized. Bracing herself for more demands from Randall, she picks up the phone.

But the screen doesn't say *Titania Randall*. It says *Leah*.

For a single traitorous moment, relief floods her body. It would be so good to talk to someone who understands what's happening, someone with whom Courtney can share her frustration and confusion and fear. Courtney's thumb twitches reflexively toward the ACCEPT button before she has time to think better of it.

"What the fuck is going on?" Leah says. "My neighbor just broke into my apartment and bit my fucking hand. I had to shoot myself up with the antidote in front of Wendy, and now she knows."

She's angry. Courtney should have expected that. Leah is the type to lash out, not take responsibility. She's calling to lay this whole mess at Courtney's door. "Wow. That sounds stressful," says Courtney, her voice carefully neutral. "Who's Wendy?"

"My . . . ex-girlfriend." Courtney hears the pause before *ex*; she's pretty sure Leah almost said "my girlfriend." Which is fucked-up. Not because Courtney is jealous, obviously. But if Leah slept with Courtney while she's still in love with someone else . . . she just shouldn't have, that's all.

"Well, I'm very sorry that happened to the two of you," Courtney says. "Do you need stitches?"

"Do I—probably, but that's not the fucking point," Leah says. "The point is, you never told me people would start biting."

"How was I supposed to know what your neighbor would do?" Courtney asks. She puts the phone on speaker and turns back to the closet. She needs to find something to wear to the press conference that will look professional and not show sweat. God, she shouldn't have agreed to an outdoor media appearance in July. What is this, her first day?

"Are you fucking kidding me? Stop playing dumb," Leah says. "It's the goddamn zombie apocalypse out there, and you started it. Did you know this was going to happen?"

"Nope, had no idea about the zombie apocalypse," Courtney says lightly. The more emotional Leah gets, the easier it is for

Courtney to retain control of the situation.

"There's more antidote, right?" Leah says. "You've gotta, like, make an announcement. Hand it out to people. You could do it at the health center, it could still be good publicity—"

"Leah," Courtney says, gentle, but it cuts Leah off like a knife. Silence hums between them, and Courtney feels her skin prickle with goosebumps. She should turn down the air conditioning.

"You're not going to do *anything*?" Leah finally asks. Courtney feels a pang of—not guilt, certainly; that's a useless emotion she doesn't indulge. Pity, perhaps. She feels sorry for Leah, wallowing in the fantasy that someone will save her from the mess she's made.

No one saves you but yourself. Courtney knows that better than anyone.

"What *we* are going to do," Courtney says, "is devote ourselves to supporting and rebuilding our community here in San Lazaro. I'm holding a press conference this afternoon to discuss—"

"Rebuilding," says Leah. "What you fucking demolished in the first place. And then you'll pat yourselves on the back for being fucking philanthropists." There's a rough, wet noise that might be Leah trying to swallow back tears. "Samantha was right about you."

"Congratulations to Samantha," Courtney says, unable to fight the edge creeping into her voice now. "I'll give her a gold star next time I see her."

After a long silence, Leah says, "You won't see her." Nothing else, and it takes Courtney a second to understand what she means.

"Oh," Courtney says. Something twists deep inside her. "I'm—"

"If you say you're sorry I'm going to kill you," Leah says, and the worst part is that there's no anger in her voice, only grief.

Courtney doesn't say it. Why should she? She's not sorry. She didn't kill Samantha. She looks down at her hands, which are clean and well-moisturized. Her gel manicure is pearly pink, not a single chip.

It feels strange, knowing that Samantha is dead. She never liked the woman; loud, aggressive, confrontational, and crass, always trying to undermine Seabrook's careful plans. There's nothing about her Courtney will miss. Still—she *knew* her. Courtney wasn't expecting people to die this weekend, certainly not people she knows.

"You could still stop it," Leah says in that same quiet voice. That same deep sadness, as if she knows it won't work but nevertheless feels compelled to try. "Before it gets worse. You could tell people. You could save people."

Courtney contemplates a black dress, then decides against it. Today is not the day to look funereal.

"Please, Courtney," says Leah. "I know you want to fix this. You're one of us, for fuck's sake."

Courtney doesn't register herself crossing the room and grabbing up her phone, but suddenly it's in her hand again. "No, I'm not," she says, her voice coming out choked and painful. "You need to get that through your head, Leah. I am not one of you. I never was."

"But you could—"

"I don't want to be." She's so angry her hands are shaking. Where did all this rage come from? "You think just because you made me come a few times I want to join your little clubhouse? You think I've spent my life waiting for some fat lesbian with ridiculous hair to guide me out of the closet? You want to *fix* me?

You want to teach me to love myself? Please." Courtney laughs, a high mean laugh she doesn't recognize. "I love myself enough to pick the winning team, babe. I have no interest in getting sucked down with the rest of your little gang of degenerates, demanding that everyone call me brave just because I let you eat my pussy."

"Jesus, Courtney."

She gasps for breath, her heart pounding, and adds, "And just for the record, even if I was a dyke and screamed about it to anyone who'd listen, I'd still never be seen in public with you." She gives Leah a moment to respond to that, but there's only silence on the other end of the line, so Courtney hangs up.

For a few seconds, she just stands there by the bed. Sweat cools on her skin as the air conditioner roars. "One," she says out loud, then stops, takes a few breaths, and starts over when she's sure her voice will be steady. "One. Two. Three." She counts all the way to twenty-five. Then, calmer, she returns to her closet. She runs her fingers over the row of blazers and dresses, letting the feel of the fabric ground her, return her to herself.

CHAPTER 15

The Pride festival is in Salt River Park, just south of downtown in the half-gentrified former warehouse district. Neither Logan nor I want to ride in the back of the truck alone, so we cram into the cab with Beau. It's a crowded, bumpy, rattling ride. Aurelia brings up the rear on her giant bike, and I keep sneaking peeks in the rearview mirror because her stoic leather-vested presence makes me feel safer. Logan fidgets and taps his fingers on his knees, nervous energy bubbling over. Beau glances at us and laughs.

"Sorry," she says when she sees our faces. "It just occurred to me that you two have never gone to Pride prepared to fight for your lives before. This is just like old times for me."

"Well, that's fucking dark," Logan mumbles.

"Is it?" Beau shrugs. "I think I'd rather show up with guns blazing than walk in peacefully and drink the poison they sell in a rainbow can."

"That was extremely on the nose," I say.

"I'm an old dyke and I'm probably about to get eaten by

zombies," she says. "I don't have time for subtlety."

The streets of San Lazaro are postapocalyptically empty. We drive along the parade route, but I don't see floats or crowds. More windows are smashed this morning, and more cars are haphazardly crashed or abandoned on the side of the road, some of them still protruding into traffic. Beau's truck has no air conditioning and it's so hot I could throw up. There are clouds piling in sticky meringue peaks along the horizon, but above us the sky is clear and hot and blue-white as the center of a flame.

"Where is everyone?" Logan says.

"Dead, infected, hiding, or blissfully unaware," Beau says, ticking off the options on her fingers.

We cross a bridge over a dry creek. A month from now, during the rainy season, this will be a tributary to the Salt River, but right now it's just a ditch, banks lined with scrubby little trees. The wide road curves and dead-ends at the park, a quarter mile square of cactus, rock gardens, a rusty playground, and, on the far side, an incongruously beautiful flagstone amphitheater.

In between us and all of these things, there's mayhem.

The park is arrayed with kiosks and booths for selling T-shirts, greasy festival food, and lots and lots of Seabrook, but all those stations are unattended. No one is waiting in line. No one sells tickets or overpriced bottled water. No emcee strides the stage. No one waves signs or chants slogans. I expected a scene like the one at Hellrazors last night—entertainment on the verge of disintegrating into chaos. But the last vestiges of a good time were chewed up and spat out long before we arrived. Here, there is only carnage.

"We're too late," I say quietly.

The park is mercifully less full than I expected, and it must be because the uninfected, if there are any left, have already fled.

Everyone who remains is clustered in twos, threes, fours, little knots of violence arrayed across the flagstones like weeds pushing through sidewalk cracks. They're tearing each other apart. I see fists flying, fingernails shredding flesh, hair ripped out in clumps. I see people taking bites out of each other, still alive or not. Wherever I look, deep red pools of blood stain the pale red stones.

The vehicle entrance to the park is entirely blocked off by two police cars, presumably the cops assigned to monitor and/or protect the festivities. I see a cooler lying open on the grass, leaking melted ice like blood from a wound that's already mostly bled out. Cans of Seabrook, some full and some empty, glitter in the sun. Of course the corporate sponsors made sure the cops were well supplied with refreshing beverages.

To the right of where the cars form a blockade, two officers in uniform are gnawing on opposite ends of what might be a human leg. I try to think of something else it could conceivably be and reach the unfortunate but inevitable conclusion that it is, in fact, a human leg. My desire to vomit is not going away.

With the road blocked, Beau swerves onto the grass, hopping over the curb with a groan from her suspension. Behind us, Aurelia takes the same route but more smoothly. Then Beau slams on her brakes and the truck skids, spraying rocks with its back wheels. Aurelia curves gracefully around us and brings her bike to a cinematically perfect stop. I only realize this as the jolt of adrenaline that squeezed my heart like a fist slowly abates and I have a moment to process my surroundings. Lying on the grass is a human body in shorts and a pink crop top. The truck was almost on top of the person before Beau saw them and reacted. From here, it's impossible to tell if they're breathing.

I try to jump out of the truck, but there's six and a half feet of

Logan in my way. "Come on," I shout, shoving him.

"Excuse *me*," Logan says in a snippy voice, like I cut him in line at the coffee shop. Then he opens the door and climbs out. I half jump, half fall out behind him. Beau races around the car to join us.

I drop to my knees next to the body on the ground, gravel scraping my shins. It's someone I vaguely recognize, a trans guy I've seen at parties.

"He's not breathing," Logan says.

I don't want to leave someone lying dead out here, but I don't know what we can possibly do with him. Before I can come up with an idea, I hear a low, grumbling noise. I look over my shoulder and see a tall white guy with a scruffy beard. He's ten feet away and his eyes are fixed directly on me. His beard is stained with blood.

"Oh, fuck my life," I say quietly.

Bloody Beard lunges toward me. Logan yanks me by the arm and I leap out of the way.

I still have the handle of the truck door in my hand. As I jump to the side, the door swings open hard and hits Bloody Beard in the side of the head. The sound is a horrible cacophony of metal and bone and ripping skin. Blood pours down his face, and a flap of his cheek peels back and hangs loose, beard and all. He roars in what sounds more like rage than pain.

The roar rises into a screeching whine and I realize I'm not just hearing the dying man. Logan is still clutching my arm, and this time it's my turn to pull him out of the way.

In a blur of red paint and black leather, Aurelia's bike flashes between me and Bloody Beard. He whips around, trying and failing to track her movements with his bleary eyes. She does a tight, perfect figure-eight turn and zooms back the other way, passing between us again. This time Bloody Beard loses his balance and reaches back toward the cab of the truck to steady himself. The door is still hanging open. Without giving myself time to reconsider, I throw myself forward and slam it on him with all my weight.

His body is trapped at an awkward angle between the door and the frame, so the sharp edge of the door hits him diagonally across the chest. I'm pretty sure I feel ribs break, but he doesn't cry out in pain, only grunts at the impact.

He snarls at me, one arm free and reaching around the door, trying to grab whatever part of my body he can reach. At the same time, he pushes back against the door. Despite his numerous injuries, he's bigger and stronger than me, and I'm not sure how long I can hold him like this.

Then Logan is beside me, adding his weight to mine. I hear something snap in Bloody Beard's chest as our combined mass bears down on him, but it's still not enough.

"We have to hit him again," I pant. Logan nods. "Let off, then slam it at the same time. On three, okay?"

"Like one, two, three, shoot, or one, two, shoot on three?"

"Jesus Christ. Shoot on three," I say. "One, two—"

On "three," Logan and I simultaneously stand up, removing our weight from the car door. Bloody Beard shoves it open from the inside, but in unison, we throw ourselves at it again. The infected man has changed position just enough that this time, the corner of the door catches him across the throat. There's a heavier, meatier crunch than the first time, and blood spouts from a ragged hole in his neck. Bloody Beard looks more annoyed than horrified as he chokes, flails, dies.

I hear a shout, and then the door of the pickup truck is wrenched out of my hands and I'm falling on my ass into blood-soaked dirt. Scrambling to my feet, I realize Beau has slammed the truck into drive and stomped on the gas, tearing across the park with Bloody Beard's corpse hanging from her passenger door. Then she slams to a halt and reverses hard. As Beau screeches back toward us, the last strands of flesh and tendon connecting Bloody Beard's head to his body snap, and most of him rolls across the grass.

"That was decisive," Logan says admiringly. Aurelia swerves across the grass and stops beside him, pulling off her helmet.

"This is worse than I thought," she says. I can hear something straining under her fraying calm, a frantic snarl trying to break free.

"Do we make a break for it?" Beau asks.

"What, run and hide?" I say, and I want to so desperately it makes my chest ache with shame. "We came to save people. We came here to *fix* things."

"Wendy," says Logan. He looks at the park all around us. "We can't fix this. You were right, it's too late."

I look around and see ripped-open bodies, empty faces, mouths full of blood and gristle. We came here to rescue the uninfected and confront Seabrook, but neither of those are anywhere to be found. It's just us and the plague-ridden, here in the sweltering sun.

The lumbering remains of what used to be our community have registered Beau's truck as a new and stimulating addition to the tableau of devastation, and they're making their way toward us. There's no path out of the park that doesn't involve cutting through human bodies. On the far edge of the square I see a few of them staggering away from the rest of the crowd, out into the streets. I think about where they might end up, remembering Emmy and the child she attacked, and the possibilities threaten to choke me.

All these people poisoned, twisted until their animal urges are the only thing left. All these lives destroyed. It's too late to bring any of them back, and it's too late for Sam and Jacquie and Mike, and in another minute it will be too late for us, too.

I look back at Logan, at Aurelia, at Beau. *I want to go home*, I think again.

But I don't have anywhere to go.

"We can't fix it," I say. "But maybe we can stop it here."

"Atta-fuckin'-girl," Beau says immediately, and claps me on the back. Aurelia's eyes burn with a fierce light I've never seen in them before.

"What do we do?" I say. Bravado is one thing, but I'm not exactly qualified to strategize a final stand.

"We fuck them up," Aurelia says. "As much as we can until we can't anymore. Anyone have a problem with that?"

"I'm solid," says Beau. I see Logan clench his jaw, but he nods too.

"This is really not how I expected this weekend to go," I say.

"No," Logan agrees, his voice shaking. "I'm just here for the fireworks."

My heart stutters. "Where?" I ask Logan urgently.

He stares at me, confused by the sudden shift in my tone. "Here. At Pride." He glances at Beau and Aurelia as if looking for backup. "I was going along with your bit. It was a gallows humor thing."

"No, I mean—" One of these days I'm going to shake him until his teeth rattle, then kiss him just as hard. "Where are the fireworks?"

"Over by the stage." He points across the park to the amphitheater, a hollow of red stone like a mouth in the earth.

Aurelia's head whips around to stare at me, her hair fanning out behind her. "Fireworks," she says. That dangerous glow in her eyes only gets brighter. "*Fireworks.*"

"Fuck yeah," Beau says, catching up quickly. "We'll hold them off for you."

Aurelia nods, revs her bike, and takes off, narrowly avoiding a snarling man in a fraternity T-shirt.

"Weapons," Beau snaps at Logan and me, and we jump into action.

Back at the house, Aurelia said, "No guns for you two. We don't have time to teach you how to be anything other than a public health hazard."

"But you trust us with fucking *spears*?" Logan asked, brandishing something that would look medieval if it weren't so viciously sparkling clean.

"You're not gonna accidentally kill someone on the other side of the street with that," said Aurelia.

"Maybe just each other," I muttered to Logan.

Now, he goes right for the spear, leaving me to contemplate a range of choices with which I'm more likely to poke out my own eye than turn back an onslaught of the undead. Then I see something buried under the weapons, way in the back of the truck bed with Beau's toolbox. I'm hardly the kind of lesbian who knows her way around a Home Depot, but I worked a landscaping gig one summer before I discovered that nannying and petsitting could get me into air-conditioned houses. I wasn't great at it, but I do know how to handle a chainsaw.

As I drag the pull cord, its deep chuckle is echoed by the lower, louder roar of Aurelia's engine. All across the park, people turn from what they're doing to look at her, then stagger in the direction of the noise. They've been tearing each other apart, and most of them are wounded, bleeding, dragging mangled limbs and shredded flesh behind them. I could easily believe they're corpses that learned to walk. They trail after Aurelia, breathing dust and exhaust, stringing out behind her like grotesque baby geese.

Shit. The plan was for the rest of us to keep them occupied while Aurelia does her thing, but instead they're fixated on her. I think back to last night at the bar, how all the fighting stopped when Beau opened the emergency exit and the alarm began to blare. It's the noise, I realize—their attention is drawn to whatever's the loudest, and right now that's Aurelia. She's faster than they are, but that won't buy her enough lead time if every zombie in the park is heading straight for her.

"Hey!" I slam the body of the chainsaw against the side of the pickup truck. The clang is earsplitting. Several people turn their bloodied faces back our way. "Come on," I say to Logan.

"What are you doing?" he asks.

What I'm doing is trying to climb into the back of Beau's pickup truck, while holding a running chainsaw. I am not succeeding.

"They go toward noise," I say, gesturing to the crowd staggering in Aurelia's wake. "We have to make some kind of diversion to draw them away from her, so she can get the stuff set up."

"I can make way more noise than that," Logan says. "If we can get over there." He points across the park, past all the fighting and corpses, to the stage on the far side of the amphitheater, decked out with a massive SEABROOK PRESENTS SAN LAZARO PRIDE banner, along with stacks of amplifiers and speakers. If everything hadn't gone to hell, that's where he and the rest of the drag queens would be getting ready to perform right now.

I see what he's getting at, and it's perfect. The only problem is crossing the park. My gambit with the chainsaw was moderately effective; the infected are looking our way. There are a lot of them.

"Fuck. Okay," I say. "Beau, can you get us across the park?"

"Hop in," she says, climbing into the driver's seat of her truck.

Instead of getting into the cab, Logan boosts me into the bed, hands me the chainsaw, then climbs up after me. He holds the spear above his head and yells, "Come on, bitches!" I brace my feet and rev my chainsaw. Beau nudges the gas and we roll forward.

Logan takes the right side of the truck, and I take the left. A white woman with icy-blond hair grabs the side of the bed and tries to swing herself up. I swing the chainsaw blade, meaning to decapitate her, but instead I slice a line through her body at shoulder level. The rattling, splintering sound of chain gnawing through bone reverberates through my own skeleton. Her shoulders, neck, and head slide sideways, and I think for a moment of a plaster bust falling off a shelf as she tumbles to the ground in pieces.

We're probably going only ten miles an hour or so, Beau keeping an eye out for any more human bodies strewn across the flagstones. It's slow enough that the zombies can sort of keep up, surging and clawing around us, trying to pull us down. I risk a glance across the park and see that a few of them are still following Aurelia, but most have shifted their focus to us. They stumble and fall and clamber over each other to keep pace with the truck. I jab at them with my chainsaw. Some of them flinch. Some don't. Their blood spatters my face and arms.

Something grabs my leg. I look down and see a kid, probably no older than sixteen. They're hanging half in and half out of the truck, feet flailing in the air, jaws gaping as they attempt to chomp into my thigh.

I scream and reflexively try to bat them away. The chainsaw bites through the top of their skull, coming dangerously close to my own leg. As they die, their muscles spasm and I feel the tender skin behind my knee give way to a sharp fingernail. "Fuck!" I shout, nearly losing my balance as Beau swerves. Struggling to stay upright, I drop the chainsaw. It falls off the truck and into the crowd, knocking one back as they try to grab for me.

"Goddammit!" I throw myself flat in the bed of the truck, the sun-hot metal searing my skin. Logan is still on his feet, but he's barely holding back the chaos on his side of the truck, wielding his spear like a bat because he doesn't have enough room to stab with it. I grope for another weapon.

Above me, Logan yelps in surprise. I look up and see that someone has a grip on the handle of his spear and is dragging on it, throwing Logan off-balance. He should drop the spear and grab something else, but in the chaos and dread he's reflexively clinging to the only weapon he has, caught in a vicious tug-of-war.

The truck is slowing down, veering from side to side as Beau tries to find a path through the crush of dead-eyed, bloody-mouthed bodies. Logan loses his grip on the spear and sways dangerously as he gropes after it, leaning too far over the edge of the truck. Abandoning my search, I throw my arms around his legs and drag him backward, and he falls in a heap on top of me. His elbow lands on my solar plexus. Someone screams—maybe both of us.

As Logan struggles to his feet and reaches to help me up, I realize the truck has stopped moving. Beau's path must be completely blocked. A man has a hold on the side of the truck and is trying to vault himself into the bed. The only reason he hasn't succeeded yet is that one of his arms is mostly detached at the shoulder.

Grabbing Logan's outstretched hand with one of my own, I close the other around the first thing I can reach. As he pulls me up, I'm already swinging from the shoulder, bringing one of Aurelia's swords around in a gleaming arc and burying it, with a noise like chopping wood, deep in the man's neck. Reflexively, the dying man grabs the blade to pull it from the wound, and in doing so lets go of the truck and falls.

But there are more coming. If we don't drive, we'll be overwhelmed by them in moments. "Beau!" I shout, glancing toward the truck's cab.

Beau is leaning out the window with a big fuck-off gun. Beyond her, I can see that the infected are crowded so tight in front of the truck there's simply no way through or around them. Aurelia is almost to the other side of the park, only a few still following her. We wanted to create a diversion and it worked. Only now it's starting to sink in that we might have sacrificed ourselves so Aurelia's plan could succeed.

I look at Logan and see that he's thinking the same thing. There are too many of them. Well, if we're already dead, we can at least buy Aurelia the time she needs.

Logan grins at me as he picks up a baseball bat. I kind of wish I could spare a few seconds to kiss him. But instead, I brace my feet and raise my sword.

In a clear voice, Logan shouts, "Category is: zombie-killers, motherfucker!"

"Let's go!" I scream, not quite as loud as Logan but at least my voice doesn't shake.

Then the ten zombies closest to us burst into flames.

CHAPTER 16

Fire. Out of nowhere, vast and roaring and consuming the bodies trying to climb the sides of the truck in one hungry bite. The flames leap hungrily from one body to the next, faster than I would have expected, almost faster than my eyes can follow. The infected don't scream, only stagger and fall.

I gape at the spreading inferno, my whole body numb from shock, barely even feeling the heat blazing through the already torrid air. Logan yanks me backward and I slump against him, registering only a few seconds later that he's probably saved me from having my face scorched off.

What breaks me out of my trance is the sound of Logan laughing.

"Yeah!" he whoops. "Get it, bitch!"

I blink and look around. What could he possibly be excited about? First zombies, now fire; we've gone from doomed to fucked. But then I follow his gaze and see the most beautiful thing I've ever laid eyes on: a neon pink and green pizza delivery car. With some kind of jury-rigged flamethrower mounted on its hood.

"Sunshine!" I shout over Logan's elated howling. How did they know to come? Or did one of these shambling corpses order a pizza before they died?

They wave to us through the open window. Then they pull on something inside the car—there are a lot of wires and things sticking out of the dashboard that were definitely not there before—and the big metal tube on the hood spews flames again, swallowing another half dozen bodies. The rest of the ravening horde have noticed the big, loud, hot thing and, as it seems they always do with whatever catches their attention, they're ambling straight toward it. Thank God this, at least, was something the zombie movies mostly got right: the infected are very, very stupid.

The stink of burning meat threatens to gag me, but I swallow the smoke and bile. The crowd is thinning out in front of Beau's truck as more and more of our attackers divert their attention to Sunshine and their fire-breathing car. Maybe we can make it through to back up Aurelia after all. I bang on the truck's back window to get Beau's attention, but she's already on it.

"Hold on!" she yells back to us. A burning hand reaches out to me, a hideous parallel to the way Logan extended his hand to help me up a moment ago. I stare at it, watching the fingernails blacken and crumble to ash.

The truck lurches forward. Logan and I sway and clutch each other and don't go down. The burning hand disappears below the horizon of my vision, and as I spare a parting glance at Sunshine I realize with a start that there's someone else in their passenger seat.

Pale round face. Midnight hair, deep blue.

My heart surges toward her like the ocean at the moon.

"Leah." Her name forms on my lips but if I say it aloud, no one hears it, not even me. Beau hits the gas and the car leaps across the scorched and bloodied expanse of the park, leaving Sunshine, Leah, and a cloud of reeking smoke behind.

"Leah's back there," I shout in Logan's ear. If this is the end of everything, I want her to be the one beside me. I want to protect her, or, failing that, I want my death to momentarily delay hers. It's a stupid, useless impulse, but it's what my guts are screaming at me. Nothing that's happened between us matters, not the sex, not the betrayal, not any of the betrayals before that. I would die for Leah.

"She'll be fine," Logan says. "Sunshine's got her." The fact that he's clearly right, and Sunshine is far better equipped to protect her than I am, in no way assuages my desire to leap from the truck and sprint across the park to drape my body over Leah's. But there are dozens if not hundreds of infected people in the way, and many of them are on fire. I stay in the truck.

With most of the infected making their way toward Sunshine's car and the growing fireball, it only takes us a minute to get across the park to the outer rim of the amphitheater. Aurelia's bike is lying on the grass. Beyond it, the semicircular amphitheater descends into the earth level by level until the stage rises up again at the far, flat end. Aurelia is crouched in the backstage area, slightly below ground level and partially shielded from the rest of the park by a big, curving white screen that serves as a backdrop for the stage. There are still a handful of people following her, but they're stumbling over each other trying to climb down the stairs. It would be hilarious if it weren't so grotesque and sad.

Logan jumps out of the truck and reaches out a hand to help me down. I ignore it and jump the same way he did, immediately regretting it when the jolt of impact lances through my shins. Beau leans out the window, aiming yet another big fuck-off gun at the clamber of people on the stairs.

"I've got you covered," she says, and I get the weirdest feeling that she's enjoying herself.

"I love you, Beau," I say, suddenly terrified that I'll never see her again.

"Move your ass," she says, which I take to mean that she loves us too.

Logan goes first, and I wonder if it's some kind of chivalrous bullshit, but I'm not about to argue with him right now. Honestly, I don't mind having a human shield. As we move down the wide risers, a few of the infected catch sight of us and veer our way.

One comes galloping up the stairs on all fours, but Logan has a clear shot and swings his baseball bat like Lori Petty. It connects with a crack that hurts my teeth, and the figure topples backward.

Another semi-human lumbers toward us, but before they're even in batting distance a bullet singes the air and blows a hole in their head. Between Logan's long arms and Beau's great aim, we make it all the way to the stage without me having to decapitate anything.

A short, narrow staircase to one side of the stage leads up again from the flat bottom of the amphitheater to the backstage area. Aurelia is crouched among the speakers and cables, hard at work. I stand over her with the machete, ready to fight off anyone that comes close, but for the moment we're alone up here. "What can we do?" I ask.

"Make them come to us," she says without looking up.

Of course. Sunshine's distraction has worked too well—we

need the zombies inside the amphitheater. I look at Logan. Logan looks at the stage, and the tiers of stone seats beyond it. "This was going to be my dream gig," he says.

Despite everything, a smile breaks across my face.

It only takes a moment to plug in what we need. I station myself at the sound board. I don't have a microphone, and Logan doesn't need an introduction anyway, but I still shout with all the strength in my lungs: "Please welcome Dahlia DePravity!"

I hit PLAY, Logan stands center stage, and in a rich, husky voice that carries from the giant speakers and across the whole park, Britney Spears informs us that there's only two types of people in the world.

The thing is, we don't really need Logan onstage for this to work. "Circus" blasting across the grass, amplified so loud it sounds like Britney is singing from inside the earth itself, would probably be more than enough to get the zombies' attention.

But it's Pride weekend. And this is the grand finale.

Logan is breathtaking. Even in a borrowed T-shirt and cutoffs, no wig or makeup, none of Dahlia's signature gothic flourishes—he owns the entire stage. His body moves sinuously, stretching out to its full, astonishing length, then curling back in on itself only to explode along a new trajectory. He jumps, I swear to God, higher than my head, and lands like he's made of nothing but air.

"You better work!" I holler. Logan flashes a smile at me, spinning on one foot like a ballerina, his head flicking around to find me again and again.

It dawns on me that I would die for him, too. The knowledge feels different than it did with Leah, not a desperate flash but a grounding weight in my core, roots unfurling from the bottom of my feet. I'd let my body be torn apart if it would save Logan. Or

Aurelia, or Beau. I want to make it through this, but even more, I want them to make it. My friends. The people I love.

"Set to jet," Aurelia says in my ear. The heat of her breath makes me jump. She holds up what she's been working on for the last ten minutes: a cluster of fireworks the size of my head, all tied together with a complicated labyrinth of fuses. Logan's sole, vital contribution to the Pride programming: an explosive finale.

I look out over the crowd. The zombies are coming. Drawn to the sound, to the vibrations in the earth, they stagger across the park and spill over the rim of the amphitheater, first a trickle and then a stream. They fall down the stairs and stumble over each other, and some of them don't get back up, and the rest of them don't notice, and they just keep coming. I see Sunshine's car zigzagging across the grass, engine snarling, spitting flames, and realize they're herding the infected toward the stage—toward our trap.

"Wait," I say to Aurelia. Just another few seconds, just enough for a few more bodies to meander into the blast zone. Just enough for Logan to get to the break in the song.

"*Let's go*," Britney murmurs so loud they can probably hear it in Phoenix. Logan does a walkover into the splits, then springs back to his feet, moving so perfectly to the rhythm of the song it's like the beat is coming from his body. Aurelia produces a lighter. I expect her to flick it to life, but instead she holds it out to me. Of course: Aurelia builds the trap, Logan is the bait, but I'm the one who gets to set it off.

God, it's so hot out here, I think. Clouds have covered the sun—or maybe that's just the smoke from Sunshine's impromptu cookout—but the air is still as warm and heavy as bathwater. I've never seen a zombie movie where people sweat as much as Aurelia and I are right now.

The throng of infected is pouring into the bottom of the amphitheater now. In another few seconds, they'll reach Logan. Still a few stragglers at ground level, but I'll have to trust that Sunshine and Leah can take care of it, with Beau's help.

I take the lighter from Aurelia's hand. Her nail polish is chipped but still beautiful, iridescent gold sparkles over a black base coat. I roll my thumb and a flame springs up, a point of even brighter heat within the crushing summer. I stifle the urge to flinch away from it. Aurelia's empty hand is still outstretched. The fire shimmers off her fingernails.

I touch the lighter's flame to the longest wick.

"Logan!" I scream. "Run!"

Without even pausing for thought, Logan pivots and leaps, throwing his whole body toward Aurelia and me. Britney is still singing, but I can't hear her clearly over the hammering of my pulse in my ears. Aurelia winds up like a professional softball pitcher, and I see every muscle in her arm in perfect detail as she throws the bundle of fireworks with all her strength. Not waiting to see it land, she turns and runs alongside Logan and me. The concrete lip of the amphitheater is waist-high above the stage. Logan and Aurelia both vault it easily, then reach back in unison to haul me up.

We make it three more steps before the world explodes.

It's so loud I don't hear it so much as feel it in my skeleton, a shock wave that knocks me face down on the dirt just beyond the stage. My blood crashes in my veins like it's trying to escape. I think at some point I scream, but I can only tell because my throat aches; the sound is indistinguishable from the cacophony.

I roll over and struggle to sit up. Something hurts, but I'm too overwhelmed to figure out what. The ongoing sounds of smaller explosions crackle and fizz in my ringing ears, and the bowl of the amphitheater overflows with bright lights in rainbow colors. Sparks and ashes swirl through the air as the explosions finally taper off.

There's a pressure on my arm that I finally identify as Logan, trying to pull me to my feet. "Look," I try to say, pointing as though he might have missed the incendiary spectacle. Below us, the amphitheater is a bowl of fire and flesh, bodies torn and scorched beyond recognition. The air stinks of acrid smoke and burned meat.

"I know, dude," he says. "We gotta—"

A spark lands in front of me, just between my splayed legs. It ignites a blade of dry grass. Without thinking, I slam the heel of my hand over the incipient fire, hissing at the slight burn.

"You gotta get that looked at," Logan says.

I hold my hand up. "It's not a big deal."

"Not your hand," he says. He crouches down next to me and cups my chin, turning my face so he can see it better. "I think your nose is broken."

Oh, that's what hurts. Now that he mentions it, the throbbing of the world does seem to radiate out from the center of my face. I bring my hand to my nose experimentally, and immediately flinch away from the burst of pain. "Fuck." My fingertips where I touched my nose are covered in blood. There's blood on my lips too, I realize, in my mouth and running down my chin.

And so what? If I come out of this weekend with no worse than a broken nose, I'll feel so lucky I'll buy a lottery ticket.

I push to my feet, ignoring the way my head briefly feels too heavy and full of water. "It hurts, but it's not gonna kill me," I tell Logan.

Aurelia is a few yards past us, farther from the cloud of gray smoke that hangs over the amphitheater. She's walking unsteadily, favoring her left foot, but the look on her face is one of grim satisfaction.

"Hey, we did it," she says.

"Yeah," I agree, although part of me wonders what, exactly, we did. The things—no, the people—chasing us are dead, but the poison that created them is still out there. Seabrook could be making more as we speak. And even if they're not, we still just blew up a huge portion of our own community. It's hard to feel victorious.

The three of us walk back around the half-circle crater, pausing every few steps because Logan's bare feet are a bruised and bloody mess. The smoke is dissipating, revealing what's left in the amphitheater. I glance at it for barely an instant and have to turn away. *Burned minestrone on the bottom of the soup pot* is what I think in that instant. I might have seen something moving, but I don't dare look again.

At the apex of the amphitheater's curved edge, Beau is waiting for us, sitting on the hood of her truck. She's ash-streaked and grimy in a way that looks artful, like the end of a disaster movie when the hero is disheveled but still hot. She hops down from the truck and throws her arms around Aurelia, then Logan and me.

"I heard that boom and I was afraid y'all hadn't made it," she says. The look on her face doesn't match the casual tone of her voice.

The pizza delivery car is approximately perpendicular to Beau's truck, surrounded by a scar of blackened grass and torn earth. Sunshine unfolds out of the driver's seat to greet us, but Leah stays in the car.

"Damn," says Sunshine, slow and easy like they're reacting to a cool skateboarding trick. "Fucked them right up."

"Thanks," Logan says with a grin I recognize as the one that got me in bed with him. "I choreographed it myself."

Aurelia hip-checks him, directing her smile toward Sunshine as well. "Thanks for rounding them up for us."

"How did you know we needed help?" I ask, even though I'm pretty sure I know the answer.

Sunshine nods toward their car. "Your girl called me. Said bad shit was going down and that you needed all the bodies you could get."

I see Logan's and Aurelia's faces as they glance at Leah, then back at each other, and carefully *not* at me. Sunshine, apparently not noticing the tension, waves to Leah cheerfully.

"I should probably," I say, and don't finish the sentence because I don't know how. Instead, I walk toward Leah, feeling the heavy slowness that sometimes comes in dreams.

She rolls down the window—Sunshine's car is old enough to have a hand crank, operable even when the engine is off—and looks up at me, saying nothing. I lean over and gaze in at her.

"Thanks," I say. My mouth tastes sour and full of smoke. Leah's cheeks are pink and shiny from the heat.

"For what?" she asks, and I get the feeling she's testing me somehow.

"For showing up, and bringing Sunshine," I say. Leah nods and breaks eye contact, and I think I've given her the wrong answer.

"Least I could do," she says.

"No," I say without thinking. "You could have done less." The corner of her mouth quirks, but otherwise she doesn't respond. I stay like that for a long moment, waiting for her to meet my eyes again, or say something else, or for a walking corpse to bite my face off and save me from this sweltering silence, but no such luck.

Finally I straighten up and turn back toward the others. Only then do I hear the car door creak open, Leah's feet on the hot flagstones as she follows me.

"You want to clean up your face?" she asks. Without looking at her, I nod. She passes me an alcohol wipe and I dab at my nose with it as gently as I can, which only makes me scream a small amount.

Logan has salvaged a cooler from one of the abandoned drink kiosks and is pouring half-melted ice over a smoldering cholla that must have caught stray sparks from Sunshine's flame-thrower. Beau is lugging another cooler over. She's walking odd-ly, carrying all the weight on one side of her body, and I can't understand why until I remember her broken ribs.

"You okay, Beau?" I ask.

She drops the cooler and straightens up, glancing at me like she's embarrassed to have been caught stumbling. "No worries," she says.

Before I can ask a follow-up question, Aurelia screams "*No!*" in a full-on horror movie soprano. I whip around, expecting to see a zombie chomping into someone's jugular, but all I see is Sunshine bending over another cooler. They look up in surprise as Aurelia dives on them, slamming into their back and sending them tumbling. An aluminum can falls from Sunshine's grasp and crunches on the flagstone, spraying fizz from a jagged hole in its side.

"What the fuck?" Sunshine asks, as close to angry as I've ever heard them sound—maybe a quarter past perturbed.

"You can't drink that," Aurelia says. The can spewing like Linda Blair reads SEABROOK in big, looping orange cursive.

"Why?" Sunshine already sounds calmer, curious rather than indignant, even though they're still sprawled on their ass with hard seltzer dripping down one calf.

"That's the shit that turns people into zombies," Logan says.

Sunshine squints. "The bubbly water?"

"Yeah," says Leah, who's now standing next to me. Sunshine hasn't moved to get up yet. "There's a compound in it that impedes rational thought and causes hyperaggression." I see Aurelia give Leah a long, considering look, and I tense up. I'm not sure Aurelia would be in the wrong, morally, if she decided to throw a punch at Leah right now. But I also know that if she tries, I'll do what I can to stop her.

"That's fucked-up." Sunshine finally gets to their feet.

Beau holds out the flask I didn't realize she had on her. "Here, if you need a drink."

Sunshine grabs it and takes a deep swig before any of us can warn them. They breathe in deep and let it out in a whistle. "Damn, that's good shit." They hand the flask back to Beau while the rest of us stare at each other, stunned. "So all this fuckery is because of a bad batch of liquor?" Sunshine asks. Aurelia's jaw tenses, but she doesn't say anything.

I glance at Leah, not sure what to say, but she doesn't flinch. "It's not a bad batch," she says. "It's intentional. The company put it in there."

Sunshine nods, eyes unfocused, rubbing their chin thoughtfully. "It's poison," they say, halfway between a statement and a question.

"Basically," says Leah.

"So those were all poisoning victims," Sunshine says, in the same not-quite-questioning tone. "All those people. That we killed."

"Yes, they were." I hear the strain in Leah's voice, but I have to give her credit: she still doesn't hesitate or even drop her gaze.

"That's fucked-up," Sunshine says again.

"You're not wrong," Logan says.

"I mean, I always figured the zombie apocalypse would start in my lifetime," Sunshine says. "I just assumed it would be, like, a bug-escaped-from-a-lab kind of scenario. Incompetence rather than straight-up evil."

"It was some kind of conspiracy," Aurelia says. "They created a crisis, and then positioned themselves as the response to it. Although I do think they must not have realized it would get this bad."

"Yeah," Beau agrees. "It's hard to imagine spinning this into good PR for anyone."

"Bet you they'll still try," Aurelia says.

"Excuse me," says Leah. Without waiting for anyone's response, she walks quickly away from the rest of us, heading back toward the amphitheater. I wonder briefly whether I should follow her, but this seems like a moment she might want to be alone, grappling with the weight of her own culpability in all this. I'll give her some space, I figure, and go after her if she doesn't return in a few minutes.

When Sunshine's car roars to life behind me, I realize I should have been expecting it, but it's too late to do anything differently. Leah has already revved the engine, sprayed gravel around the rim of the amphitheater, and screeched out of the park.

CHAPTER 17

"Hey, that's my car," Sunshine says with mild surprise. "What's she doing?" The last part, for some reason, is directed at me.

"So she's just bailing now? After everything?" Aurelia says, and I can hear the rage she's been struggling to keep in check.

"Since when do I know what Leah's thinking?" I ask defensively. But fragments of conversation echo in my mind. *Poisoning victims. Straight-up evil. PR opportunity.* I imagine Leah alone in her apartment with the corpse of Mrs. Delgado, dialing Pizzapocalypse and asking for a ride straight into the middle of the flesh-eating swarm. Staying in the car, out of the way, demanding no one's attention, but still here because she needed to be. I look in the direction Sunshine's car disappeared, around a corner into the warren of warehouses, and try to map out what lies that way. I remember what I said to her before I left: *You didn't try to stop it.*

Is she trying now?

"I think I know where she went," I say.

No one hears me, because Logan and Aurelia are both

yelling—not at each other, just in each other's direction since Leah's not here. "Hey," I try, but they talk right over me. Sunshine notices, though, and flashes me a grin that conjures their namesake.

They cup their hands around their mouth and, with far greater resonance than I could possibly produce, shout, "Please be quiet!"

Everyone falls silent and stares at Sunshine, including me. It takes a gesture from them to remind me that it's my turn to speak. "Leah's going to the Seabrook brewery," I say.

Logan's jaw drops. "That bitch is switching sides again?"

"No, goddammit," I say.

But Beau got there as soon as I said it. "Bringing the fight to them."

"I think so."

"With what weapons?" Aurelia asks.

I gesture to Sunshine. "Have you seen their car?"

Aurelia winces. "Good point."

"There's more stuff in the trunk, too," Sunshine says proudly.

It's not that I've suddenly developed an aversion to violence after helping blow the whole Pride finale into Campbell's Cream of Zombie, but unlike the staggering hordes of the undead, Seabrook will see Leah coming. They have security. They have thinking, strategizing human beings. They have more guns than Sunshine and Aurelia put together. I respect what Leah's trying to do, but I don't see any way she's going to come out of this alive.

Unless we stop her in time. "Beau," I say, but once again she's already done the math. She's moving toward her truck at an easy lope; despite her shorter legs and broken ribs, I scramble to keep up. I jump into the passenger seat just as Beau guns the engine, and Logan, trotting behind us, barely has time to dive for the bed of the truck before we're picking up speed. Through the side-view mirror I can see Aurelia swinging a leg over her bike, Sunshine climbing up behind her.

"What exactly is your plan here?" Beau asks, bumping over the curb and onto the road.

"Open to suggestions," I say. She doesn't reply.

The streets are still mostly empty. I see a few cars abandoned like Jacquie's, a few more wrecks that no one is coming to clean up. The rush of triumph from blowing up the amphitheater has dissipated, and now I wonder how much of a dent we actually made. There are far more infected in San Lazaro than the ones Aurelia's explosion wiped out.

For a sick, dizzying moment I wonder if we're the last healthy humans left in town, but I push that thought away. Surely not. There's no way it could have gotten that bad that fast. If we don't see anyone on the streets right now, it's just because they're staying indoors, where it's safe and air-conditioned.

Clouds gather overhead, but the early afternoon sun is painfully bright behind them, a gray veil spiked with ultraviolet that makes my head throb. We come around a corner and see the Seabrook brewery looming over what's left of the warehouse district, a chrome and glass hulk three stories high. It hurts to look at. There's a metallic tang in the air like the promise of lightning, or it could just be the taste of blood lingering in my mouth.

Sunshine's car is parked half on the curb, Leah standing next to the open driver's side door. In front of her is Courtney, the brand ambassador I saw at Hellrazors, pristine in a pencil skirt and silk shell. A microphone, speaker, and several rows of folding chairs are set up on the sidewalk in front of the massive floor-to-ceiling windows that make up the whole side of the building. Inside, clearly visible from the street, the pipes and kettles of the brewing equipment shine in silence. No one moves across the floor on the other side of the glass. The brewery seems to be empty. I can see the photo op Courtney's setting up, her own sleek figure foregrounded against all that impeccable machinery, but whoever the intended audience is for Seabrook's next attempt to rebrand the zombie apocalypse, they haven't arrived yet.

As I expected, Courtney is flanked by four security guards, each of them with guns on both hips. I don't know anything about guns, but these are bigger than the one that killed Sam. Sunshine's car is rigged with flamethrowers, but I have no doubt Courtney's backup dancers will vaporize Leah if she looks like she's reaching for the dashboard. That's assuming Leah even knows how to work Sunshine's Mad Max weapon system.

Before Beau even has the truck in park, I'm jumping out the door onto the asphalt.

"It's gone too far, Courtney," Leah says loudly. Neither of them glances at me as I scramble up beside Leah. "You've lost control."

"We at Seabrook grieve alongside our community here in San Lazaro, and we're here to help rebuild," Courtney says with a sparkling catalog smile.

"What community? You trashed this whole town," I say. "Whatever happens next, it's going to happen to you too."

"We've got new locations in Denver and Portland, and grand openings in three more cities next year," says Courtney. "And after facing down domestic terrorism in a red state for our socially conscious business model, we look forward to being supported and welcomed in more progressive areas."

"So that's it?" Leah says. "You set San Lazaro on fire and just leave us to deal with it?"

"Our new community health center will be on the front lines

helping our friends and neighbors deal with the aftermath of this difficult time," Courtney chirps.

"You fucking psycho," I spit at her. A squeal of tires makes me look over my shoulder. Aurelia's bike has come around the corner only to be cut off by a car with a corporate security logo. I can tell Aurelia is yelling at the security guards, but I can't hear what she's saying.

Courtney focuses on me for the first time. "Wendy," she says, as if remembering something. "From the bar, right?" She looks back at Leah. "I see it. You two would be cute together. I hope you can work it out." I can't help but glance at Leah at those words. I see her eyes darting toward me, too, but we both look away quickly.

"In the meantime, though, I need to finish setting up for my press conference," Courtney says, ostentatiously checking her watch. It's probably an expensive watch.

"No, listen, fuck you," says Leah, refocusing on Courtney. "You're not going to get away with this. We're going to tell everyone. Seabrook is going down."

"Please do spread your conspiracy theories far and wide," Courtney says. "I'm sure you can get the 'jet fuel can't melt steel beams' people on your side." I really wish my phone wasn't smashed. This would be a great time to surreptitiously record her.

"Do you know how many people we killed at the festival grounds?" Leah snarls.

"Those were your people, not mine," Courtney says with a shrug. "Doesn't hurt my bottom line a bit."

"That's not what I mean," Leah says. "I mean we could just as easily do the same to you."

I'm not sure she's right about that. It's one thing to swing a chainsaw at someone screaming nonsense and trying to bite your face off. In that park, the infected became a nearly faceless horde, a sea of madness and violence surging all around us. It was horrible but uncomplicated: shut them down before they killed us. They didn't deserve it, but neither did we. This is different. Courtney is still a person, sentient and aware. I wouldn't shed a tear if she were killed, but I'm not sure I can be the one to do it.

"Well, I wouldn't love that, but big picture, it still wouldn't make much of a difference," Courtney says. "I'm replaceable. You'd just generate more press for Seabrook." She adopts a singsong, faux-sweet voice. "If only you'd had access to community mental health resources, this terrifying violent outburst could have been avoided." Dropping the affected voice, she adds, "Besides, these guys would blow your head off before you laid a finger on me."

Leah looks at Courtney, at the security guards behind her, and then at me. I can tell she wants something from me, but I don't know what to give her. We're cornered. I don't see how we can win this.

Leah's eyes are frantic. She looks back at the security guards, and I follow her gaze. Then I realize it's not the guards she's looking at, it's the building behind them. The giant panes of glass, reflecting the gray and swirling sky. Behind them, the brewery itself, all gleaming pipes and vats like the churning guts of a robot. This is where they make the poison.

I nod at Leah. I get it now.

"Listen, you hateful bitch," I say, stepping forward so I'm between Courtney and Leah. "What the hell is wrong with you? Don't you understand that you're killing people?" I move closer, into her personal space. Courtney doesn't back up, but in my peripheral vision I can see the guards placing their hands on their weapons, angling their bodies toward me. Adrenaline sings through my exhausted body once again.

"You think you'll get away with this, but you won't," Logan says behind me. "It's all going to come out in the end."

Courtney rolls her eyes. "And then what?" she says, sounding bored. "We'll pay for what we've done, just like every corporation that ever poisoned a river or used sweatshops? You're too old to be that clueless."

"She kind of has a point," Beau says. "Individual people might face consequences, but the company itself, pretty much never."

I know she's right, but in this moment I have no problem making Courtney a scapegoat. I see the smirk on her face and I think maybe I could kill a thinking human after all. I take another step toward her, knowing the guards have their weapons trained on me, fighting the ferocious instinct to turn and run. "Maybe Seabrook won't pay for what they did," I say, low, so the guards can't hear it. "But *you* can."

Courtney laughs in my face, close enough that I feel the heat of her breath. "Sweetheart, if you think—"

Behind me, a roar like an awakening dragon as Leah revs Sunshine's car to vicious, gleeful life. The driver's side door slams shut from the momentum as the car leaps forward. The guards whip around, but they're too slow; the car is a moving target, a streak of neon pink and green across the pavement toward those massive panes of glass.

The car hits the window in an explosion of glittering shrapnel, throwing sprays of light in every direction so that for a moment I can't see Leah at all. Then my eyes adjust to the vast dark openness where the brewery's wall used to be. Inside, Leah screeches to a stop, tires skidding on the smooth concrete floor. Her arms and back are dappled with blood, but from this distance it's impossible to discern where it's coming from.

I start to run toward her, my vision so tunneled I completely forget that Courtney is standing directly in front of me. She's half turned to see what Leah's doing, but as I move she whips back around and throws an arm across my path. I crash into her. We both stumble and sway, leaning into each other in a terrible imitation of slow dancing, but don't go down.

I wrench free of Courtney's grasp and can't figure out which way to go. Everyone is shouting and screaming. One of the security guards has Logan pinned on the sidewalk, and another is grappling with Beau, but the other two are moving toward Leah, guns drawn. I turn and see Aurelia and Sunshine running across the street toward us. The security guard from the patrol car chases after them, shouting, the car still in the middle of the street with its door hanging open.

"Why are you doing this?" Courtney shouts in my ear, and she has the nerve to sound genuinely indignant. Past her shoulder, through the empty eye socket of the shattered window, I see Leah twisted around, reaching into Sunshine's back seat.

I expect her to emerge holding guns, but what she pulls out instead makes me leap backward, pulling Courtney with me by the front of her shirt. Leah swings the car door open and climbs out, almost leisurely, one hand held high, as Courtney yanks free and aims a fist at my head. Ducking her punch distracts me so that I don't actually see Leah pull the pin and throw the grenade.

All I register in that first instant is noise and heat and danger, the shock obliterating all order and sense. Then the sounds resolve into a series of explosions, like beads on the necklace of some ancient goddess of war.

The brewery—all the kettles and pipes, the steel and glass—is burning wreckage. That was the sound that drowned out the world. But there are still explosions going off all around me, and it takes another second to identify them as gunfire.

One security guard is still on the ground with his knee on Logan's back, but the other four have abandoned their pursuit of Sunshine, Aurelia, and Beau to fire at Leah. There's smoke and shards of glass everywhere, and my eyes can barely focus on anything, but I think I see Leah drop down behind Sunshine's car inside the brewery. I can't tell if she's using it as a shield or if she simply fell.

When the shooting stops, the street is horrifically silent: the silence of everything being erased, the silence of the end of the world. Courtney is still blocking my path, but I throw her aside like she's made of paper and run—Do I fly? Do my feet touch the ground at all?—toward Leah.

The pizza delivery car is bullet-spangled and spurting fluid from I don't know where. Inside the brewery, several things are on fire, and more fluids are gushing from the remains of the brewing apparatus, its robot heart now crushed and bloody. The smoke mixes with the too-sweet smell of fake fruit syrups to create a perfume that reminds me viscerally of the scented candles my mother liked to light around the house.

I kneel beside Leah and see immediately that she didn't crouch behind the car for shelter; she fell here, inert as a pile of rags. Her body is ripped in a dozen places. My mouth opens in what feels like a scream, but I still don't hear a sound.

Unbelievably, Leah struggles up to her hands and knees, but her arms give out and she falls again. She rolls onto her side and grins at me. "Got it before they got me," she says. There's blood on her teeth, blood on her shirt too, holes in her skin and in her clothes.

"Jesus," I say, trying to cover her wounds, which are much more numerous than my hands. I can't tell which ones are superficial and which are really bad. "Where's your bag?" I know she has pads in there, maybe some bandages too, things I could use to stanch the bleeding, but I don't see her bag anywhere. Did she have it at the park? Did she leave it in Sunshine's car, or all the way back at her apartment? I stand up to scan for it and find myself staring into the barrel of a security guard's gun.

I feel my heart cough and sputter like an engine failing to turn over. My body wants to kick into overdrive yet again, to speed up my pulse and spike my energy, but I'm simply too wrung out. I just stand there staring at the security guard, a white man with a sunburn across the bridge of his nose, waiting to see whether he'll shoot me. He seems as uncertain as I am.

"Wendy." Leah's voice is wet and thick. I drop back down to my knees beside her, ignoring how the sunburned guard's gun hand twitches at my sudden movement.

"I'm here, I'm here," I say, stroking her head. Blood stains her blue hair black.

"I did it," she says. "Fucked up their whole, you know." She gestures with her chin. "Whole fucking deal. The works. All the booze spraying out like . . ." Leah tries to make some kind of exploding noise but it frays into coughing.

"Okay, you did great, baby," I say, trying to keep the terror out of my voice. I haven't called her *baby* in months. I look up at the security guard, his gun still aimed somewhere above my head, where my heart was a few seconds ago. "We have to get her an ambulance."

He stares at me like I forgot to say *Simon says*.

"Don't bother," Leah says, and coughs again. Blood flecks her lips. I've seen enough movies to know that coughing up blood after an injury is a bad sign. "It's inside."

I look around frantically. Sunshine and Beau are yelling at the security guard who's still pinning Logan to the sidewalk. Aurelia is trying to get to Leah and me, but there are more guards in her way. Courtney is on this side of the shattered window now, but she just stands there, looking thunderstruck. For all her big talk, I suspect she never planned to see the gory outcome of her plans this close up.

"Courtney," I say, and my voice comes out thin and desperate. "Help her." She blinks at me. "Fucking help her, call someone, get her to a doctor—"

"Wendy," Leah says. She lifts her hand like she's going to pat my arm, but she doesn't make it. Her hand flops back down to the floor, limp and spattered with blood. "Chill, okay? There's no point. I told you. That stuff was spraying like Old Faithful."

I almost ask her "What stuff?" but of course I know what she means. The Seabrook seltzer, the poison, the plague. I'm crouching in a half-inch puddle of it, and there are open wounds all over Leah's body. The Seabrook is mixing with Leah's bloodstream, inside her body and out.

"Actually feel it," she muses. "It's all fizzy. Inside."

"The antidote?" I ask.

Leah flails an arm out. "Where's my bag?" she asks, looking mildly annoyed.

I raise my head and see Courtney, still standing in the same place, twisting her head from side to side. "Courtney, goddammit, call her a fucking ambulance," I scream. I feel my pockets for my phone, even though I know it's gone.

"There's nothing an ambulance can do for her," Courtney says, like she's reading the words off a page.

"Wendy," Leah says. "They're okay. I didn't."

"What?" I don't understand what she's saying.

Her jaw works as though she's trying to chew through something tough. "No, I didn't—I don't . . ." Leah's face crumples in frustration. "Don't let it through," she pleads.

I remember Jacquie's not-quite-comprehensible words, hot in my ear at Hellrazors. Is this the symptoms starting, or just blood loss making Leah incoherent? As I watch, a red dot appears in the white of Leah's eye, like a drop of ink spilled onto paper.

"Don't let it through," she says again, and it's almost nonsense but I know what she means.

"I won't, baby," I promise.

Leah closes her eyes. She almost looks peaceful for a moment, until a shudder goes through her and her teeth clench in pain.

I look up at the man with the sunburn. "I don't suppose you'd loan me your gun real quick. I'll give it right back." That finally jostles him into enough awareness that he re-aims the weapon at my head. I look around for other options. Most of the broken glass from the windows didn't make it this far into the building, but there's a good-sized shard near the security guard's boot, an uneven triangle with one point that looks viciously sharp. I pick it up gingerly, trying to avoid the edges. It's heavy.

"Leah," I say, but she doesn't open her eyes. I love her, still. She trusted me with this. I can be worthy of her trust, just this once, this last time and for all time. I hold the shard of glass in both hands and lower it until the stiletto point is just above Leah's throat. She twitches but makes no move to block me. I'm not sure whether she still knows I'm here.

I can do this. I breathe slow, steadying. I feel the floor under me, sticky with blood and alcohol, rough with broken glass. The air smells wet and electric. I can do this. I press the glass into Leah's throat.

I can't do this.

My body shakes with the thunder of a sob I can't let out. Leah's eyes are still closed. I can't breathe, my chest too tight, my skin too hot. I grip the makeshift knife too tightly, and it bites into my fingers. A drop of blood wells up and falls onto Leah's throat, rolls down, painting a thin red line as though instructing me where to cut.

I can't.

It's taking all my strength to hold myself in place, to refrain from jumping to my feet and running.

I'm already on the verge of screaming when I hear the gunshot. My scream might actually break free before the bullet leaves the chamber, but it's so close it's impossible to tell. The side of Leah's head bursts in blood and flesh and the smell of burning. It's the amphitheater explosion in gruesome miniature.

I flinch backward, dropping the shard of glass. Before I can do anything else, someone has an arm around my waist from behind and is pulling me, gently but implacably, away from Leah. Leah's body, now an object, a discarded possession whose owner will never reclaim it. It doesn't even occur to me to fight against the grip. After a moment I realize it's Aurelia.

Courtney stands a few feet away, her gun lowered to her side, wiping her eyes with the back of her hand.

I want to scream again. I want to throw myself at Courtney, take the gun she killed Leah with and turn it on her, or maybe on myself. I want to scratch her eyes out of her face and let blood wash away her useless tears. I want to fall on my knees and thank her for rescuing me from what Leah asked me to do. I don't do anything.

Aurelia keeps pulling me away. My feet scrabble at the sticky floor, then the threshold of broken glass where the full-length window used to be, then the pavement outside. Courtney gets smaller and smaller, my eyes stinging the longer I stare at her without blinking. I don't look at what's lying at her feet.

As we step out under the sky, I feel the first drop of rain, warm as blood, on my face. In the distance, thunder groans like a reluctant waker. Logan is back on his feet, road rash on his forearms and the side of his face. He moves toward Aurelia and me, Beau and Sunshine close behind him. We cluster together as if to shelter each other from the oncoming storm. The security guards belatedly circle around to put themselves between us and Courtney, mercifully blocking her from my view.

"You're going to have to leave," one of the security guards says. "The police department is overloaded right now, but in their absence we are authorized to take any necessary actions in the interest of public safety."

"Authorized by who?" Aurelia says. I hear the danger in her voice. The raindrops come faster, rattling off the hot pavement. Warm mist rises around our ankles.

Instead of answering her, the security guard repeats, "You need to leave the premises now."

"Leah," I say desperately. My throat feels like it's the first word I've said in a long time.

Logan puts his hand on my arm. "We can't do anything for her now."

"We can't just leave her there." I stare at the three guards, their guns pointed at us, the barrels like a second row of dead, empty eyes. "What are they going to do with her?"

"It doesn't matter," Beau says. "She's not in there anymore."

It matters to me. I feel Aurelia's body coiled behind me, like a bowstring pulled back, and I know that if I throw myself forward she'll come with me, even though she's the one who just dragged me out of there. If we move, the others will follow. We could rush the guards; there are five of us and four of them, if you count Courtney. We could force another firestorm. Maybe we could get to Courtney.

But what difference would that make?

I'm so tired. I want to go home.

The rain is coming down harder and harder. Soon the streets will be flooded. I close my eyes and tilt my head back, breathing in the smell of the open, gushing sky.

LEAH

Leah doesn't want to die.

She thought she was going to die a few hours ago, when Mrs. Delgado's teeth broke through her flesh. A little while after that, she thought she was going to die when she called up Sunshine and asked for a ride to Salt River Park. When she stole Sunshine's car and headed for the brewery, she was pretty sure she was going to die. When she drove through the plate-glass window, she knew for certain she was going to die. It felt right, in the moment her foot slammed down on the gas pedal, to offer up her own life in trade for all the suffering she'd caused. It felt like a closed circle. It felt like the only way she could apologize to Wendy, to Aurelia, to Samantha most of all. She squeezed her eyes shut and made up her mind to die.

And now she's dying, and she doesn't want to.

It's not fair that she's dying. It's not fair that it hurts so much. It's not fair, when all she ever wanted was to help people, to lift up her community, to save . . . to save . . . she can't remember now. Something seeps in around the edges of her vision, of her memory, a red-black stain that swallows what it touches. But Leah knows she's a good person, that she did her best. She doesn't want to die before seeing her good work take root and grow.

She's lying in a sticky puddle. Some of it is blood, and some of it is sweat, and some of it is something else that smells vicious and stings when it creeps inside of her. She licks it from her lips and tastes fake sweet, the flavor of some fantastical cyberpunk fruit. A half-forgotten instinct tells her not to swallow, not to take this sugar poison deeper into her body, but reflex and thirst are stronger. She gulps the fake fruit taste with her own spit. It doesn't soothe the burning in her throat.

Wendy's face rises over her like the moon. She's crying, Leah sees with a little twist of satisfaction. Wendy will miss her. Wendy is sorry. Leah's sorry too, of course she is, her repentance is so immense inside her it feels like a second skeleton, showing through all the holes in her ragged skin, but—it feels good to know that Wendy's sorry. After everything Leah has done, everything she's been through, Wendy owes her at least that much.

At her apartment, Leah has succulents in pots on the windowsills. They'll live a long time without water, drinking the sun through glass, for weeks or maybe months. The thought makes her stomach cramp. Bile rises up her throat, but she has no strength to eject it. She lies still and swallows and swallows, even though it hurts. Her fucking plants are going to outlive her. Wendy is going to outlive her.

It isn't fair. Leah doesn't want to die. Why does she always have to be the one who makes the hard choices, the sacrifices no one else can bear? What was she trying to prove?

She wants to live. She wants to hold Wendy as she shakes and sobs, to kiss forgiveness into her hair. She wants them all to understand what she was trying to do, to thank her, to love her. She doesn't know if anyone has ever really loved her, and now it's too late to ask.

The red-black stain is everywhere, or maybe it's just in her eyes. She tries to remember how the jade plant on her windowsill looks in the sunlight. What is that color called? She can't see Wendy anymore. She hears voices, but they're very far away. She's alone in here, red and black like the inside of a throat. She doesn't want to die alone. She doesn't want to die.

CHAPTER 18

SAN LAZARO, AZ—Following the domestic terrorist attack on the San Lazaro Pride Festival last Sunday, the city's LGBTQ community is rebuilding with the help of Seabrook Beverages. Seabrook, the corporate sponsor of the festival at which more than 100 people were killed, has pledged to donate a portion of its profits to the families of the deceased and to pay the medical bills of survivors. In addition, to honor the lives lost, the company is moving forward with plans for the Seabrook Community Health Center, which will provide culturally competent services including mental health support, STI screenings, and reproductive health care. Around the country, LGBTQ people and their allies have responded with open hearts to the tragedy, resulting in a massive increase in sales of Seabrook beverages.

Investigations into the attack on San Lazaro's gay community are ongoing, while State Senator Titania Randall is urging other metropolitan areas to cancel their Pride celebrations due to safety concerns. The person who set off the explosion in Salt River Park Amphitheater during the Festival, killing at least 120 attendees, including five police officers, has not yet been identified. In addition, the widespread appearance of neurological symptoms in surviving attendees has caused some to speculate that bioterrorism was involved, and that a broader conspiracy is at work. However, these symptoms could also be related . . .

"Thanks, I hate it," Logan interrupts. I shrug and stop reading, hand Aurelia her phone back. In all the apocalypse, I haven't had a chance to replace mine.

"So in a moving tribute to the people they killed, they're going to . . . keep doing the thing they were already planning to do," Aurelia says.

"Neurological symptoms," Beau says, shaking her head. "Domestic terrorism. This is so fucked-up."

"Are you still trying to post what really happened?" Logan asks Aurelia.

"I gave up," she says. "Every time I say anything it gets flagged for potential misinformation. I sound like a crackpot. I mean, would you believe it if you weren't there?"

"We can't be the only survivors," I say. "There must have been other people at Pride who didn't get killed or infected. They can't keep this hidden forever."

"They've gotta be laying the groundwork for something bigger," Beau says from her spot on the couch. "Tell everyone it's terrorism, then start rounding up the terrorists. I think what we've seen so far is only the beginning."

"You heard about the Pride festival in Silver City being canceled, right?" says Logan. "Because they're concerned about violence. The homophobes are going to use what happened here as an excuse to shut down every Pride they can. For our own protection, of course."

Beau nods. "That Randall psycho is on every news site saying Pride is a public health hazard. Wonder if that was part of the plan all along."

"And it's spreading," I say. "There are stories in Tucson and Yuma and up in Prescott. Violent altercations, biting, vomiting blood. There was even one in Las Cruces."

Aurelia peers through a gap in the cardboard we've taped up over the windows. "Doesn't necessarily mean it's the same thing."

"No, I guess it could be from the other zombie plague," I agree.

"There's another zombie plague?" Logan says, sounding horrified. I press my lips together to keep from saying something regrettable, but when I look at him, he's barely suppressing a smirk.

Is he fucking with me?

I don't have time to ask. Aurelia turns abruptly away from the window. "They're here."

My heart races. We all jump to our feet. Because it's her house, Beau is the one to stand at the door and look through the peephole. The rest of us stare at her, watching the set of her shoulders until, with one decisive nod, she tells us it's time.

She yanks open the door. Sunshine stands outside it, drenched from only a few steps through the rain from their car, the neon green of their polo shirt visible under what appears to be a blood-stained Kevlar vest. They hold a stack of pizza boxes balanced in one hand and a small crossbow in the other.

Beau takes the pizza while Aurelia hands over some cash, along with the tip: a mason jar of Beau's moonshine. Sunshine twists the top off and takes a sniff. My eyes are watering from across the room, but they just sigh in appreciation.

"Thanks," they say. "It's been a day."

"Stay safe out there, kid," Beau says. Sunshine salutes and turns back toward their car. They'll be back after their shift, since Beau's has become our shared home base for decompressing from the ongoing apocalypse and strategizing how we're going to survive it. With social media hopelessly censored, we're working on finding other ways to let people know what's really happening in San Lazaro. Aurelia is teaching Logan and me how to use guns. We're not grieving yet. I think once we let ourselves start, none of us knows when or whether we'll be able to stop, and right now we just don't have that kind of time.

Just as Sunshine steps off the porch, a long-haired person three-quarters of the way to a corpse emerges from behind their car. The person takes a few uncertain steps, weaving from side to side, splashing in the pond-sized puddles that line the driveway. Then their eyes lock on Sunshine and behind them, the house.

"Ah, balls," Sunshine says. They fire the hand crossbow, but, perhaps unsurprisingly for someone whose main weapon is a car, their aim is kind of shit. The bolt goes wide and thunks into the heart of a saguaro on the edge of Beau's driveway.

"Y'all, a little help here?" Sunshine asks, but they don't need to bother. We're already grabbing our weapons. Aurelia, whose gun never leaves her hip these days, is out the door first, with the rest of us close behind her. A tall woman with blood oozing out of her mouth—unclear whether it's her own—is coming up the driveway now.

"Okay," I say, shoulder to shoulder with my friends, holding a machete high. "Let's do this."

Acknowledgments

The Z Word began as my NaNoWriMo project in 2020. While I didn't finish the first draft in a month, I did build up the momentum that eventually carried me to my first published novel. I owe so much of that momentum to my NaNoWriMo group chat, Billie Wood, Maggie Down, and Karrie Waarala. Thank you all for being there at the inception of this book and cheering for it from the very beginning. I wouldn't have gotten here without you.

Dane Kuttler, thank you for being the first person to read a complete draft of this book, even though you hated horror back then. Your encouragement and love have carried me through every step of this writing process, and I could not be more grateful for your friendship. Don't fist me.

To Kate McKean, my incredible, tireless, and brilliant agent, thank you for sticking with me through the doldrums. I know zombies aren't what you signed up for, but I appreciate you rolling with it. And I'm so grateful that you saw something in the early, messy draft of this book that was worth your time and energy.

Jess Zimmerman, you have put so much into this book. I am beyond proud of what we've made together, and I know it's orders of magnitude beyond what I could have achieved on my own. Being edited by you is an honor. (And also a lot of work, but in a good way.) Thank you so much for believing in the book this could be, and bringing it into existence.

Thank you to everyone at Quirk for being a joy to work with and championing *The Z Word*.

Hailey Piper, thank you for reading this book when it was a novella's worth of hot mess, and never wavering in your belief that it would go places. You inspire me to make horror gayer.

No one can survive the process of writing, editing, submitting, and publishing a book without some trusted friends who will listen to you bitch and moan. While many have taken up this mantle for me, I need to especially thank Moses Netz and Matthew Lyons for always having my back and reassuring me that you cannot actually die of waiting for an email.

Thank you to Jana Clark for the day we threw writer's block out the window. Everything I've ever written or will ever write is in some way indebted to you.

To Doc Luben, Mickey Thompson, the Outlaw Bitches—Teresa Driver, Maya Asher, and Kelly Lewis—Laura Lacanette, and the rest of the Tucson crew, thank you for all the inspiration and all the parties. If you danced in my kitchen, puked in my sink, or peed in my driveway between 2007 and 2010, you are part of this book and part of my heart.

Thank you to all the artists whose music contributed indispensable Vibes to my writing process, especially Nova Twins, Sleater-Kinney, Janelle Monáe, and Britney Spears.

Thank you to librarians everywhere, especially those at the Denver Public Library Pauline Robinson branch, my beloved neighborhood library, and the Sam Gary branch, where I wrote several major parts of this book.

Thank you to Heather Mahoney, always. I wish you could read this one.

To my parents, Michelle Miller and Ranger Miller, and my stepmother Dot Miller, thank you for your tireless love and support, and for reading everything I write even when it's . . . like this.

Thank you to Kara for giving me great book recommendations, and to Kevin and Sam for always taking mine. I really won the sibling lottery three times in a row, and I love you all so much.

Thank you to my Bunny and my Bear, the two most brilliant, creative, gorgeous, and hilarious children on earth, for all your patience when Mommy was working on her "edit-book." You are my world and the inspiration for everything I do. I hope you love this book when you read it sometime in the mid-2040s.

No one has dedicated more time, energy, hope and faith to this book than Charlie King-Miller. My gratitude to you is beyond what words can express (and you KNOW how I feel about words). Thank you for believing I would get here, even when I didn't. I love you past the crab.